THE RISE OF GERRY LOGAN

BRIAN GLANVILLE

THE RISE OF GERRY LOGAN

ff

faber and faber

This edition first published in 2010
by Faber and Faber Ltd
Bloomsbury House, 74–77 Great Russell Street
London WC1B 3DA

The right of Brian Glanville to be identified as author of this work
has been asserted in accordance with Section 77 of the
Copyright, Designs and Patents Act 1988

A CIP record for this book is available from the British Library

ISBN 978-0-571-26919-8

For Pam

It was the openness of the face that struck me most, more even than its intelligence. Openness, in the sense of wanting to know, was what really set it apart from all the other faces in that dressing-room. They were heavier, of course, they hadn't the same friendliness, the unexpected welcome, but above all, they were closed, they didn't aspire. They knew what they knew, and that was enough; they knew it at twenty-five, which was *his* age, they'd know it at thirty-five, and they'd know it still—no more, no less—at forty-five. But his greeting had more than friendliness, it had eagerness, too, as though he might find through me some part of what he wanted to know.

Of course, I had seen his face before, but always in newspaper photographs, or at a distance, on the field, set in the tension of the game, so that the impact now was new and undiluted. His hair was thick and straight and very blond— I remember thinking how attractive he must be to women, though he was too boyish to be handsome—and there was a tremendous *freshness* about him; red cheeks, as though he'd come straight from a farm, not a football field; eyes blue and clear and effervescent. His body, as he sat there wearing only his football shorts, looked almost slight, strengthening the impression of boyishness, belying the display of stamina he had only just given. He was thin chested, he'd escaped the squat, bull-power of the footballer's neck, his arms and shoulders were unexceptional, almost slight. Even his legs, still barred like a honeycomb by his discarded shinpads, still pink with the bruises of the game, were merely well articulated; one had to look close to see the lean muscularity of calves and thighs.

"Did you enjoy it?" he asked, in a Glasgow accent. It was from Glasgow—Third Lanark—that he'd joined the club, four seasons ago.

"Yes," I said, "I thought you had a very good game."

"Don't tell him that," said another Scot, beside him; Connor, a short, bald, heavy man, who played left-half. "He always bloody plays well, Gerry. Never has a bad bloody game."

"I can't afford to," Gerry said, "with you letting them in, up the other end," and he pulled off his shorts, with a certain, useless modesty, then made towards the steam and the singing of the bath.

"Don't listen to him," said Connor, wryly. "He'll write your report for you, and *he'll* be the only one that played."

"It's written," I said, and left the dressing-room, getting a dour good-bye from Wakeman, the manager, raincoated and withdrawn in a corner, as though the match, the team itself, were none of his affair. How did he and Gerry get on, I wondered; chalk and cheese.

A month later, I was to be told, told as one was told so many things, in the Great Terminus Hotel, hard by King's Cross Station. In its stuffy, over-heated corridors, its prosaic meals, its cosy obsolescence, the Great Terminus always seemed to me a home from home for cautious clubs from the North, unwilling to commit themselves by venturing farther into the glittering treachery of the metropolis. Here, the very whistling and shunting of the trains assured them that escape was near at hand.

I had come to see the manager of Leicester City, had pushed my way through the Saturday morning crowd of small boys with biros and devoted scrapbooks, before I saw Gerry in the vestibule. I'd forgotten Jarrow were in town. He greeted me with the same spontaneity he'd shown before, and again I felt flattered; embarrassed, too, in confessing I'd come to see someone else. But he didn't seem bothered. "Come on and have coffee," he said, guiding me briefly, by the arm. "Leicester are still having breakfast in the restaurant. They eat like they play — they're a dull team."

He led the way past the lounge where directors — unmistakably — sat plump and hearty over morning coffee. One of them called out to Gerry as we passed: "All right,

Gerry?" and Gerry answered quietly—even primly—"Yes, thank you, Mr Burns.

"It's to show he knows me," he said, passing on. "If we lose today, he won't say a word to me, all the way back to Jarrow."

He opened a door into one of the numberless, proliferating smoking-rooms with which the place was honeycombed. It gave, like the rest of them, an instant impression of green beige, a whiff of the cold, stale ghosts of a thousand cigarettes. "We'll get a bit of peace here," he said.

He was wearing the blue, crested blazer, the habitual grey flannels, of the club. Even so he contrived, with his brisk white collar, his green, striped tie, to seem better dressed than the normal footballer. "The directors get on my nerves," he said. "When it's trips to London, they all want to come, there's no escaping them. When it's Liverpool or Bolton, you're lucky if you see a couple."

"It's an outing for them," I said.

"Yes, at the club's expense. I wonder how many bottles of whisky they'll get through in the week-end?

"They're all living on the club," he said. "This one's a solicitor, so *he* does the legal work, that one's a surgeon, so *he* takes out all the cartilages, the other one's a builder, so *he* looks after all the club houses."

"Aren't you happy there?"

"I'm *happy* enough," he said, and seemed to cut off from me, in a moment's hermetic silence. "Happy for the present," he said. "Jarrow's not big enough for me, Brian. I don't mean to say that I'm too big for it; I only mean to say, Jarrow's a small town, and it's always going to be a small town; there's not enough there, however well you play. Sooner or later I want to come to London, only I don't want to leave it too late. I want to come when I think I'm at my peak."

"And aren't you now?"

"Not yet," he said. "I've things to learn still, and I think I'm better off staying where I am, until I've learned them."

"What sort of things?"

"Pacing myself, for one thing, because if you can't pace yourself, how can you hope to pace a game? Then there's other things that seem like little things, only they're big things, because the higher you go in football, the more you're playing against people who are as strong as you are and as clever as you are and as experienced as you are, the more it's the small things that make the difference. I don't think you can learn many of them in this country, though, I think they've been forgotten. You'd have to learn them from the Continentals, from people like Puskas and that big Austrian —Ocwirk. I've seen them when they've come over here and I've seen them on the television and now and again I say to myself, that's the way I'd like to play."

His frankness was deeply beguiling; it gave the impression one had been admitted to a tiny and exclusive club.

"Then another thing," he said, "this is a transition period for me. I'm changing my style, I'm tending to lie deeper, I'm getting more interested in making goals than scoring them. When I was eighteen and I started playing for Third Lanark, there was nothing in the world like scoring a goal, it was a marvellous feeling. Now I don't get the same kick any more; I think it's a sign of maturity. Like Alex James, he scored goals for Raith, he scored less goals for Preston, and for Arsenal, he didn't score at all, it didn't interest him. Well, if I *am* changing my style, it's better to do it before I get to London, before I'm in the goldfish bowl, and people are expecting too much. Mind you, I haven't told Billy Wakeman about it, because if I don't tell him he certainly won't notice and if he doesn't notice, then he won't worry. All Billy's concerned with is how he stands with the directors, and all the directors are concerned with is whether we win matches."

I had noticed myself that he was changing his game. He'd come to Jarrow as an opportunist, gliding into good positions near goal, making them for himself with elegant, wasteless ball control; a graceful swerve, a sudden burst of pace. He played well upfield, beside the centre-forward, expecting the ball to be purveyed for him, though even at this time one could see the tactician masked by the scorer; a sudden reverse pass, expertly concealed, a through pass, perfectly timed. He had just lost his place in the Scotland team; I asked him if he thought this was why.

"I'm playing for an English club," he said, "it's a wonder they ever picked me at all; maybe it's because I didn't go too far across the border. It's amazing how many good players turn into bad players as soon as they get to England, and how they turn into good players again, the minute they're back in Scotland."

I had to leave him, then, to keep my appointment. "Come over whenever we're in London," he said. "It's nice to have somebody to talk to."

Whether or not his change of style had cost him his place for Scotland, it was certainly the cause of his quarrel with Jarrow, a quarrel which blew up within mere weeks of our conversation. Jarrow, it seemed, were unwilling to serve as his laboratory. There were the usual statements and counter-statements in the Press:

LOGAN MUST PLAY OUR WAY SAYS JARROW CHIEF

CITY SAY, WE WON'T SELL LOGAN

There were the interviews with the manager—Wakeman —"We are acting in Gerry's best interests. His value to any side is as a striker," the counter-interviews with Logan himself. "A player has got to develop. If Jarrow won't allow me to develop, then I've got to get away, to protect myself."

But Jarrow, plainly, would hang on to him like bulldogs; he was all they'd got, their one authentic star; the local papers, I heard, were full of urgent letters; peace must be made, Logan must at all costs stay.

"Football's all they've got," he told me, when we met in the great, grey Tottenham Hotspur car park, before a match. Hangers-on surrounded us, a pop-eyed urban chorus, swarthy and unabashed, annotating and explaining.

"They're fanatics, honestly. They come up to me in the the streets, they say, 'You're not going, Gerry, are you? You wouldn't let us down?' and I tell them, 'Jarrow are letting *me* down,' but they can't see it."

One sighed, and resigned oneself to deadlock, the inevitable war of attrition. In those days, before the footballers' revolution, the New Deal, a player was bound to his club like a Russian serf; if they would not give him a transfer, he could whistle for it, and if he refused to "sign on" again at the end of a season, he could whistle for it without wages.

But in Gerry's case, they had caught a Tartar; he turned it into a persecution, a martyrdom, a lone crusade; he wrote a bevy of signed articles in the *Newcastle Chronicle*, the *Sunday Sun*, even the *Daily Express*.

"People keep telling me, you can't fight the system, the system will always win. All I can say is that if this is the system, the system is rotten, and so is the game."

The club directors, clearly, didn't know if they were coming or going; provoked beyond restraint, they would from time to time erupt, like small expostulations of marsh gas.

"If Logan knew what was good for him, he'd sign on and shut up."

"If Logan goes on like this, he'll talk himself out of football."

"I've got no respect for them, Brian," Gerry said—once more, at the Great Terminus. We sat in the coffee lounge; Burns strode portentously by us, as though we were not there. "He thinks he's hurting my feelings," Gerry said. "If he only knew : it's a bloody relief not to listen to him !"

"Will they ever let you go?"

"They'll have to let me go," he said, serenely. "A player that won't play is no use to anybody." And a player who isn't paid? I wondered, but he instantly divined the thought. "I can keep going, don't worry. If they think they can starve me out, they'll think again. I'd never have begun it if I hadn't something up my sleeve; they're not going to make *me* another Mannion."

"I'm glad," I said, remembering the Mannion affair, which had also, in its time, aroused the North East; the great player—greater than Logan was, now—who refused to sign on again for Middlesbrough, held out a few, sad months, then was forced to come to heel, to return to the same, undifferentiated pittance.

"If you win," I said, "you'll strike a blow for all of them. But they'll only yield to force; it's the old story, isn't it—capital and labour."

"It is," he said, "but it shouldn't be. They *treat* us as labour, but what we are is entertainers. In America, they recognise that. These baseball players get entertainers' salaries, they have entertainers' status. Over here, they treat professional players like a lot of peasants."

"You can be their Wat Tyler," I said.

GERRY LOGAN

I WONDERED almost as soon as I went to Jarrow, have I made a mistake, and before I'd been there a season I *knew* I'd made a mistake. Glasgow wasn't London, but at least it was a big city, even if in some ways it had a small city mentality, but Jarrow was just a little town in every way, and at the back of everything there was the depression, the Jarrow marchers; either the people that remembered it or the people that were too young to remember it and didn't want anyone else to remember it, either.

Jarrow was ugly, too, it was even uglier than Glasgow— so were Sunderland and Newcastle—and they hadn't got the *size* of Glasgow, nor the character. At least in Glasgow you had the hills, and some important looking buildings, and at least you could get out quickly to the country, but here you didn't want to get into the country, it was all cluttered up with pit heads and those great, black mounds.

I was happy enough at Cathkin, anyway, I'd just had my first cap for Scotland and the lads there were mostly lads that I'd grown up with. Now and again, I'd maybe thought I wouldn't be staying there forever, but that was something in the future; it was a shock to me when they had me in the office and said, "This is Mr Wakeman, the Jarrow manager, and his Chairman and Vice-Chairman. We've agreed terms, and now it's up to you." Then our own manager took me aside and he said, "Look, it's not that we think we can afford to get rid of you, we can't, but financially, we can't afford to keep you, either."

I said, "I'd like a day to think it over," and then Wakeman got hold of me and he said, "Listen, if you're worried about whether there's going to be anything in it for you," and I said, "I never even thought about it," which was true. Only now that I did think of it, I couldn't just ignore it, because my mother was ill at the time, she needed to go away,

16

and my father could only work a couple of days a week in the shipyard. Personally I didn't like it, I hated the whole situation, the way they made you into a sort of a conspirator if you took anything from them, which should have been yours by right, in any case. So I talked to my mother and father about it, and they said, "You do what you want, Gerry," but I could see what they were thinking, because there were five of us children altogether and I was the only one that was earning apart from my sister Peggy, who only brought in six pounds a week.

So I spoke to Mr Wakeman the next day, though honestly it choked me, really, and I said, "Well, I've considered it, what's it worth to me?" and he gave me this sort of a look and he said, "Four hundred," and I said, "I'll have to talk it over with my parents," meaning it, and he said, "All right, then, five hundred," and that made me really despise him.

He and one of the two directors went back that day, but the Chairman, Mr. Steele, stayed on to finish off the deal. I believe they paid twelve thousand, so five hundred wasn't bad, considering all I was entitled to officially was a tenner. This Mr. Steele amused me, he was a pompous little man with a gold watch-chain and a little pot belly and he walked around like a turkey-cock, talking in this funny North-East accent that I hadn't heard before. I could tell he fancied himself the big noise in the club, he kept telling me how lucky I was to be coming to Jarrow, what a great history they had, the times they'd won the Cup and the times they'd won the League, though as far as I could tell they hadn't won anything since 1930. I could see I was meant to think that they were doing me a favour by signing me, though I'd looked at the English League table and saw they were only four places off the bottom, and I wondered whether maybe this was the reason he kept talking about the past.

The deal went through on a Wednesday, and he wanted me to play in a match that Saturday, so we left on the Thursday morning. I met him at the station, by the platform, and he huffed and puffed a bit and then he said, "Here's your ticket," and he handed me a green one, second class, and I looked at his and saw it was a white one—first class, and I thought to myself, I'm good enough to play for him, but I'm not good enough to travel in the same compartment, and all the way to Jarrow I sat there wondering if there was any way I could get out of it, and if there wasn't, then the first chance that came, I'd be away.

When I turned up for training the next day, though, I found most of the players thought he was as big a shit as I did; they said, "What did you get out of it?" and when I told them, they said, "It must have nearly broken his heart, he hates parting with a penny, no wonder he gave you a second-class seat, it's a wonder you didn't have to travel with the engine driver."

He was a local builder, they told me, he'd made a packet in the war, and the other one that had come up to Glasgow, the Vice-Chairman, Mr. Gray, hated his guts; there was a terrible feud between them. In fact they told me it was Gray that wanted me, not Steele; as soon as he knew Gray was keen, he'd done everything he could to oppose it, but the Board had outvoted him. But I didn't like this Gray much better than I liked the Chairman; to me he seemed a loud mouth, he was full of promises the whole time—"We'll look after you, we'll find you a nice flat here, we'll see you're all right if the club stay up this season"—but I had a feeling that he wouldn't keep them, whereas the other fellow wouldn't even make them. Gray was a butcher, he was a big fellow with a big stomach, and he had the sort of personality to go with it; his line was, he didn't know anything about football, he left it all to the manager, and I wondered if that was the case why they'd had seven managers at Jarrow in the last five seasons, because they couldn't *all* have been sacked by the Chairman on his own. In fact what it seemed to me Gray was saying was, "Look at me, *I* don't interfere, but *he* does."

Billy Wakeman, the manager, had been a Jarrow player himself, just before the war; he'd played for them at Wembley in the Final, and he'd had two or three games for England. He'd been a wing-half; he was before my time, but they told me he'd been a dour sort of player, always grafting but

18

never doing anything brilliant, which is what I would have expected. He'd lasted two years so far as manager, but if the club went down, he'd go down with it, and although he never said much, I could tell that I was the one he expected to save him his job. You'd see so little of him, you'd wonder did he do anything else all day but sit in his office and worry.

The training was all under Ronnie Castor, the first team trainer, and all it consisted of was running round the field, round and round until you thought you'd start to go mad. At Cathkin I'd still been a part-timer, I was still at the technical college, learning engineering, but here they'd talked me into going full-time and just taking night-classes, and I wondered was this the sort of life all the English footballers had, day in, day out? I asked the other players but they didn't seem to see anything unusual in it. One of them said, "Ronnie's not bad, he doesn't work you like some of the others do," and another one said, "You've got to get fit, haven't you? You've got to be able to last on the heavy grounds," and I hadn't any answer to that, then, but later on I started thinking, "Fit for what?" and "What's the point of being able to keep on running when you don't know what to do with the ball when you've got it?"

Once I got a ball out myself during training and I started kicking it up against the fence around the terraces, but Ronnie shouted at me, "Put that fucking thing away," and in the end I took to coming back on my own in the afternoons, and doing a bit of ball practice when there was no one to see me.

The first game I played, that Saturday, was a home game, against the Arsenal, and I didn't play well. I'd been told it was all much quicker, and it *was* quicker, but not so much the pace as the speed of thought. You'd see what you believed was a gap, and then you'd go towards it and it wasn't a gap, because somebody else on their side had seen it, too. As it happened, I was lucky, because in the first five minutes I got a goal and that was what I'd been brought there to do, that was what the crowd wanted, although it was a goal that anybody could have scored. Our left winger crossed the ball, their goalkeeper was slow in coming off his line, and I just headed it in, just by the near post. Afterwards I realised it was just as well, because they could be a vicious crowd, and if they got their knife into a player they could make life impossible for him. I've seen some young boys that they've ruined there who might have made good players. I didn't do much else but score, but in the end we won it by 2–1 and everybody was delighted; even Billy Wakeman had a smile on his face, which was something I'd never seen before.

Gray came up to me in the dressing-room and he said, "Good start, good start," and I didn't say anything, but I remember thinking, if that's what he calls a good start, then he's not hard to satisfy. We stayed up, though, we won enough games for that, and by the end of the season I was finding it easier. I could see the other players were mostly very ordinary, the only thing they'd got that I hadn't got was experience of this quicker sort of game.

In April, they chose me for Scotland against England, at Wembley, and it was very exciting, not just the match, but because it was my first time in London and I thought, this is the place for me, this life here is what I want, so that going back to Jarrow was a terrible disappointment. I think I made up my mind then that sooner or later, I'd end up in London.

What it had was this vitality, wherever you went, you felt that things were happening, there was adventure. Even where we stayed, at King's Cross, it was dirty and ugly, like Jarrow, but there was life. The first few times I came down to play, I'd leave the hotel straight after breakfast and I'd get in a bus or maybe in the tube and just go round the city. The more I saw of it, the more it appealed to me; the parks, and the big shops, and the buildings like Westminster Abbey, and streets like Fleet Street and Knightsbridge and Park Lane.

Now and then, I'd be down long enough to go to a night club. I wouldn't drink there, and I wouldn't dance much, but the whole atmosphere was exciting, the music and all the good-looking women, there was an elegance about them you never got in Glasgow or the North : the feeling that this life was going on, and it was something maybe I could join in.

When the end of the season came, I waited and waited, but I got nothing; when I saw Gray, he always seemed to be running away from me. Not that I was really surprised, because he hadn't kept his other promise, either; I hadn't got any flat, I was just in lodgings with two of the other players; it wasn't bad, but I'd been better off when I was home. In fact I went home for the summer and I was tempted not to come back again; I didn't think that Jarrow City could teach me anything. As far as I was concerned, it was a bad club with bad players, and if I stayed there too long, they'd drag me down to their level.

I talked to my father and my mother about it, and in the end I decided, I'd give it a little while longer. It was my mother I listened to more than my father; she's always been a very dynamic woman, and it was she that encouraged me in my football, she'd come to all my school matches and afterwards to see me in junior football and she used to say to me, "It's what you enjoy most, if you're good enough, why not do it?" whereas my father was more cautious, he wanted me to have a trade, and that was why I took up engineering. I don't want to say I didn't get on with my father, but it was my mother who was the strong personality in the family, the old man would come home and either he'd be tired and go to sleep in a corner with the newspaper over his face, or else it would be Saturday night and he'd go out to the pub with the boys. Football didn't much interest him, only his job and whether he could keep it, because in between the two wars he'd been out of work as much as he'd been in, and this was one of the most terrible things that could happen to anybody.

But the more I watched him, the more determined I was that I wasn't going to be in the same position, I was going to get away from Clydeside and even get away from Glasgow if I could, I was going to be my own master. I could tell this was what my mother wanted, too; she was an independent person herself, and she wanted me to be free as well, and I think she realised that football was a *way* of getting free, long before I did, because at this time, I felt crushed by it.

When she said, stay with Jarrow, I listened to her, but

when my father said, stay with Jarrow, I knew it was from fear, just in the same way he might have said, don't change your job, it's dangerous, you may not get another.

My mother said, maybe it's better for a while to be a big fish in a small pond, if you went to one of the biggest teams, Manchester United or the Wolves, you might get lost, and anyway, there's one thing, you're out of Glasgow.

That was something else in which she and I were on one side and my father was on the other; all this stuff about belonging to Glasgow. He was proud of it, but it never meant a thing to me, and as for my mother, she came from a village in Renfrewshire and she'd always hated the whole city. Glasgow to her meant a hard life and ugliness and unemployment and drunkenness and for me she wanted something different.

So I went back to Jarrow, and things began to go a little better for the team, it was more enjoyable, and then something else happened to me, something more personal, that gave me a stronger reason for staying. In fact the end of it all was that I got married there.

MARY

OFTEN you think of things, if it happened again, would I do it? I sometimes think it of Gerry and me, only at the time, I didn't stop to reason, it was too strong, it just carried me along.

The first time he played at Jarrow, the first time I ever saw him, he *looked* different from the others, so young and slim, he was more like just a boy. He kept dashing and darting after the ball, he didn't seem to care how many were in the way, and all I could think of was I was afraid he was going to get hurt. I couldn't see his face well—it wasn't just that, at all—it was something about . . . everything, the way he stood and the way he moved, I can't properly describe it. To tell the truth, I wasn't really that interested in football, I went because Joe used to take me, he had these two season tickets, and he was so keen on it, he just took it as a matter of course I was as interested as he was. It was typical of him, really.

People said afterwards, why did you marry him, weren't you in love with him? and you couldn't explain to them that you *were* at the time, or maybe what you were in love with was the idea of being married; then you change and he doesn't change and—well, other things—and that's when everything starts to go wrong.

I wanted to meet Gerry, and I knew I would sooner or later, because often Joe travelled to away games, and when he did he'd be with the team party, because his father had something to do in business with Mr. Steele, the Chairman. Sometimes he'd talk me into going with him, but mostly I'd get out of it, because I hated the journeys, stuck all day in the train, and the directors were a lot of dirty old men, I thought, winking at you, and putting their hands on you, whenever they could.

But when they were playing in Birmingham, I said I'd come. There was nothing behind it then, honestly, I just

23

wanted to meet him, there was something drew me to him; you felt when you saw him play you wanted to look after him.

Meeting him on the train, at close quarters, you felt the same, only he was much more sure of himself than I thought he would be, he had this way of looking straight into your eyes when he was talking to you, and I liked the way when he disagreed with anyone, he'd come straight out and say so.

Joe started talking to him about the team ought to have done this and the team ought to have done that and he wouldn't have any of it, he kept on contradicting him, and I could tell Joe was getting angry, he was trying to impress me how much he knew about the game and how he could lay down the law even to the players. I don't remember saying much, myself, or Gerry saying much to me; he was very polite, and I liked the Scottish way he had of talking. I didn't care what he was saying, I just felt I could sit there listening to his voice, I didn't know how much listening I'd have to do, later. Once I thought I caught him glancing at me when he thought I wasn't looking, but I couldn't be sure, and afterwards I kept thinking, did he or didn't he, but on the way back after the game we neither of us had a chance to speak to him, he was with the team the whole time—only I noticed where they were all playing cards, he was on his own and reading a book.

Joe was saying he was too big-headed and that he'd still got a lot to learn; it was always the same when anybody got the better of him, there was something mean about him and I loathed it.

The first time I was ever alone with Gerry was on another of these journeys. Joe and he and I were at a table together in the diner and Joe went out for a moment and left us. I'll always remember, Gerry turned to me at once and said just like that, "I want to see you tomorrow, have tea with me in Newcastle," and it was a shock for me, I was so surprised and so pleased as well that I couldn't answer him. Then he said, all terribly intense, "Will you?" and this time I managed to say yes, I would, and he said, "There's some things I want to talk to you about."

So I met him in Newcastle, it was in Binns, I think, I drove there in the car we had, and I was twenty minutes early and I was sitting there and sitting there wondering, would he come, and when he did come he was right on time—he was always right on time—and he sat down and the first thing he said was, "You don't love your husband, do you?" and I was that surprised again I didn't know how to answer him, it was this way he had then of going direct to the point and taking the wind out of your sails. I know I ought to have got angry with him, but all I could say in the end was, "What makes you think that?" and it sounded so silly I was ashamed, but the thing was, I'd never even thought about it.

He said, "It's obvious, just looking at you, he's a closed person and you're an open person," and I said, "Is that what you wanted to talk about? Is that what you got me here to tell me?" and he said, yes it was, because he just had to know, did I love Joe or didn't I? and I couldn't look at him, I just said at last, "What right have you to ask me?" and he said, "That means you *don't* love him, if you did you'd never hedge like that," and I began to be a bit afraid of him, he was so direct, he was like a terrier, just going on and on and on and never letting you alone. Another thing was, I was getting frightened there were people there that might know him, because it's such a small place really, Newcastle—and Jarrow even smaller—and Joe was well known because of his father and the business and all. So I said to him very quietly, "What if I love him or I don't? What's it to do with you?"

I suppose what I hoped he'd say was, because I love you myself, but he didn't, you'd never hear a thing like that from Gerry, he just said, "Maybe it's more to me than you think," and I had to be content with that. When he left me he squeezed my hand a moment, that was all, then he was away before I could even say to him that it was best he didn't come back with me in the car.

After that I kept wondering and puzzling what he wanted, would he phone me, would he ask me out again, but it must

25

have been a week before I heard from him, and then the phone went one afternoon and a voice said, very short, as if the person was disguising it, "Mrs. Burrows?" and I *knew* it was him, and I said, "Yes?" and then he came through in his own voice and he said, "It's Gerry. Meet me tomorrow at Seaburn."

So I drove up there, through Sunderland, and I met him in front of a café, it was like a detective film—he turned up with a hat on, I'd never seen him wear one before—all pulled down over his eyes and his coat collar turned up and when I saw him I laughed at him, I couldn't help it, but he said, "It's no joke if they recognise me, it'll be no joke for either of us," and then we went walking along the beach.

I don't know what I expected him to do, try and kiss me, perhaps, or something, but all he did was talk, he talked and talked, we must have walked up and down that beach for hours. He talked about what he meant to do in football and what he thought of Jarrow—the club, the team and everything; what he thought of the directors and the manager and how he'd noticed me because he saw I was sad, I was a *different* sort of person, like he was, and I thought, is that what you brought me all the way here for, to talk about yourself, and yet you couldn't help being fascinated, he had such a flow of words, I'd hardly ever heard such a flow from anybody, let alone a footballer, and I said to him, "You've missed your profession; you ought to be on the wireless or a writer," and he said that was what he wanted to be; as soon as he had the chance, he said, he wanted to combine them with his football.

He was going to put everything right in football, every blessed thing, and after a time I started feeling about him just like I had when I first saw him on the field almost like a mother, really, sort of wanting to protect him, because even I could tell that half the ideas he had, he'd never be able to put them into practice. I didn't know then, of course, that this never mattered as far as Gerry was concerned, he's never changed in that, putting ideas up just for the sake of putting them, so that one day he may say one thing, and a few days later just the very opposite.

Just as we were going up the promenade, it was as if he suddenly remembered, and he took hold of me and he kissed me on the mouth, very quickly, like he was saying, that's what I'm meant to do, so I'll do it.

This time I drove him part of the way home, then left him at a bus stop, and the rest of the way back, on my own, I was half fascinated and I was half furious, thinking, a good listener, that's all he wants, that's all I am to him, nothing else. Yet I couldn't help feeling glad it was me he'd picked, because I knew he was going to be all the things he said, I knew it was more than just hot air.

We met once a week after that, nearly always on the same day, very nearly always at the same place, until he started getting worried somebody would notice us, and then we changed it. He'd kiss me more often, now, he'd kiss me when we met — very off-hand, though, like it embarrassed him; just a peck, really, as though he was doing it for me, not for him. Once he asked me, "Why haven't you got any children?" and I didn't know how to answer him; in the end I said, "Joe doesn't want them," which was true, only it wasn't really true. He'd say, "There's no hurry," or, "Might as well wait until the old man takes me into full partnership," but I knew deep down if I'd really insisted, if I'd really wanted to, I could have talked him round. I suppose the point was, really, I didn't want them, because once we had them, I was tied to him.

I asked Gerry, "Do you want children when you marry?" and he said, "If I marry." I said, "That makes you sound very young, when you say that," and he was furious, he hated ever being reminded how young he was. He said, "You're not so old yourself," and I said, "I'm twenty-three, that's two years older than you — and anyway a woman knows more at that age, a woman grows up quicker," and he said, "Rubbish! Women just get more things happening to them, that's all. They may get married earlier and have children earlier, but that's all there is to it. A man makes more of what has happened to him, because he thinks about it."

It must have been about the third or fourth time we went out that he told me he was more or less engaged to a girl in Glasgow; he'd been going with her for the last two years. "Well," I said, "you're a fine one, making dates with a married woman, and all the time you've got a fiancée!"

"She isn't my fiancée," he said, "there's nothing settled, nothing at all. I could never marry her, I've outgrown her, she belongs to something I've left behind." And I remember when he said that, he picked up a stone from the beach and threw it out to sea, he fairly flung it, as if he was throwing *her*, and I looked at the expression on his face and there was something hard about it, something set. I said, "You'll be saying the same about me, I expect, very soon."

"No, I won't," he said, "you've got something to offer me," and again I had this feeling of being half furious because everything had to be *him*, and half happy with it, as a compliment. I said, "What about this business of going to London? You won't want me then, you'll want somebody smart! You'll want a London girl!" But he said, "London or not London's got nothing to do with it, it's a question of understanding. I feel you understand me; when I'm with *her* I feel she doesn't, she listens but she doesn't hear."

I was beginning to wonder was he shy of women, but one day as we got back into the car he kissed me, and as he moved away I made believe I was excited, I put my arms round him and wouldn't let go and kissed him, you know, properly, and I'll always remember that moment, it was a terrible moment, would he kiss me back or would he pull away again, and then he kissed me back and put his hands on my breasts, and I wanted to stay and stay, but he said, "Quick, they're watching us!" and broke away. But when we'd driven only a little distance he said, "Go up that turning there and stop the car." It was a little country road and I stopped the car and God knows how long we were there.

But in one way he was still the same. It was somehow the wrong way round, it was me that was leading on and him

28

that was drawing back, until I thought I couldn't bear it any longer and one day we were in the car and it was getting dark and I didn't mind what, I just wanted him to do it, and we were there and I was saying, "Now, now! Please, now!" and I'll never forget, he shouted out, "I can't, I can't, I've got nothing!"

Now I'm older, I look out for things like that more, you've got to take notice of these moments, when people tell you things; they warn you when they don't mean to. But I explained it away, just like I'd explained the other things away, and if the same thing happened now, I wonder would I have been any cleverer.

Joe found out of course, it wasn't all that long. He was waiting for me when I got back one evening, when I'd been with Gerry in the car. I suppose I must have looked all hot, and my hair all over the place—he never usually got home so early.

He said, "Where have you been?" and before I could answer, "You've been with Logan, haven't you? You've been with that bloody little Scotch bastard." I said, "What makes you think that?" I was playing for time. And he said, "Because everybody knows, that's what. You've been seen with him all over the bloody place, Jarrow, Seaburn, Newcastle." I think he really wanted me to deny it then, so that he could kid himself it wasn't true, but I told him, "What if I did? I like to talk to him." He said, "That's it, is it? You go off to Seaburn to talk. You go sneaking away in my car, telling me a pack of bloody lies to get it; just to bloody well talk."

I said, "I won't listen to you when you talk like that, I'm going up to bed."

Up in the bedroom, I could hear him downstairs, thumping and banging about, and it must have been midnight before he came up. He didn't put on the light; he was blundering about the room, undressing, and I could tell he must be drunk. I was lying there on the edge of the bed, it was a double bed, pretending I was asleep. I'd been wondering and wondering what to do, what I could say, because the stupidest thing about it was there was nothing in it, if I'd left it to Gerry there probably *would* have been nothing in it then but talking, and even as it was, you couldn't say we were serious. He'd said I understood him, yes, but he'd never said he loved me, he'd never made me any promises. I hadn't told him that I wanted to go away with him, or anything.

And perhaps that's where it might have stood, just up in the air, until it fizzled out, if Joe hadn't kept on and on. The moment he got into bed he said, "Mary, are you awake?" and then, when I didn't answer, "You're to stop seeing him, do you understand me? I'll not be made a bloody laughing stock. It you see him again, you'll answer for it."

I still didn't say anything, and then I was sure he was drunk, because he did something he'd never have done otherwise, he leaned across and shook me by the shoulder. I shouted at him, "*Let* go," I was so furious, and he said, "Oh, you are awake. Well, you heard what I said, keep away from him." I told him, "I'll do as I please." I was so mad with him, I didn't know what I was saying. "If I want to see him," I said, "I'll see him."

So he started shouting at me, "You'll not stay in my house, then, you can bloody well get out, you can get out tomorrow," and I said, "I'll get out *now*," and I jumped out of bed and turned on the light and I was beginning to dress—I really meant what I said, though I'd no idea where I was going—but when he saw I was serious he climbed down, he started saying, "Don't go now, you can't go out at this hour," and I said, "Why can't I? Are you afraid what people will think?" and he said, "You just tell me you'll stop seeing him, and there's an end of it."

"Oh," I said. "You're changing your tone a bit, aren't you? Right up to a minute ago you were carrying on like you thought I was going to run away with him, or something."

"No, no, I don't think that," he said. "It was just the shock, that's all. I admit I went too far. It was suddenly being told, like that."

Well, I didn't really want to go out, so I let him persuade me. I put my clothes away again, and when I got back into bed, he tried to kiss me, but I wouldn't have it, I just pushed

30

him away. He said, "Mary, Mary," and he put his arm round me, but I just lay there stiff and in the end he took it away and let me be.

For the next three days we hardly spoke to one another. When he did try, I'd just answer yes or no and carry on with whatever I was doing. I was desperate then, really, I was caught betwixt and between, I didn't know what to do with myself. I knew that Gerry was right now, that I didn't love Joe, and I knew I was in love with Gerry, but what was I going to do about it? I didn't think he loved me and I was afraid to tell him Joe had found out, I was frightened he wouldn't have any more to do with me.

I didn't see him the next week, I just sent a note to his lodgings, "Can't come," written in capitals, so it might have been from anybody. A few days later he rang me up, he said, "Why didn't you come to Seaburn?"

"I couldn't," I said, "something happened."

"Well, why don't you come today or tomorrow?"

"I can't," I said, "and I can't come next week, either. Don't ask me why—there's a reason, but I can't tell you."

"Has he found out?" he said, just like that, and I said, "Yes," and then I was terrified, I was waiting and waiting, and I had this awful feeling right there in my stomach, is this going to be the end of it, won't he have anything more to do with me, and then at last he said, "I suppose it was inevitable. I should have expected it. What is he going to do?"

And I was crying, I could hardly speak, I said, "He said if I go on seeing you he'll throw me out," and he said, "We've got to talk about this, Mary," and then it was as if I'd come alive again, I was so happy I started crying again, I hadn't lost him, I hadn't, and I said, "Come round now, we can talk here," and he said, "Don't be crazy! Come to your house?" and I said, "He's away, he's away all day," though it wasn't true, and when he did come round, I caught hold of him and I just pulled him up the stairs and we made love there, right on the bed; I'll never forget it, never.

GERRY

I THINK, looking back, my mother was right, Jarrow *was* a good place to start, but not just from the football point of view, from the point of view of life, as well. It was a sort of interim period that gave you a chance to make up your mind what you wanted from the game—and what you wanted outside the game, too. I was still very young, remember, and when you're young you don't know your own strength, you want to keep testing it all the time, and at the same time you don't know the *other* people's strength.

I'd thought at first English football was going to be much more highly organized, on the field and off it, and when I found it wasn't, I began to think, well maybe it's me that's wrong, maybe that's all there is to football, and yet inside me I knew that there must be something more. For instance, it wasn't only the training that disappointed me; I thought there'd be a lot of concentration on tactics, and the team talks amazed me. We had one every week, in the boardroom. Billy Wakeman would come in and he'd sit at the top of the table, and he'd say, "Well, this week, boys, it's Preston. You know who the danger man is, it's Finney, and Tom—Tom Johnson was our left-back—I want you to stick to him like glue, where he goes, you go," and Tom would say, "Yes, Boss," and then Billy would say, "Well, I think that's about all, then. Go in hard for the ball and don't let them settle down and we ought to be able to do it."

And I'd sit there, and I was too shy to say anything at first and I'd think, there *must* be more than that, he *can't* have finished now; what about *us* playing football, why has it always got to be how we're going to stop *them*—and anyway Preston have ten other players, what are *they* going to be doing while Tom's following Finney all over the field and getting pulled out of position?

Now and again some of the older players would ask a question, but on the whole it was just this, "Yes, Boss," all the time, as if they'd given it up as hopeless, and if there was any discussion it would be among ourselves, in the dressing-room, or maybe in the train. We had one or two players who did know the game, they weren't deep thinkers about it but they were shrewd—like our left-half, Sammy Connor, who'd played a lot of times for Scotland. He was quite an aggressive type and sometimes he'd disagree with Wakeman and even argue with him, but it would always end up the same, with Wakeman saying, "I'm the manager, you'll play it *my* way; if we don't get results, I'm the one that carries the can."

I asked Sammy once, "Is that all a manager ever does?" and he said, "He's there to answer the fucking telephone and buy the train tickets for the directors," and it was terribly disillusioning. I'd thought of managers as very wise and terribly experienced, weighing things up all the time and then coming out with great decisions, and here was this man who kept his job by sitting at his desk and saying nothing.

I'd got an idea that Sammy was wrong—at least, I *hoped* he was wrong—that there *were* other managers who really managed, like Chapman before the war, and Busby and Rowe and Cullis, but now I wasn't certain any more, and that was a terrible feeling at that age. You felt adrift, you were all alone, with nobody to help you or turn to. The thing that saved me then was just playing, because I loved it and nobody could take that away from me; in fact I sometimes think we talk too much about the game, because however much you theorise and discuss, these are only side issues. You go into football because you enjoy playing, and once you're on the field talk is useless, it can't do anything for you; you can't talk your way past a full-back or talk the ball into the net. But the trouble is that while *you* may enjoy it, the farther you go, the more you meet people that want to kill your enjoyment, because they're using football for their own purposes. Sometimes they don't even know they're doing it, and these are the most dangerous of all, because they kid themselves they're acting unselfishly.

Another thing at that time was I didn't find it easy getting adjusted to the life. I was used to being busy all day, and three or four nights a week I'd fit in my training, but now, after the morning was over, I'd have all the day to myself, and there was too much of it. I wondered what the other players did with it. I supposed they must be learning some sort of trade, like I was, but the more I studied them, the more it seemed to me they did nothing with it. There were one or two exceptions; Sammy Connor ran a little sweets shop and Dan Morrison, the right-back, used to coach in the schools, but mostly if you wanted to find them it would be in the billiard parlour or a café or a cinema, or if they were married, just at home, sitting in the house, and maybe helping their wives a little. This frightened me at times, because I thought, am I going to get like that, and if I do get like that, what happens to me when I have to finish playing? None of the others seemed to mind, and I must admit it only worried me occasionally myself; I was still very young. But even the older ones were come-day, go-day, they all seemed to expect to stay in the game as managers and coaches and trainers, even though it was obvious the game just wasn't big enough to take all of them.

The first season I was there, we had a big centre-half called Charlie Brixton. He'd been a first team player for four or five seasons, but now he was over the hill, he must have been 33, and he was playing in the reserves. At the end of the season, they put him on the transfer list at £5,000, and it must have been a terrible blow to his pride. He was a local boy, one of the real Geordies, he used to be a miner. He said, "Bugger them, I'll play for someone else, then," but no League club would pay that price, so in the end he said, "Bugger all of them, I'll play outside the bloody League," and he went to one of those little, local miners' welfare clubs. He said, "I'm all right, I'll play till I'm forty," and when he said it I wanted to ask him, "But what'll you do *after* forty?" but I couldn't make myself.

The lodgings I was in I shared with two others, both young

34

players, like I was. One of them was the goalkeeper, Reg Topham, he was a young Welsh lad who'd come to us from Newport County, very big and strong and didn't say very much, nor think very much, either. He could do brilliant things in a game, but *he* couldn't tell you why he did them, and he could do some shocking things, as well. In a Cup tie we played, the first one I ever had for Jarrow, we were playing Chelsea, at Stamford Bridge, and leading 1–0 with two minutes to go, when Chelsea got a penalty. Reg saved it, it was amazing for such a big fellow how he could move at times—he flung himself right across the goal and pushed it round the post—then just as we were waiting for the whistle, he misjudged a lob from twenty yards and it sailed into the net over his head, so we had to replay.

The other boy was Frankie Jordan, and he and I were more the same type, we both liked to talk about the game. Frankie was our right-half, playing behind me; he was a Londoner, and he had a Londoner's quickness, he liked to question things. He'd come to Jarrow from Brentford, in an exchange deal, and now he wished he could go back to London. He and Reg would go around a lot together, and I was really the odd man out. They'd go to the pictures a lot with one another, two or three times a week, and at least once to the dance-hall. I don't think Frankie liked dancing all that much, he went because Reg went and Reg went because he was sex crazy. He'd never talk about anything else; the ones he'd had and the ones he was hoping to have. Sometimes he'd say to me, "What's the matter with you then, Gerry? No bloody cobblers, or something?" and I'd say, "I'm perfectly normal, Reg, it's you that's bloody abnormal, they ought to pay you for performing and give you back your amateur status as a footballer."

"Well," he'd say, "I know you're bloody engaged, man, but she's in Glasgow now and you're in bloody Jarrow, you can't let her have it by post." Then Frankie would say, "He does it quietly, Gerry does; while you're talking, he's doing, Reg."

I suppose there was some truth in that, to the extent that

35

I've always thought sex is something you keep apart, it's something that belongs to you, not you and twenty different others. In Glasgow I'd been going with various girls, sometimes two or three at a time, but lately, before I'd come to Jarrow, I seemed to be getting tied up more and more with just the one; her name was Jean Crawford, and actually that was one reason why I was glad to leave. She'd got to the stage of talking as though it was all settled I was going to marry her, and I'd no intention of marrying her, I'd never even hinted that I would, and the longer it went on, the worse it was going to get. There never was a woman yet that didn't have this in the back of her mind the whole time, this feeling that sex is a bargain, she gives it you because she expects something in return, and what she expects is you'll give her the rest of your life. I couldn't see this, to me it didn't seem a bargain at all.

So I got away and now and then I wrote her a letter, gradually easing off, though, so by the time I got back to Glasgow, she was prepared. Besides, by then there was this thing between me and Mary, and that was a reason I was glad to leave *Jarrow* at the end of the season, because that was getting out of control as well, I wanted some time to think about it. Marriage was something I wasn't prepared for, in fact to tell the truth one of the things I liked at first about Mary was that *she* was married, then before I knew it, things had started happening that I never meant to happen, and it was out of control. She'd say to me, "Do you love me, Gerry, do you love me?" and I didn't *know*, I still didn't know, even by the time May came, and yet there was all this talk about marriage and leaving her husband—they had separate rooms now, and they hardly even spoke to each other. She said to me, "Joe wants to see you, he wants to have it out, I think you should see him," and I'd say, "I don't want to see him, there's no point, it would just end in bad blood." I wasn't afraid of seeing him, what I was afraid of was the position I'd be put in if I did, committing myself before I meant to be committed.

It was all over the town by now, and things were very

36

difficult; I knew I'd have to resolve it one way or the other. The boys were on about it all the time, "How's Mrs. Grange, Gerry? Was she good last night? Does her old man make you tea in the mornings?" I didn't like it because it was cheapening *her*, and whether I loved her or not, I respected her. I knew on the train, the first time we ever met, that I attracted her, and that her husband bored her. He bored me as well, he was one of those typical local businessmen, very dogmatic about things he knew nothing about, very intolerant, and if he wasn't on the Board of Directors yet, he probably would be one day.

But then the whole thing went faster than I bargained for, and back in Glasgow I tried to work it out, shall I stop seeing her, or shall I marry her, because there wasn't any other alternative, apart from leaving Jarrow. One day I'd decide one thing, the next day the other. I thought I *did* love her, but I wasn't sure. I knew she could help me in a lot of ways, she was intelligent and she believed in me, and she was an adventurous type of person, like I was. She'd take chances and let *me* take chances.

The day after I was back in Jarrow I had a note waiting for me at my lodgings from him, Joe, demanding that I come and see him. I rang him at his office and he said: "You'd better come over here and see me now," and I said, "No, you come over and see me," because I wasn't going to let him dictate what happened, I didn't want him sitting behind a big desk while I was kept standing there like someone he employed. So when we did meet in the end it was in a pub, we sat at a table in the corner of the bar, and every now and then his voice would raise and people would start looking round, and then he'd lower it again, which was one of my reasons for choosing there, because he couldn't afford to make a scene in public.

He said, "You'd better make up your mind about my wife, because if she's going to take up with you again, she's not staying in my house, I've told her that."

I said, "Don't you try and tell me what to do and what not to do, you may bully her but you can't bully me."

He said, "So you don't deny it? You don't deny you're carrying on with her?"

I said, "I'm not denying anything and I'm not admitting anything. I agree that something ought to be decided, but it won't be decided by threats."

He said, "It had bloody well better be decided. You're making me a laughing stock in this town."

And I said, "That's what hurts you, doesn't it? Being laughed at. Much more than whether Mary leaves you or doesn't leave you."

He said, "It's none of your damn business what I feel," but that had hit him, his voice broke, and for a moment I was afraid he was going to cry, he looked so sorry for himself. He said, "I'm giving you an ultimatum: I've told her, too. You've got a fortnight to decide, then either she gives you up, or she leaves my house. If she wants you, then you can bloody well keep her."

I said, "I think you're a very small man, and I'm surprised that a girl like her's ever stayed with you."

He said, "A fortnight, don't forget it, and you may be hearing something from your Chairman, too," then he got up, and left me to pay for the drinks. That was his parting shot, about the Chairman, but it didn't worry me at all, because I'd begun to realise, when the end of the season came and I was getting goals, that Jarrow needed me more than I needed Jarrow.

There was another thing I'd decided, too, after seeing the way they threw Charlie Brixton on the scrapheap; that I was going to use football, I wasn't going to be used by it. Sometimes I'd lie in the bath and I'd look at my legs, just a pair of ordinary legs, not thin, not fat, and I'd think, is this all I've got, are these what everything depends on, and it would seem ridiculous. Or there'd be other times I'd think; what if I break one of them, what if I get run over in the street? A doctor or a businessman or a lawyer, he can break both his legs and it wouldn't affect him, but if it happened to me, what would I have?

Mind you, I'd been very lucky as far as injury was concerned, just an occasional pull. I think it was a matter of fitness and quickness; if you turned fast enough, a defender couldn't clog you, even if he wanted to, and there were quite a few that did. I must admit we had one of the biggest cloggers of all in Sammy Connor; some of the things he did used to embarrass me, I'd want to apologise for him. He was one of these Jekyll and Hyde people, off the field quite friendly and polite, you'd think he wouldn't hurt a fly, on it so hard you didn't like to play against him even in a practice game, you were afraid he'd go over the ball just from habit. In fact in one of them I swerved to go one way and went past him the other and he tripped me. I got up and said, "For God's sake Sammy, I'm in your bloody team," and he said, "Och, I'm sorry, Gerry, for a moment I forgot," and I believed him.

In our first Derby game that season, against Sunderland at Roker, I thought the crowd was going to come over the wall. He chopped Len Shackleton in the first ten minutes, just went right over the ball without even pretending to play it, and one of the other Sunderland players turned to me and said, "Did they let him out of the fucking bullring for this game, then?" I said, "Don't blame me," and he said, "You're from his bloody country, aren't you?"

These Derbies were an experience, though, Roker and Gallowgate, because football in the North-East was a religion, the people that watched these games weren't watching for fun, they were bound up in them, and if their team lost, it was a disaster. They were biased crowds all right, like any football crowd, though they hadn't the viciousness of a Celtic or a Rangers crowd; they didn't get the bottles and the razors out. If we won a point at Parkhead or Ibrox, when I was with Third Lanark, and even more if we got two, I was always relieved to get into that dressing-room all in one piece.

This Sunderland game was one we won, and I got the only goal, just three minutes from the end. Frankie Jordan had the ball and was holding it, not seeing anyone to give it to, and I ran across the defence, diagonally, and shouted for it, pulled the ball down with my right foot, turned on it, and hit it with my left, and it went in where nine times out of ten it would have gone wide, or I'd have sliced it.

That week I was really popular, all the directors wanted to speak to me, and the people were stopping me in the street saying, "That was a great goal you scored there, kiddar." The local reporter on the *Argus* did a whole piece about me the next week, how if Logan could go on playing like this, then Jarrow could beat any team in the country, and this was the beginning of a great run like they'd had in the twenties; ridiculous stuff, really, because I could just as well have sliced the ball, or, for that matter, what if it had hit the bar?

He was a funny little man, a real Geordie, he travelled everywhere with the team and it was *his* team; when they lost, he lost, and what the Chairman thought was his opinion, too. It was always. "Yes, Mr. Steele, no, Mr. Steele," except for just once or maybe twice a season, I suppose just to keep his self-respect, he'd come out with a tremendous attack on the policies of the club, usually if we'd lost at home to Sunderland or Newcastle, and then there'd be hell to pay. The directors would ban him from travelling with the team and his Editor would go round to see the Chairman and for a fortnight or so, in any case, he'd be travelling on his own, very shamefaced. Then they'd make it all up, and he'd be with us again. I quite liked him really; he didn't know the game, but there was nothing vicious about him. He was in an impossible position, any local reporter is, because when you're that close to a team, how can you be objective? Every week you've got to face the players you criticise, so what happens? You don't criticise them.

I wasn't any too sure about the rest of the Press. In Glasgow they'd nearly all been fanatics, anything Scotland did was right and anything England did was terrible, Most of them were Rangers daft, more like fans than reporters, and they hadn't much time for a team like Third Lanark. By and large, though, I didn't get on with them too badly. But down here it was different, they tried to build a journalist into a god, and some of the journalists *believed* in the god. Great posters everywhere, huge pictures of them in the paper with headlines — Bill Bloggs Says and John Willy Tells You — and this impressed me at first, I thought they must be very important men, and how lucky we footballers were to *have* such important men writing about our games; not realising that it was just a question of their circulation departments competing, and that John Willy might disappear today and some other name you'd never heard of come up just as big in his place, tomorrow.

The biggest of all was Harry Roberts, of the *Daily Gazette*; he *was* sport in the north — or at least his paper said so — and even the boys seemed to be a little afraid of him, they'd say, "Harry's here today, you'd better put on a show for him, Gerry," whereas with most of the others it was, "Oh, *that* twat."

I'd see him now and then, he was a big man and he always wore a black coat and this black Homburg hat, he looked more like a businessman than a reporter, and he always seemed to have this expression on his face, looking around, disapproving, as if it was all a bit beneath him and he was waiting for somebody to do something about it. The first time I met him he said, "Oh, *you're* Logan," and I said, "Yes, I'm afraid I don't know who you are," and this made him furious, his face went red and he snapped at me, he said, "I'm Harry Roberts," but he'd annoyed me and I said, "Oh, yes, do you work for a newspaper, then?" and he turned on his heel and walked away.

After that he avoided me for a long time, and when he wrote about me it was in a sneering sort of way; "Apart from his goal, Logan was never in the game," or, "Logan must learn the ball won't always come to him, he must sometimes look for it." But in football these things don't last very long, you're meeting the same people all the time, and after a while, when I started getting goals, he began talking to me again, this time without being so patronising, and we didn't get on too badly. I've always found the best way to have friends in this game is to be playing well, when you're playing well, everybody wants to know you, and when you're not, they walk by you on the other side of the street.

This business with Mary and her husband was on my mind all the time, it was affecting my play, and apart from that goal at Sunderland, I wasn't having a good time. Billy Wakeman had me in his office and said, "You're playing badly" — which meant the Chairman had said I was playing badly — "and you know there's this story around, about you and Joe Grange's wife." I said, "I'm not interested in stories."

"Well," he said, "if you want to get on in this game, you've got to live a clean life. You've got to dedicate yourself. Leave married women alone." I said, "That's none of your business. Outside the club, my life's my own affair." He said, "If you lose form because you're playing about, it's the club's affair as well. Anyway, I'm warning you, it's got to stop," and I walked out of the room without saying a word. I'd got no respect for him, even then, but I think I knew he was right. To play football well you *have* got to be dedicated, otherwise games lose their importance, they're just things to be got over. I felt responsible for Mary, it was I who'd got her into this mess with her husband, so it was I who ought to get her out of it, only at the back of my mind I had no idea it wasn't all that simple, that in a way I was being manoeuvred.

Every time we met we talked about it and she said, "You don't have to marry me, Gerry, I don't want to force you into anything," and I'd say, "Yes, but your marriage is finished, what'll you do when you leave?" and she'd say, "Oh, I'll do something, I'll be a secretary or work in a shop," and this would make me feel worse. The thing was telling on both of us, whenever we met it was so hurried, we were always looking over our shoulders. Once when we were playing in London she came down and stayed at another hotel from the team, but even then you had the feeling someone was watching you, you had your eye on the clock all the while.

She'd say, "Do you love me, Gerry?" and I'd say, "Yes, yes," because I didn't want to hurt her, and all the time in my head I'd be asking, "Do I? Do I?"

And then one night, when Joe was away and we were in bed at her home, I suddenly thought, yes, yes, I do, I'll never find anyone who understands me like she does, I'll never find anyone I feel as peaceful with, and I said, "Mary, I want to marry you, darling, when he comes back you can tell him," and when I'd said it, she began to cry. She cried for half an hour.

HE got his way eventually, of course; he was really the first star footballer to beat the "system". And he succeeded in the only way that was possible—by having an alternative job that paid him as much as football.

"Job" was probably a euphemism; it was a Newcastle book-maker who helped him, paying him a subsidy until it was all over—when the club realised at last they were cutting off their nose to spite their face. The whole thing had to be done cautiously; a Football Association rule forbids players to be bookmakers, and the nature of Gerry's job was carefully kept amorphous; he was "consultant on matters of football," or something similar. Jarrow protested to the F.A., who said they'd given a decision on it, but when Gerry heard this, he said merely that he hadn't signed on for the club so he wasn't a footballer anyway; that as soon as he became a footballer again, he would give up any connection he had with book-making.

The bookmaker's name was Wally Dean. I had met him only once, and then very briefly; he was the parody of a book-maker, immensely stout and very loud, saved from vulgarity by his Geordie accent, the implication that he was a noisy, earthy, three-dimensional person first, a bookmaker second. While the battle was on, I spoke to him quite often on the telephone. "That's not right!" he used to say. "That's not bloody right. Take a man's livelihood away because he won't let a lot of daft buggers dictate to him! I'll tell you this much : he's earning *more* now than he was playing football, he's earning more without kicking a bloody ball. Now then !"

I thought then that Gerry was right, but that he was lucky. For being right wasn't enough, any more than it had been enough for a Jarrow worker in the depression years; you could negotiate only from economic strength, and if you were a footballer, economic strength had to be provided by someone else.

Thus it grew clear, over the weeks, that Jarrow City had lost, that they were delaying their surrender merely to save face. First came the equivocal public rumblings. "A discontented player's no good to Jarrow," then the concession that they would transfer him, but at the sort of price—forty or fifty thousand pounds—which nobody would pay, then the negotiations. Arsenal were meant to be interested, Chelsea and Tottenham and Chiswick United—Gerry had said specifically that he'd go only to a London club. I wondered a little how much his insistence on a transfer was caused by the wish to change his style, and how much by his urge to come to London. He seemed to me a smaller Napoleon, seeking fame in the East; triumphs elsewhere were merely those of the provincial. "I've had enough of the provinces, Brian," he told me on the telephone. "If I don't get to a London club now, I might almost as well stay with Jarrow."

It seemed he would go to Arsenal, then to Tottenham. Each manager in turn went to Jarrow, each in turn came away frustrated. "He wants too much under the counter," other journalists were saying, but I didn't believe that. Perhaps he would get an illegal bonus, but it would be secondary to him. "I'm in prison here, Brian," he said. The great thing was to escape.

And at last it was Chiswick who signed him, for a fee reported to be £28,000—still far short of the existing record—they were a good club a little gone to seed, which had won the Cup once since the war, and had twice come second in the Championship. I telephoned him to congratulate him and he said, "It's because of Lionel Stone, Brian. This is a man I can respect; I wasn't so sure about the others. He's a man with ideas—I'm very excited about playing for him, because his ideas are like my ideas."

The admiration seemed reciprocal. I visited Stone a few days later, at the Chiswick ground in Milton Road. Like all football grounds, on a day when there was no match, it lay as bare and dingy as an empty stage; there hung about it a tired air of anti-climax, like some abandoned desert city. On Saturday, the crowd would bring these shabby streets alive, but for the moment they were enveloped—dull brick, the twilight windows of sweet shops, cake shops, newsagents, grocers—in the living death of the suburban afternoon. Even the footballers, trotting and shooting on the pitch, had no reality. They were ghosts, who would exist again only when the steep grey terraces, the Stygian fastness of the grandstand, were full once more.

"Gerry can do a lot for us," Stone said. "He can play it how you want it; deep and clever or up and scoring. Maybe he likes to play it a bit too much at times, but that's a good fault, as far as I'm concerned."

Stone was a Cockney and he had once played for Chiswick himself, a centre-forward who had won three caps for England. Though he must have been over fifty, his hair was still quite black and still abundant; moreover, he still parted it down the middle, in the obsolete fashion of the nineteen-thirties footballer. His face was round; plump and a little tanned, though perhaps the tan was a mere question of pigmentation, an illusion, suggested by the fact that he still seemed such a vigorous, outdoor man, someone who *would* incur the sun. And this colour in turn set off his eyes, which were grey and very pale, eyes which despite their drooping lids never seemed to blink, giving them a quality of melancholy alertness, questioning and assessing.

"No wonder he didn't get on up there," he said. "Billy Wakeman was a twat when he was playing and he's a twat now they've made him a manager. They don't want one there, anyway; they want an office boy. I'm surprised that Gerry stood it as long as he did. He's a good boy, too : I know at least one of the other clubs was willing to drop him something, but he wouldn't have it, he said, 'No, I'm coming to you, Mr. Stone.' I'd like to use him the way Hungary use Hidegkuti, deep but coming up every now and then to score goals. Not stereotyped like Manchester City use Revie, just deep all the time; there's no variety. If you get a forward who can score goals *and* make the others play and you use him

46

deep but bring him up periodically—like Hidegkuti—you take the weight off him. Don't you? You give him a surprise value."

Those were the days when it was all Hidegkuti, Puscas, Koscis; we lived in the shadow of the Hungarian trauma, the casual crushing of England at Wembley; exotic names tripped off our insular tongues as easily as "Brown" and "Jones."

"Do you know his wife?" Stone asked me, suddenly.

"No," I said.

His pale eyes became contemplative. "I think she's good for him," he said. "She knows you've got to let him go his own way, but I think she can handle him, too, and she's as keen to come to London as he is. She was married before, she's a local girl; I think it's been a bit difficult for her up there. You know that sort of place; nothing to do all day except stay at home or go to the pictures. She told me a lot of them still walked past her in the street."

"Good luck to the partnership," I said, as I left.

"All right, boy!" he said, and shook hands with me. His hand was always firm and very dry.

And so the partnership began, for it was a partnership; there was an equality about it; they were, as Gerry said, "on the same wavelength." The new style was put into effect at once; perfected, I learned, in an infinity of practice games, and very soon it brought success. The team, becalmed for seasons in the mid-reaches of the First Division, began moving quickly upwards.

Gerry was the pivot, the essential motor, of this success; his translation to a new city, into a new role, seemed to have galvanised him. Everything he did "came off," the most impudent flick, the most ambitious pass, the most narrow-angled shot at goal. I could never see him play too often; the spare, graceful figure with its absolute air of purpose, its absolute mastery of the ball, its fascinating clairvoyance. It was as though one were watching a Grand Master of electric chess. As the Master might raise his piece above the board, contemplating his next, insidious move, so Gerry would pause a moment with the ball while one scanned the field, seeking

47

what damage could be done, weighing possibilities, seeing none—or only those which were obvious. And then, in a flash, the ball was on its way, to the place that was obvious, inevitable, the moment after he had kicked it.

When he beat a man, it was with a certain weary expertise, a shrug of the feet almost, as though this were something tiresome which had to be done to clear the way for the important work of constructing—or of scoring. He never lost his temper, never retaliated when knocked flat, tripped—even when he was kicked. He would just get up with resignation, give the muddied leg of his shorts an instinctive, disgusted flick, and trot away, ready for the free kick. Haste was the ultimate vulgarity; he seemed to move in a transparent bell of timelessness, to have as many eyes as a fly, pulling the ball gently back with the sole of his boot as a man came rushing at him from behind.

Sometimes a team would try to nullify him by putting a man to shadow him, following his every step; but in that case, he and Stone between them had devised an infinity of counterplots. Gerry might play as far upfield as an orthodox centre-forward, while Charlie Barker, his inside-left, dropped back into midfield; he might even spend a whole game deep in an outside-left position, controlling play from there, while his shadow wondered hopelessly whether to pursue him or to leave him be.

"You've got to have variety," Stone said. "If they know Gerry's always going to stand around in midfield like a spare prick at a wedding, it stands to reason they'll have somebody standing with him. Gerry's strength is he can do it for you from any position. He can make a goal from outside-left or score one from outside-right, so by the time they've finished, they don't know whether they're having a shave or a haircut."

The publicity, of course, was enormous. "Gerry!" cried the journalists, "Gerry!" and bore down upon him with those transient smiles, those wringing handshakes, which tomorrow might be bestowed on someone else. It was too easy for us all, I sometimes thought; we were always on the win-

48

ning side, forever hunting with the hounds. Each victory was our victory, each triumph ours to share. He was a journalist's man, though — a journalist's dream — fluent, talkative, extrovert, invariably good tempered. Before a match, one would see him surrounded by those smiling Fleet Street faces; afterwards they would be at him for "quotes," and he would give them quotes. He was the perfect player, brilliant on the field, endlessly complaisant off it.

Now and then, I would meet his wife at matches. She smiled and said little, overshadowed by his colossal fluency, his killing charm; a slim, pretty woman with red, curly hair, intelligent brown eyes and a soft North-Eastern accent. As Gerry talked, she would glance at him from time to time with contented pride. They had two very young children — it was she who told me this, not Gerry — a girl and a boy, and the club had found them a house in Acton. "Very nice," she said. London, too, was "very nice." She seemed to be sunning herself in the new glow of it all, too contented to feel the need to talk about it.

The other players admired Gerry and responded to him, both on and off the field. Only the inside-left, Charlie Barker, was a little sour; a small, jaunty Cockney whose fair hair, receding now, stood for the waning of his star. Three years before, he had still been an England player, a "character," whom journalists were anxious to quote; quick and brash and loud, his football cheeky and inventive. "Knows it all, Gerry," he said. "You can't *tell* him nothing. We've got to play it like this, we've got to play it like that. I said, 'Listen, my old son, I was playing this game when your mother was still wiping your arse for you in bloody Glasgow; don't tell *me* how to play, or you and me aren't going to get on.' Him and Lionel's like bloody husband and wife, though. Yes, Lionel, yes, Gerry; quite right, Lionel, I agree with you, Gerry; you'd think they was on their honeymoon. I admit he can *play* this game, I admit *that*, but I ain't having him telling me how I got to fucking play it."

Nevertheless, the two of them appeared to blend together, finding on the field the common language of two gifted footballers; Barker seemed to respond despite himself, like a great musician to a great conductor.

Chiswick were now the team to see; people were trekking west, deserting Chelsea, Spurs and Arsenal. Now and then, one heard echoes of resentment. The Chiswick directors, small men with small businesses, were being forced aside—or so they felt—and needed to assert themselves. Stone would drop a hint occasionally, remarks so evanescent that one felt they hadn't been made a moment after he had made them—"Of course, with this bloody lot. . . ." or, "If I bring 'em home the Cup, they'd wonder why it wasn't filled with whisky."

"You're top of the League," I said, once, "what more does any board of directors want?"

"You don't know 'em, boy," he said.

LIONEL STONE

I'VE always said football's an easy game if you play it the right way, and when I had Gerry down there with me at Chiswick, we *were* playing it the right way. Everything was simple and everything was progressive. The first time I ever saw him, I knew he was the player I wanted. We were at home to Jarrow, and as a matter of fact he had a bad game, he was hardly in it, until he did this one thing, two minutes from the end; he made to go one way with the ball, and then he gave this reverse pass. It caught our defence completely, they were standing around like a lot of constipated camels, and their outside-left, I forget what his name was, went through and scored. And I remember I thought, any boy who can do that is a boy I'd like to have in my team, he *thinks* this game.

I knew there'd be a bit of trouble with Charlie Barker when we started these new tactics, because for the last five years Charlie had been the one that everything revolved round; now he was going to be one of the revolvers. After a couple of weeks, I got hold of him and I said, "How do you think it's working, Charlie?" and he said, "Don't ask me, Mr. Stone, I only play here."

"I'm glad you do play here," I said, "because we'd be struggling without you, boy." He said, "What me? Don't be funny! I'm just there—I don't do nothing. I'm just on the field; it's Gerry Logan does it. Every time I pick up the paper —Logan. I have to look down the bottom for the team to see was I playing."

"Now look," I said, "as far as I'm concerned, there's eleven players in this team, and between you and me, only two of them are forwards, there's you and there's Gerry. He's getting the publicity because he's a novelty, you know that as well as I do, but if you weren't there working with him, he'd be in trouble; one pass, two passes, and the whole thing would break down."

"Thanks for telling me, Mr. Stone," he said. "I'm proud to be of help to the star of your team."

"Don't you see he's helping you as well, you silly little bugger?" I said. "While they're looking for *him*, you're getting the space, you're getting more room than you've had for years; and when he's marked, it's you that's running everything."

Being Charlie, he couldn't let it go, of course, he had to keep up his usual front, but I could see I'd got through, I'd got him thinking, and after that, things went better. It could never be perfect, because both him and Gerry wanted to run things, and in fact in a football team you can only have one person who runs things, and in this case, it was Gerry. The difference between them was that Gerry wanted to run things because he thought he could see how they could be improved, but Charlie wanted to run them because he was Charlie.

I suppose the team we had in those two and a half seasons played some of the best football an English club's ever played. It was partly the style and partly Gerry, only Gerry *was* the style, you couldn't have had it without him. Charlie helped, but he was secondary, and he knew it, he was a clever little bugger, and you couldn't kid him that he wasn't number two. Mind you, even I was surprised it started working as quick as it did; I was relieved, too, because I could turn to the Board and I could say, "There you are, look what you've got for your money." As far as I was concerned, he was a bargain at £28,000, he'd have been a bargain at double that, but getting them to spend money was like opening a tin with a toothpick. Jarrow wanted forty thousand at first, and that was terrible, they wouldn't hear of that, they just weren't interested any more, and I told them, "Look, they're only kidding, *they* don't want £40,000, or rather they may want it, they don't expect it."

In the end I would have lost him if it hadn't been for his wanting to come to me; Arsenal and Spurs were both ready to go to £30,000, but he wouldn't have them, and our Board said their limit was £25,000. I said, "I can get him for you for twenty-eight—that's saving you two thousand; twelve thousand on what they were asking originally. If you don't pay it, he'll go to White Hart Lane or to Highbury and we'll have him on the doorstep as a reminder. Anyway, what can you buy with two thousand pounds today? You can't buy a third team player."

Well, they hummed and hahed and had this bloody meeting and that one and in the end they said, all right, twenty-eight thousand and not a penny more, as though they were doing *me* a favour. As a matter of fact, the Chairman wasn't too bad, he was a clean old man and when you could make him understand what you were doing, he'd usually stand by. The niggers in the woodpile were Dawson and Pyke, they were both villains; the difference was Dawson looked like one but Pyke looked as if he wouldn't say boo to a goose. Dawson's hats were the giveaway. I don't know where he got them; whether he had them made specially for him or whether he'd bought them off a Chicago gangster somewhere; they had those great big broad brims, and the first time you set eyes on him you'd say, this is a villain if ever I saw one, and then you'd think, no, he can't be; if he was, he'd never allow himself to look like that—which perhaps was his plan, maybe that's what you were meant to think. I was told he came on the board years ago when the club was struggling, and he put in a few hundred pounds; he was a business friend of the Chairman, he had this furniture factory in Uxbridge. When he talked, it was like he was choking to death, he had this wheeze in his voice, and his skin was a terrible colour, almost yellow, so you'd think to yourself, *he* won't last the winter, but he always did, so there was times you'd think instead, maybe I won't last it.

Pyke was a little fellow, he was a retired schoolmaster; the first time I met him I quite liked him, I thought, *he* won't do you any harm. He was always talking about old players who'd played for the club and matches he remembered I'd had with them, and I thought, he's an old man that really likes his football. Well, he did like his football, because when

there was football he knew there'd be whisky and he wouldn't
pay for it, the club would. Dawson was worse—there was
more of him, so I suppose it stood to reason there was more
capacity. I reckon if either of them swallowed a match after
a home game, they'd go up like a petrol pump—and they
didn't do badly on trains to away matches, either. They'd
had five managers before me in the last five seasons, so I
knew there must be something wrong with the Board. I don't
know, all the managers may have been bad, but if you average
out they had a season each, that don't give you much time to
find out.

Anyway, we won the Cup my first season, that was one bit
of luck; we weren't a good team but the ball ran for us, and
we'd got Charlie Barker playing really well, then; I reckon
he was at his peak.

They were all delighted then, of course; marvellous, marvellous, we must give you a bonus, go along to the bank and
see what we've left you, and I went along to the bank and
saw what they'd left me—it was a hundred quid. I reckoned
later on that might have been their way of telling me I wasn't
worth as much to them as I thought I was.

After that, we had the usual ups and downs; you know,
why isn't so and so in the team, why don't you pick so and
so, until you say, look if I'm the manager, I pick the team, if I
don't pick the team, I'm not the manager. But you can't do
it too often, not unless you're getting results. They were
purring at first when Gerry came into the team, you would've
thought that they'd talked *me* into having him. Gerry asked
me early on, "What are they like, the Board?" and I said,
"You'll find out. You ask them for a new pair of laces." I
thought I knew them pretty well by then, but I can see now
that I didn't; I was, I don't know, I suppose I was naïve. I
knew they were full of their own importance, I knew they
liked interfering, I knew they were mean, I knew they'd
ponce on the club for everything they could get, especially
in bottles. What I didn't know was the lengths they'd go, not
when we were losing, but when we were *winning*.

If I'd been wise to it, I would have got the first hint one day after we'd beaten Everton, at home. We were a bit lucky, really; Gerry got a kick just after half-time, and it looked as if we'd draw until we got a penalty we'd never have got away from home. Little Pyke came up to me in the boardroom and he said, "Do you think these are really the right tactics, Lionel?" Well, I couldn't believe my ears at first. I said, "Well, if they aren't, Mr. Pyke, I don't *want* to find the right tactics, I'd rather go on being wrong—we've won the last six in a row."

So he shook his head in this way he had, just like a bloody schoolmaster, and he said, "Too much depending on one man, Lionel, too much depending on one man." I should have walked away, really, and not said anything, but I couldn't take that, I said, "You show me a successful team that hasn't had a key man. Arsenal had Alex James, Spurs had Alf Ramsey, Manchester United had Johnny Carey."

"I don't like it, Lionel," he said, "I don't like it"—you might as well have saved your breath—"Gerry gets hurt today, and the whole team breaks down. It loses all its rhythm."

"Any team that has a man hurt loses its rhythm," I said. "That's something you've got to be prepared for. That's football."

"We're too vulnerable," he said, "I don't like it. One man doesn't make a team."

"Well, I'm sorry, Mr. Pyke," I said, "but I'm afraid I think one man *does* make a team. You look at our team before Gerry came along, and look at it now, now we've got him." Mind you, I knew as well as anybody else that if Gerry got a bad knock and was out of the side, we'd be struggling, but as I said to Pyke, that was a risk you'd got to take. I'd built the style round Gerry, so no Gerry, no style; Charlie Barker could do a bit, but he wasn't Gerry. Pyke was typical of these people that learn a few phrases about football and never go beyond them, they mouth them without thinking what they mean : "One man doesn't make a team," and "Never change a winning side," and all the rest of that bloody twaddle.

Then Dawson started, he started at a board meeting, they

called me in to, he said, "Logan's a fine player, but we've got to take care we don't spoil him. There's forty other players on the books, we don't want to upset them."

I said, "Would Mr. Dawson mind explaining what he means by that?" and he stood there like a great gorilla and he said, "It's obvious. If a player thinks the whole club revolves round him, he's going to get too big for his boots. He's going to become impossible."

"Well, Gerry's not too big for his boots," I said. "I've never known a footballer so keen to learn about the game. He's thinking about it and perfecting his game all the time. Anyway, what player's been upset? You name him : nobody's come to me."

He backed down then, of course; he just said something vague about he knew what was going on. I said, "There's one or two moaners, I agree; you know who they are and I do" — I was thinking of Charlie Barker, of course — "but they'll moan anyway, they don't need an excuse. One or two had their nose put out of joint a bit when Gerry came, but now everything's fine, as long as you leave them alone and don't encourage them."

"I don't encourage them," he said, which meant to me that he had done.

"I didn't mean you personally," I said. "I meant anyone."

Gerry kept out of trouble after that, and we mostly went on winning, and I thought, that'll shut that up; but it didn't. The next thing that happened was someone brought me a copy of the local paper with an interview with Pyke in it. According to the reporter he'd said, oh, yes, he was glad we were doing so well, but he still felt worried, because it wasn't really a team effort; it was all coming from just one man. He thought we were working towards the right tactics, he didn't think we'd got there yet; but he was sure Mr. Stone would keep hammering away until we had.

Well, the first thing I wanted to do when I read that was ring him up and tell him what to do with all his bloody suggestions, and say that so far as I was concerned, this *was* the tactics, and if he didn't like them, he could find another manager. Then I thought no, that would be playing into his hands, and in any case, maybe he *hadn't* said these things; I knew what reporters could be like. The only thing was, they were nearly word for word the same as what he'd said to me. So I didn't do anything at first, I just thought about it, I thought about it from one angle, and then I thought about it from another. I'm bad like that, things upset me; it's ridiculous when you've been in the game as long as I have, but I don't know, I just expect people to behave to me the same way I try and behave to them, and when it's in your own club, even more so.

My wife started asking me what was the matter, she said, "You're moping about the house as if everything was going wrong, when everything's going right, what is it?" But I couldn't tell her; that was another fault I had, I suppose, keeping things to myself, brooding on them. I'd got so locked up in the game that I'd lost touch with what was going on at home; my wife would say, "Barbara"—our daughter—"wants to go to another secretarial college, she isn't happy at this one." And I'd say, "Does she? Well, let her," but my mind wasn't on it, I'd be thinking, can I get hold of this player, or, how am I going to get a decent price for that one? You realise these things when it's too late.

So I did nothing for a time, and then another interview came out—in the same paper—saying much the same thing, really; just after a Cup tie when we'd won at Bolton, and I thought the team had played about its best football of the season. I couldn't take it any more; I went along to the next board meeting and I brought the paper with me, I slammed it on the table, open at this page, and I said, "Would Mr. Pyke mind explaining this?" And old Pyke looked at it like he'd never seen it before and said, "Good Lord, am I supposed to have said all this?"

I said, "Yes, and it's the second time, too."

"Great exaggeration," he says, "great exaggeration. Just a few harmless remarks I may have let drop after the match, and they've made it into this. We ought to take their Press facilities away."

"Do you mean to tell me," I said, because I'd got to the point I didn't care now, "that you didn't say *any* of that? That he's misquoted you? Because if he has, he's done it twice, and we ought to have him along here and face him with it."

'I don't think that's necessary," he says, and he keeps looking away from me and down at the table like a crafty rabbit. And Dawson joins in and says, "No, I don't think that's necessary at all; you've got Mr Pyke's word, and that ought to be enough for you."

I said, "Can I have Mr. Pyke's word that he approves of what I'm doing, and that he'll back me up as long as we keep getting results?" and Pyke snuffles, "Yes, yes, of course, just a misunderstanding, just a misunderstanding." And I said, "Good. I'm glad it's worked out like that, gentlemen, because to tell you the truth I came in today prepared to give you my resignation."

The old chairman says, "Resign? Don't talk about resigning, Lionel, we're all delighted with you here, delighted, aren't we?" And some of the others said, "Yes," but I noticed Dawson and Pyke didn't say anything. I was foolish, really, because all I was doing was building up trouble for myself; as soon as they had the chance, they'd come down on me—and anyway, I should have known Pyke would never have the courage to admit it, he'd never have a showdown. His way was to go sneaking round behind your back, and scheming.

I spoke to Gerry, I said, "How do you get on with Pyke and Dawson?"

"All right," he says. "They come up to me and say, 'Well played, but you should have done this,' and I say, 'Yes, maybe you're right, maybe I'll try it next time,' because it's no good trying to explain to them."

"Good boy," I said, "you keep on like that."

"Why?" he says. "Have they been saying anything?"

"Only giving interviews behind my back saying that the tactics are all wrong," I said, "but don't you worry. You keep on doing your job out there, and I'll look after them."

Well, he was like me at first, he couldn't believe it, he said, "I thought this sort of thing went on at Jarrow, but never here."

"You've got a lot to learn," I said. "I've got a lot to learn myself. Just keep on being polite to them, that's all. They're both old, they can't go on forever."

But privately I took it a lot harder than that. It spoiled everything for me, everything we did, I had it in the back of my mind, those bastards will still be trying to stir it up. And I began to realise they hated Gerry, too, they hated him because he was exceptional. If he had a bad game — and he had to have one now and again — you'd see them in the directors' box and they were grinning, I'm not kidding, out and out grinning, turning and talking to each other every time he put a pass wrong or made a balls-up of a shot. In the board-room now, when I was asked to be there, they had a new line; they weren't criticizing the tactics; they were knocking Gerry, only doing it in a crafty way — by praising Charlie Barker.

Dawson would say, "I thought Charlie had a great game on Saturday, eh? He's a new player this season. Everything's Logan, Logan, Logan, but if you ask me, they're overlooking the man that's really doing it." And Pyke would say, "Quite right, quite right, I agree with you, George. Charlie's been a wonderful servant to this club. I'd like to see him given a little more acknowledgement."

Well, that was another trap for me, because if I said, "Don't you think I acknowledge him?" he'd say, "Not you, Lionel, not you, I'm talking about the Press," and then he'd dart one of those little looks of his at Dawson as if to say, "There you are!"

I'll give Charlie this, he didn't play up to them, he had about the same opinion of them as I did. In fact he'd take the micky out of them, I'd hear him say, "Thank you very much, Mr. Dawson," or, "That's very, very kind of you indeed, Mr. Pyke; I never knew you cared," and of course they had to take it, they'd have looked silly, otherwise.

I didn't tell Gerry any more about what was going on, because he was a sensitive boy and I didn't want to upset him. But it was wearing me down, I didn't know how long I could stand it, and then I'd think, if they're like this when we're on top, what'll they be like if things go wrong? As I said, I should have ignored them, but I couldn't, the thing kept preying on me, I couldn't get it off my mind.

GERRY LOGAN

LONDON was what I'd expected. It wasn't *all* that I'd expected, because it couldn't be, when you come to a new place you read into it all sorts of things you're hoping for, and they may be the kind of things you'll never find in any place. But there was the *size*, for one thing, you felt there were possibilities there, there was this feeling of space you never had in Jarrow, and never to the same extent in Glasgow. The great variety of people too; instead of meeting just footballers and directors and journalists, you'd meet people from every walk of life, band leaders and singers and film stars and boxers and all kinds. Then, you didn't have the feeling any more you were being watched the whole time, and this made it much easier for Mary, because I knew in Jarrow she always had this feeling people's eyes were on her all the while.

Wakeman had said, "You'll be a little fish in a big pond when you get to London," and I said to him, "I don't mind that, at least there'll be room to swim."

This feeling of being anonymous didn't worry me, because if you were anonymous, you were free.

We had this nice house in Chiswick, a club house, much more modern than the one we'd had in Jarrow, in fact I think it had only been built ten or twelve years ago. It had a garden front and back for the children to play in, and everything inside was very bright and very contemporary-style; the wallpaper, the decorations, and everything. But the main thing was I was happy with United, and that was thanks to Lionel Stone.

He didn't disappoint me, in fact the longer I played for him, the more I admired him, the more I found there was to learn from him. There was this contact between us, out on the field I sometimes thought I knew what was going through his mind, I knew what he would want me to do, as though we were using radio. It wasn't that he forced me to do anything, just that our minds seemed to work in the same way, it was a perfect combination. He wanted me playing deep, and of course I wanted to play deep. I wanted to direct the play.

We tried out this new idea in practice, with me there in midfield as a sort of lighthouse, beaming passes everywhere, and sneaking up every now and then to have a crack at goal myself, and it seemed to be working wonderfully. The only question was, would it work in a proper match—and the answer was yes, because the first match we tried it, we won by five goals, and after that, we were away.

We have a very good team, I don't think we had a great team. Lionel always thought it was the tactics made the players, rather than the players being brilliant and the tactics following, and I agreed with him. We had a strong defence before I got there, two very good wing-halves, Len Johnson and Harry Mould, and an exceptional goalkeeper, Johnny Watson, he was England's goalkeeper then and he deserved to be. In the forwards, there was only one I called exceptional, and that was the inside-left, Charlie Barker. I'd always admired him when I played against him, because he was trying to do unusual things, he was an unorthdox player, and so was I.

When I got there it wasn't easy at first, because he'd been cock of the walk a long time, he'd been used to running things, and he didn't like someone else coming along and running them instead. He was a typical Londoner, an East End boy, he'd got all this Cockney humour and bravado. They'd made him into a character and he had to be a charac·ter, both on the field and off it—it was expected of him. Underneath all the wisecracks, though, I thought he was a bit confused; he was thirty-one now, and a lot of his speed had gone, he was trying to adjust the pace of his game, to do things by thinking instead of just by instinct, and it wasn't easy for him.

The first day I met him he said, "So you're the bloke that's going to put me in the shade, eh?" I said, "I don't know what you mean. I've come here to play football. Nobody told me anything about shades."

He said, "Another of them clever buggers. All right, I know it, I don't need no telling. I'm over the old 'ill, you're the boy that's going to run things, now. I wish you luck, son. You'll need it with the shower they've got here; there's only two of them know how to fucking trap a ball."

"Well," I said, "I think I know how to do that, but as far as I heard, I was going to play with you, not instead of you."

He said, "I'm glad to hear you say that, Gerry, I can't tell you how glad I am, son, but I'm afraid there's other people here got different ideas to what we have."

Then things came off and I started getting publicity and it was difficult again, there were days I'd come in to train and he wouldn't speak to me; I behaved as if I didn't notice it. Another day, especially on a Monday, he might say, "Hallo, Gerry, I see you won again," and I'd say, "We won, Charlie," and he'd say, "You won, you mean, don't you? I read the papers yesterday and this morning and no one else was fuckin' playing."

At times it would show on the field, he'd have the ball and I'd be in a good position and I'd call for it and he'd just turn his back on me and go running on. Sometimes he'd lose it, but sometimes he'd finish up by doing something good, and then he'd come strutting by me like a little turkey cock, not looking at me, but as good as saying, Just leave me alone, I know what's best.

It was a pity, because I liked playing with him, he knew what the game was about, he'd take up good positions automatically. The other three forwards were different, one was a coward, and the other two would give you everything—but with them it was everything or nothing; flat out all the time, like bloody madmen. John Wilton was the outside-right, he was from Bristol; if you gave him the ball in front of him, he'd go through a wall to get it, but that was all he could do; he'd got as much brains as Barney's bull, and Dave Brent, the centre-forward, was the same. Mike Smithson, the outside-left, had got brains, but he used them most of the time to keep himself out of trouble. He was a London boy, like Charlie, and they'd been playing together for years, they'd a good understanding.

Sometimes Charlie would shout at him, "For Christ's sake stop poncing about on that wing, Mike, and get the fucking thing across," then Mike would sulk, and it might be ten minutes before he'd start trying again. He was very slight, that was part of his trouble, you'd never have taken him for a footballer, with all this black hair combed into waves; he must have gone through a pot of Brylcreem a week.

It was Mike as a matter of fact that introduced me to Sam Cowan, and that made a lot of difference to me, he opened a new door in my life—into the show-business world. Sam was a music publisher, he had an office in the Charing Cross Road, and he was Chiswick mad, he'd follow us anywhere. I'd wondered who he was, seeing him drive up in this great big red American car, and talking to the boys. He was a little, square, dark man, and he always had a big cigar in his mouth. I asked Mike one day, "Who's the little dark guy with the big car and the cigar? The one that looks as if he might be a Jew," and Mike said, "What, Sam Cowan? Don't you know him? Yeah, he's a bit of an old five to two, Sam, but he's all right. You want to go out with him one night; all right for crumpet."

Although I'd asked was he a Jew, I didn't mean it in a derogatory way. At that time Jews were just strange to me. I'd known very few of them in Glasgow and none at all in Jarrow, but now in London I found I met a lot of them and I liked them. They were individuals and they had this vitality about them and this generosity. I admit it surprised me at first, because to me a Jew had always been someone who was tight—and here were people like Sam coming along and spending pounds and pounds on parties for the players. He had this big flat near Marble Arch; he was married, but his family lived down in Bournemouth, and when you went there you'd meet singers and comedians and dancers and sometimes film stars, and I got in with them, we had a lot in common. They were individualists and I was an individualist, we both had this same attitude of wanting to be independent, only I envied

64

them in a way, because they were more independent than I was. They could argue about their contracts, and I was tied down by mine like every other player, with the same ridiculous maximum wage, which was seventeen pounds a week, then, and less in the summer.

I used to talk about it to this singer, Jenny Cunningham; she wasn't well known yet, but at that time she was making her way, she was singing with a dance band. I'd tell her what the position was and she'd say, "It isn't fair"—she went to football quite a lot with Sam and some of the others—"you're the best man in the team, they all rely on you, why shouldn't you get more?" and I'd say, "I don't know whether I'm the best man, but I'm the one that's supposed to keep the attack going. But you'll not change it, I'll tell you that; you're up against mean men, small-minded men. They're the people that control the game."

I admired Jenny, because she'd done what she wanted, and she was going to succeed, you could tell it even then. Her father was an accountant somewhere in the Midlands and he'd tried to stop her, but she wouldn't let him, she was a determined girl. She had this tiny little flat in Camden Town that she shared with a friend, it was barely big enough for one of them, but it didn't worry her, because in her mind she wasn't living in that flat, she was already living in the West End. I admit there were times when it irked me; I had just as much ambition, but I'd have to stay forever where I was, earning the same money—apart from these little bits I made on the side, from newspaper articles and maybe television.

Mind you, though I went to these parties, it was always tomato juice or orange squash; I'd never drunk, and I never wanted to; and I hadn't smoked, either. This was something some players couldn't understand, they'd think you were trying to be superior to them. Charlie Barker once said to me. "He's too bloody good for us, Gerry. Don't smoke, don't drink, reads books. You're too bleeding good for this game, mate." I said, "I don't try to stop you smoking, Charlie, so why do you want me to start?"

Charlie was nervous, he needed his cigarettes, before a

game he might smoke two or three, but as far as I was concerned a footballer's body was his instrument. You may be the best violinist in the world, but if you leave your violin out in the rain, you'll still make a noise like hell. So if your body's your instrument, why take chances with it? Make it last as long as you can and as well as you can. Some players say that a few pints of beer don't do any harm, because in training the next day they'd sweat them out in ten minutes, but to me that was only their way of being able to live with themselves.

Perhaps with me it was a reaction, I don't know, perhaps it was because my father drank a lot. He wasn't a drunkard, but as far back as I can remember, as a child, he'd come in and he'd kiss me and his breath would have this smell of beer; or maybe, if he had a job and it was a good job, it'd smell of whisky.

I wouldn't want my children to drink, either, so maybe that is the reason behind it. They were both very young when we got to London. Janey was eighteen months and Duncan was barely six months, but you could see already that one was completely different from the other. Janey was a thinker and Duncan was going to be a doer. Janey was a very placid baby, we had no trouble with her, she hardly ever cried in the night and she was just happy to sit there and watch what went on. But Duncan was more like me, he was all energy, nervous energy and physical energy, too; he was sitting up and crawling before we knew it, and in the night we'd have to get up to him four and five times; it got so I was turning up for training with red circles round my eyes, and the boys would stay, "Where have *you* been, then? Who have *you* been stuffing?"

Physically Duncan looked like me, too, he had the same very fair hair, but Janey was darker. I wouldn't say she was like her mother, because Mary isn't a placid woman, but she was more like her mother than she's like me, so that when she took sides with her I wasn't surprised, I expected it.

Mary was as happy as I was, coming to London. She'd come to the matches, whereas in Jarrow she'd stay away because she felt embarrassed. She got on quite well with the other

66

players' wives, and in the evening when we could get a baby sitter we'd drive into town and go to the pictures or a theatre, maybe. I suppose those two years or so were really two of the best in my life; everything was going well, the football, life in London, everything : I even got my place back for Scotland.

Not that I enjoyed playing for Scotland; the best part about it was being selected, there was no real fun in the matches. When we were young in Glasgow, we were always hearing about the Scottish tradition, how the only real football was Scottish football, ball control and short passes and keeping the ball on the ground, but as we grew up we found there *was* no Scottish football, or at least nobody was playing it in Scotland. Rangers were the worst of all; the great club with a great history, Alan Morton and Davie Meiklejohn and all the rest of it—and out on the field it was nothing but power and speed, big strong wingers and long balls, they were a team I hated to play against, because everything was physical, you never learned anything. And when you played for Scotland it was the same, because the selectors were as Rangers-daft as the reporters, and they knew even less about football.

I remember my first foreign tour, we went to France, Italy and Austria, and I was dropped after the first match in Paris; we lost, 3-1. One of the selectors came up to me and said, 'We're no' very pleased with you, Gerry. Ye were fiddling an' fiddling with the ball like one of these Continentals. We put you in to score some goals."

"Well, I'm sorry about that," I said, "but to me being compared to a Continental forward is a compliment, after that game. I wish I *could* play like some of those fellows. And as for fiddling, you can't give a ball when there's no one to give it to, and you can't score a goal when you never get given it yourself in a scoring position."

He didn't like that, he said something about English football having spoiled me, and as I was saying, I didn't get a game again that tour. But I'd meant what I said about the Continentals, and in Turin when I saw this Boniperti and Lorenzi, I thought it even more. They had this different rhythm, their whole way of running was different. Everything we did was so hurried, and everything they did so relaxed. I liked the travelling, too; Paris after Jarrow was fabulous, I couldn't believe a place like that existed, and in Turin I liked the friendliness of everybody. I envied these people like Boniperti who could live there and play football there; I suppose it was from that time I had it in the back of my mind, maybe some day I can play there, too.

About the middle of the season, Lionel Stone made a remark to me that surprised me, about not getting on with two of the directors, Pyke and Dawson were their names; he thought they resented both of us. I hadn't talked much to either of them, personally; Dawson was a big, surly fellow, he always struck me as being a pig, and Pyke was like a little weasel. But they didn't seem to interfere like the directors did at Jarrow; as far as I could tell, they kept in the background more, so that what Lionel said was a shock. Apparently it was the style they were against, me lying deep and purveying balls, and Pyke was having this campaign, dropping a hint here and a hint there in the newspapers; it seemed crazy to me because we were winning, and I don't think I really took it seriously, even though I noticed they were paying a lot of compliments to Charlie Barker, "Great game today, Charlie," and "Well done, Charlie—back in your old form."

The other boys didn't like either of them, even Charlie hadn't much good to say for them. "Two very good judges, Mr. Pyke and Mr. Dawson," he said. "Know a good footballer when they see one, they do; won't have none of them fucking ballet dancers like this Logan. Pyke come up to me on Saturday and he said, 'I liked the way you distributed today, Charlie,' and I nearly said, 'You must mean in the first half, because when you been in that boardroom at half-time, you can't see the bloody second half.'"

One of the local reporters, Tom Goodman, told me to keep an eye on Pyke and Dawson, he said, "They're dead cunning, both of them, and they've both got it in for Lionel, so naturally they'll have it in for you."

I said, "Got it in for Lionel? What, after what he's done for them this season?"

"Yeah," he said, "that's what I mean, that's why," but even then, I didn't take any notice. I thought that year we were going to be the first team to do the Cup and League double this century; there was only Manchester United that was near us in the League, and as for the Cup, I couldn't see who could beat us, home or away, provided we hadn't any injuries. We got through the first round okay, at home to Birmingham, then for the second round we had to travel to Milltown; they were halfway down the Second Division.

When we heard it, Lionel said, "It's a sod of a draw, they kicked their way through the last round and they'll try and kick their way through this one, only don't go saying I said so, Gerry, or there's one or two of them'll jump off the train before we get there."

So all he said in front of the others was, "Could be worse, lads. If we don't do it there, we should piss it in the replay."

The first minute of the game, I picked up a ball in our half, and their inside-left came belting in at me from behind and laid me flat. I got up and I said, "You dirty bastard, that's how you're going to play, is it?" and he said, "What's the matter? What are *you* bloody crying about?" The referee was yellow, he was a homer. He gave us a free kick, but he didn't say a word to the player, so right at the start they knew they could get away with it. We weren't allowed to play football! I had two men on me the whole time, digging at me whenever the ball came near, and when I went up and Charlie Barker went back to do the deep stuff, he was kicked as well; and once you kick Charlie you upset him completely; he's not thinking about the game any more, he's thinking about revenge.

Lionel came into the dressing-room at half-time, when there was still no score, and he said, "All right, lads, you've just got to play the referee as well. Don't lose your heads, don't retaliate; you'll never beat them at that game, and they'll never beat you at football. You've just got to carry on as if it wasn't happening, and if we only draw with them today, we'll tear them to bits in London."

But Mike Smithson had swallowed it already, Charlie was

more interested in the man than in the ball, and I got a kick soon after we came out again that had me limping all through the rest of the game.

They beat us by one goal, just a few minutes from time; their centre-forward came through on the right wing, he pulled a ball back across the goal, Jack Pollard, our centre-half, went in to head it away and was nudged, so it dropped right at the feet of their outside-left, and he banged it in.

After the game I was disgusted. Their bloody villain of an inside-left came up to me and wanted to shake hands, but I turned my back on him and walked away, and when the crowd saw that, they booed me. As far as they were concerned, they'd won, and this inside-left was a hero.

On the way back in the train, Lionel Stone hardly said a thing. He was a very emotional man, I knew that; this tough way of talking he had was misleading, and losing this match had hurt him. He was at a table with three of the directors, and I was at the table across the aisle, and I could hear most of what was said. Little Pyke was one of the directors, and I remember being astonished, because I almost had the impression he was glad. He was saying, "Ah, yes, that's all very true, Lionel, but I've kept on telling you, haven't I : we're vulnerable. We make it easy for them. A ruthless team like that, they kick Logan and where are we? We're out of the game. I'm not defending it, mind, I'm not defending it, we ought to report them : but that's the size of it, you can't deny it."

I was afraid Lionel might blow up then, but he just sat there, saying nothing, wearing this brooding look, and I thought what a little shit this man Pyke was.

After that, we went on and won the League, and Lionel was happy. We had a banquet at the Savoy, and he made a speech, saying everybody had done all he asked them, but he didn't think anyone would disagree if he said the transformation came when I was signed from Jarrow. He said he thought the tactics we'd worked out had proved themselves by results, and that anyway tactics weren't something you kept in a bottle, they had to be based on the players you'd got. He'd been given a lot of good advice, and he was always grateful for advice, but as long as he opened the paper on Sundays and saw Chiswick's name at the top of the table, he didn't think he was going to take it.

I saw Dawson and Pyke, and they turned and gave each other a look like a couple of conspirators. I thought then I wouldn't like to be Lionel, if things started going wrong.

CHARLIE BARKER

WELL, you know who made Chiswick United, don't you? You know who was the man behind their scintillating run? I was *playing*, yes! I mean, I used to look in the papers at the teams at the bottom of the report and see my *name* there, but otherwise I might have been playing for Leeds United.

Gerry was all right really, when he stopped rabbiting about how to play and how not to play, and teaching his bloody grandmother to suck eggs, and got out on the old field. I blamed Lionel Stone more, for letting him get away with it, he was more like the assistant manager than a player, and he wasn't even the bleeding captain, the captain was still Tom Roach, our left-back. Tom was easy going, though, as long as he had a quiet life, he didn't worry, so in fact there was two captains in the team, one that talked and one that tossed up. As far as I was concerned, I didn't listen to either of them, because I reckoned I knew the game a lot better than they did.

There's no doubt Gerry made a lot of difference to the team. Until then, I'd been on me own, I'd been on me own ever since Des Cochrane got transferred to Bury; they reckoned he was over the hill, and blimey, you should have seen some of the others they give me to play with. When I give a ball, I knew nine times out of ten I'd never see it again. With Des, you knew if you found a space and you called you'd get it.

Like I say, when it came to theory, I thought Gerry talked a load of bloody rubbish, but he could play this game, there wasn't no denying that, and if he got nearly all the credit, I suppose it was natural, really, with a new man. A lot of the others was impressed with him, they hung on every bloody word, especially the younger ones. Jimmy Rawlings, the right-back, he said to me, "Great thinker about this game, isn't he, Gerry?" I said, "Great bloody talker you mean,

72

don't you?" Still, when he saw he couldn't get away with it with me, he give up trying. I don't say all of what he said was bollocks, but three-quarters of it was; his trouble was he got carried away, he went on just for the sake of talking.

Once he said, "Frank Brennan of Newcastle's a bad centre-half."

I said, "I don't know. He takes a bit of fuckin' getting round."

"Yeah," he says, "but his distribution's terrible."

"A centre-half's not there to distribute," I says. "He's there to destroy."

"That's where you're wrong," he says. "If a centre-half just destroys and can't distribute, the ball simply comes straight back again. He might as well stay at home."

"Well, I wish old Frank Brennan would stay at home," I says. "We might get a few goals then, and all."

"You're too conventional," Gerry says.

"Look, don't mess about," I said. "What's a centre-half's job? He's there in the middle to stop things. He's a *negative* player. You want a big, tall bloke that gets his nut to everything in the air, and stops them coming through on the ground. In the old days, yes; the *attacking* centre-half — but the way you're talking, the best centre-half would be a tiny little bloke like Tommy Harmer that wouldn't ever get the ball even if he *could* distribute."

But Gerry went round and round and on and on, because you'd never hear Gerry admit that he was wrong. He was the one that knew; he was always right, Gerry. It was the same with crumpet — Gerry was different from everyone else. There was this singer, Jenny Cunningham, he met her at one of Sam Cowan's parties, I'd been to quite a few of them meself. He was a bit of an old Jew-boy, Sam, but he was all right; he was Chiswick mad, and he'd go anywhere to see us. This Jenny Cunningham, I'd fancied her meself, but when Gerry got on to her, he was on the crest of the wave, everything in the papers was Gerry Logan and the Logan Plan till you didn't know if you was playing for Chiswick United or Logan United.

Anyway, we had him on about it, 'Married man, two kids," and all that, "you ought to be ashamed of yourself." His wife was a good-looking girl, too; he'd met her up in Jarrow and she'd been married to one of the directors or something. But Gerry wasn't having none of it, he'd ignore us, he wouldn't say a word, or else he'd say, "I don't know what you mean."

I'd say, "Don't know what we mean? Don't you give me that, old mate, I seen you go off in her car, I seen you *personally*."

"She was giving me a lift home," he says.

"What," I says, "your home or her home?"

There was quite a few married men in the club at the time, and most of them went off and did a bit of screwing on the side now and then, but with them, they was open about it! I mean you could make a joke of it with them, you could laugh about it, they'd admit it, but with Gerry, he always had to be better than anyone else.

As far as I was concerned, there was only one man I'd listen to in our club, and that was Lionel Stone, because Lionel knew what he was talking about. Lionel knew as well as what I did that if Gerry had been on his own, he couldn't have done nothing, just the same as I couldn't do nothing on me own before Gerry arrived—it was like talking to yourself. Lionel could be wrong at times, like everybody else; I thought personally there was something *in* what one or two of the directors said, that basing so much of the midfield play on Gerry, you left yourself wide open if he was having a bad day or if they put a couple of men on him, or if someone came over the ball. Mind you, I reckon the one what put the idea into their heads was me, because our Board was a load of twots, like every other board; I never met a director yet in this game that knew his arse from his elbow.

The first season Gerry come we won the League, and we might have had the Cup and all if we hadn't been kicked out of it. The second season we did get the Cup and we was second in the League, a point behind the Wolves, we dropped a lot of points like most Cup Final teams do, between the semi-finals and the Final. We played lively at Wembley, all along the carpet, finding the open space—beautiful. We was playing the Villa and they couldn't touch us, we just walked round them. I scored one after ten minutes, a chip from the edge of the box that went over the keeper's head and skimmed in off the bar, and Gerry headed another before half-time. It was me that started it. I put Mike Smithson away with a pass inside the back—and in the second half Mike went through on his own and scored our third. It was lovely to watch.

I reckon I was dead unlucky not to play for England again, those two seasons, I certainly didn't play no better when I was *in*, but that's the way it goes, don't it? Selectors. *You* think you're playing bloody terrible, and that's when they pick you.

The next season, things started going wrong. Gerry got injured in the second match, it was an evening match at Chelsea, and at first they reckoned it was cartilage—I thought old Lionel was going to have kittens. But even though it wasn't cartilage in the end, they're terrible things, knees, and it took a long old time to get it right. I could see by the way Gerry was playing he'd got it on his mind, he was pulling out from balls he'd usually have got, then he'd get fluid on it and he'd be out for a month or two, and I'd have to do it on me own.

By Christmas we was halfway down the table, and we could say good-bye to winning the Championship: it was the Cup or nothing. The week before, we had a League match at Everton and Gerry got another kick on the knee, it was a question would he be fit in time or wouldn't he, and we knew he had to be fit because we was away to Manchester United.

We took thirteen men up to Manchester in the train, and the morning of the match, Lionel took Gerry to the ground and give him a fitness test. I was there with them, and he didn't look right to me. At the end of it, Lionel says, "How do you feel, boy?" and Gerry says, "Not so bad."

"Well, I leave it to you, then," Lionel says.

I'm still a great admirer of Lionel, but I think he done the wrong thing this time—if you put it to a player like Gerry or me, "Will you play?" we'll say, "Yes," and I reckon Lionel knew that. Gerry says, "I'm all right, I'll play," but in the first few minutes the centre-half comes across and tackles him —strong, not dirty—and that's the knee gone again. He went to outside-right, Jack Wilkins come inside, and I dropped back to do the clever stuff; but it was no good, really, it was hopeless. I wasn't getting no response. We held out till ten minutes from the end, then Tommy Taylor headed one in against us, from a corner, and I thought, that's it. Then suddenly I put Mike Smithson through, he cuts inside the back, the centre-half comes across and brings him down, and it's a penalty.

Now, normally Gerry took the penalties, he took them quite well, he had this sort of dummy which sent the keeper one way while he put the ball the other, but I thought, not today, Gerry boy; he was hopping about on one leg there like a bloody stork. So I picked up the ball meself, because it was me that used to take the penalties before Gerry come—I'd hardly ever missed one, either—but then what happens but Gerry comes hobbling across and he says, "I'll take it, I'll take it." I says, "Look, don't be a cunt," I says, "you can hardly fucking move," but he says, "Give it to me! I'm perfectly capable." Tom Roach, the captain, could hear what was going on, but he didn't say nothing, like you'd expect, and I wasn't going to start an argument in the middle of the bloody field, so I give it to him.

Well, he puts the ball down on the spot, he goes back five or six paces, dot and carry one, he comes hobbling up to it again—it was pitiful, honestly—and then he *pushes* it, just pushes it, straight at Ray Wood, their goalkeeper. We was out.

After that, there was a right old barney. Lionel didn't say nothing in the dressing-room, just, "Hard luck, lads," like he usually did, but once we got into the coach, them two directors, Pyke and Dawson, was on about it. Why did Gerry take the penalty, what did he mean by taking it, when he wasn't fit? Why didn't he let me take it? And Lionel butted in and he said, "He took it because them were my instructions." Dawson said, "You don't mean to tell me you'd instruct an injured man to take a penalty?" Lionel says, "Gerry's the penalty taker in this team. If he was fit enough to go out for the second half, I reckon he was fit enough to take a penalty."

That shut them up for a minute, when they saw they got Lionel to deal with, then they was on about it again, talking to one another very loud; they kept it up all the way to the station, and they was at it again when we got into the restaurant car: how it was ridiculous the way everything had to revolve round one man, how this was the last straw, this proved it once and for all, and I looked at Lionel, because he wasn't saying anything, and he'd got tears in his eyes. I'm not kidding, he was really crying. Then he suddenly says, he was sitting at the same table as them, "Would you gentlemen mind saving your remarks for your next Board meeting? You're upsetting my players," and after that you could have heard a pin drop, there wasn't another word all the way back to London.

Two weeks later they sacked him; we'd lost the next two League games on the trot, and Gerry was out for at least a month. Lionel called us all together in his office and he said, "Boys, I'm leaving you. They've sacked me. I don't want to go; you're the best lot of lads I've ever worked with," and then he stopped and he was crying again.

Most of us couldn't believe it. I said, "You're joking, aren't you, Guvnor?" but he says, "No, I was never more dead bloody serious, boy." Then Gerry says, "It's disgusting, Lionel, we'll put in a petition, we won't kick another ball until they have you back again."

"No," he says, "don't do that, you'd only do yourselves harm. I'm finished here. As long as there's this Board, I'd never last."

We whipped round and we made a presentation to him; it was a silver clock, a beautiful clock, with engraved on it, "To Lionel Stone, who showed us how to play real football. From the Chiswick United players, with gratitude and admiration."

When he got that, he couldn't speak, and I'd got a bit of a lump in me throat meself, I admit it. That's what football does, though. You get a good bloke like that and there's no room for him. Sometimes I've wished I'd never fucking been a professional footballer, honestly.

MARY

WHEN Gerry said he wanted to go to Italy, I thought, maybe this was the answer. Not that I really wanted to leave England, especially with the children being so young; it was more the idea of getting away from London. London wasn't good for him, they'd spoiled him there, and things weren't the same with us.

For the first year I'd liked it, it had been exciting, all the publicity and Gerry playing so well, and meeting all the different sorts of people, but then I realised I was seeing less and less of him; he was always out at this engagement or at that engagement, and he trusted everyone, he didn't discriminate. I remember him saying to me once when we were at a West End cinema, "Look, there's Sam, there's Sam, it's Sam Cowan!" and getting all excited, and I looked and there was this little dark man smoking a big cigar, and I couldn't see what was wonderful about him.

Afterwards he introduced me, and this man took my hand in both of his and held it there—I couldn't *stand* it!—and he said, "I've heard a lot about you dear, a *lot* about you; you must both come along to my party on Saturday night." I wanted to make an excuse, but Gerry said, "Oh, yes, yes, that'll be marvellous," and I said when we were alone, "Marvellous for you—I don't want to go, what am I going to do about a baby sitter?" And Gerry got terribly excited, he said, "You *must* go, he'll feel insulted, we'll *find* a baby sitter, what about Mrs. Nicholson next door?" and I said, "Her? I wouldn't trust her to mind the cat," and the end of it was he went on his own, and didn't get back till three in the morning. Later on I used to think, perhaps I was wrong, perhaps I *should* have gone with him, but at the time I didn't understand, my mind was full of the children—they were enough for me, and I couldn't see why they weren't enough for him.

I was having a lot of trouble then with Duncan, he'd wake in the night, and nothing that you fed him on seemed to be right, but Janey was as good as gold. She loved Gerry, it was, "Daddy, daddy," all the time, she'd sit on his knee for hours if he let her.

Several other players lived round our way, and the wives and I would drop in on one another; there was Jean Smithson and Janet Roach and Ann Wilkins, it was nice to have company in the day and it was useful for baby-sitting, but we'd got nothing much in common, really. We'd talk about our children and then maybe about the club and what was happening to the team, and that was about as far as it would go.

The man I liked was Mr. Stone. I thought he was marvellous for Gerry. Gerry needed someone to look up to then, and there'd been nobody at Jarrow, he'd just despised them, but Lionel Stone was more like a father to him. He'd come over now and again, and he'd stay and stay until two or three in the morning, just talking football. It was marvellous to see the two of them, really; their faces would light up, they'd get so excited, and they'd never any idea of the time. I'd bring them in cups of tea and they'd drink them down and not even notice; they'd never even know I was there, but I didn't mind. I enjoyed just sitting there listening, watching them, even though I often didn't understand what the half of it was about.

When we'd been in London six months, Gerry's mother came down to stay with us. He got very excited about that; everything had to be just right, we had to put her in a room where she wouldn't be disturbed by the children. I said, "I'm sorry, Gerry, as far as I'm concerned, the children come first. Your mother's very welcome, but if she's coming here, I'm afraid she'll just have to take us as we are."

I'd met her twice, once at the wedding, when she and his father and two of the sisters came down to Jarrow, and once in Glasgow when we stayed there a week, one summer. I still didn't really know whether I liked her or not, though I liked his father, he was a sweet little man, and so proud of Gerry. I got the feeling that after all these years he'd been squashed by her, even though to listen to Gerry you'd have thought his mother was everything and his father was nothing. She was a strong personality, and she was still very good looking; her hair was hardly grey at all, it was thick and blonde, just like Gerry's, and she'd got the same eyes as him, only hers were so cold; she looked at you and you felt she was looking right through you.

Gerry couldn't do anything wrong for her. She'd talk about him in this matter of fact way, "Of course, Gerry did this," and "Of course, Gerry's going to do that," so I could see where his confidence came from, but she made me feel uncomfortable, you felt like she was thinking all the time, who's *she*, then? No one's good enough for my Gerry.

He was always on about the way she'd let him be free, and we had to be the same with our children, but I wasn't so sure. He said, "She left me alone, she left me to be what I wanted," and I didn't say anything but I thought, maybe she left you alone because she didn't care. He was the favourite, though, there wasn't any doubt about that. The other four were all younger than him; two boys and two girls. Jenny must have been twenty-one then, Ian was sixteen, Peter was fourteen and Heather was twelve. I'm not saying she wasn't a good mother, but you never saw her show them any affection. She was so aloof, she'd sit there, I don't know, like the Queen of Sheba, with this little smile on her face, you never knew what she was thinking, and Gerry would come into the room and he'd kiss her and she wouldn't look at him, she'd just smile and put her hand up and touch his cheek.

Ian wanted to turn professional, too; he was in junior football then and doing his apprenticeship as an electrician. Gerry was his idol, it was Gerry this and Gerry that; will you come out and show me this, Gerry? Do you think I ought to do that, Gerry? But I was surprised, really, because Gerry never said much to him, and he was such a nice lad, I think in lots of ways the nicest of the lot; there wasn't a nasty thing about him.

Gerry would say, "Do it the way you think best, Ian," or "I've no time to come out now, Ian," but Ian wouldn't mind, he'd just smile and carry on, even though you could tell he was disappointed. I said to Gerry once, "Why don't you go out and help him? You know you're not doing anything," and he said, "He's got to make his own way; I made mine, nobody helped me, and it was better for me. If he pulls himself up by my bootstraps, he'll find in the end he'll not be able to stand up by himself."

I thought at the time, well, maybe he's right, maybe he knows Ian better than I do, but now I know he wasn't right, now I know that it was just Gerry; what he had, he kept for himself.

When Janey was born, his mother came down to Jarrow. She stayed for a week to give us a hand, and she and my mother were like night and day, they took a dislike from the moment they clapped eyes on each other. My mother said, "Who does she think *she* is, then, coming in and sailing round the place all high and mighty, giving everybody orders?" But they never had a quarrel. I think Mother would have liked it, but you couldn't quarrel with Mrs. Logan; if she disapproved of you, you weren't *there* as far as she was concerned. It got to a point where *you* didn't think you were there, either. I was that glad when she left I can't tell you, even though everything she did was just so.

And it was the same when she came down to London. She'd never criticise, but she'd walk about the house as though something was wrong, as though she could see dust all over the place, or I wasn't bringing up the children properly. Janey was frightened of her; Duncan was too young to understand. She'd say, "Is grandma coming? I don't like grandma!" and Gerry would get very angry, he'd say, "Now that's naughty, Janey, grandma's very nice, grandma loves you, you must love grandma, too." But I don't think she loved them, children know when people love them. I don't think she loved anyone except perhaps Gerry, and then only in her own strange way.

The first year we were down in London I was so bound up in the children I hadn't time to think, really, what was happening. Then gradually I realised I was seeing less and less of

Gerry, he was out for this thing or for that thing, speaking at a dinner or going on television or the radio, and I suddenly got frightened, I felt so lonely there with just me and the children. In Jarrow, everything's so close, but in the suburbs you're cut off from everything. And I said to Gerry one day, "Gerry, what's happening? I see you less and less, I'm on my own so much," and he said, "I'll come home for lunch, then, I'll stop having lunch at the ground." I said, "It's the evenings, more, you're never home, you hardly seem to see the children," and then he suddenly got angry and he said, "It's for the children I'm doing it! I've got to get out, I've got to meet the people, people that can help me. Now's the time I've got to take advantage, when my name's well known."

It worried me when he spoke like that, because I knew it must be that he felt guilty, and I didn't know what he was guilty about, whether it mightn't be he'd found someone else. Then one day one of the other wives, I think it was Jean Smithson, said something just jokingly about this singer, Jenny Cunningham, how she was mad about Gerry, and I said to him that night, "Who's Jenny Cunningham?" though I knew very well, I'd seen her with Sam Cowan, at matches. And his whole face went stiff, he said, "Jenny Cunningham? What about her? What do you want to know about her?" like a frightened little boy. And I knew then, I said, "She's in love with you, isn't she?" and he said, "I don't know what you mean!" And I said, "Yes, you do; you're having an affair with her, aren't you?" and he just turned straight on his heel and walked out of the house and slammed the door.

I sat up till quarter to four before he came back, and I was crying and crying. Now and then I'd think, it was wrong of me, jumping at him like that; I didn't give him a chance. But then I'd remember his expression and the way he'd walked out, just running away from it, and I thought, what was I going to do? There was me and the two children; how was I going to live? Because I couldn't imagine living without Gerry; Gerry was still everything to me.

Then I heard him walk up the garden, and his key in the lock, and when he came in he had his mother's expression. I called it his mother's expression, all closed and shut in; I was afraid of it. He looked in at the door, but not at me, not taking any notice of me, and I said, "Gerry?"

He said, "Yes?" in this very cold voice.

I said, "Where have you been?"

He said, "I've been walking" — we didn't have a car, then — "I've been walking and thinking about things."

I said, "What were you thinking?"

He said, "That it's terrible you don't believe in me."

I said, "You know I believe in you. I've always believed in you."

He said, "Then why do you throw things at me? You've no right to accuse me like that."

I said, "If I've no right, why did you behave like you did? Why did you run away?"

He said, "I never run away. The sort of mood you were in, there was no sense in talking to you. Who told you this, anyway? Who's been lying to you?"

"Nobody," I said. "I just heard. These things get round, you know. You ought to be more careful."

I suppose what I was doing, I was testing him, because now I wasn't sure; now I could see him in front of me, I was hoping that it wasn't true.

He said, "It's a filthy lie. Here, if you don't believe me, here's the telephone, you can ring her up and ask her."

I said, "You know her number pretty well, don't you?"

He said, "Do you want me to walk out again? If you carry on like this, I *will* walk out again."

I said, "What good do you think that'll do? You might as well be honest, you *are* carrying on with her, aren't you?"

He said, "Tell me who told you, just tell me who told you!" He was shouting at me.

I said, "You'll wake the children. What does it matter who told me?"

He said, "There's nothing; I promise you! Will you believe me or won't you? If you don't believe me, what's the point of us going on together?"

So then I couldn't help it, I started crying again, and I said,

"I don't know, I don't know, it was such a shock, hearing about it," and he knelt down and put his arm round me and said, "There's *only* you, Mary, you know that, *only* you." And I said, "I deserve it, I left Joe, didn't I? I didn't think about Joe," and I went on crying, but now I was crying because I believed him, and because I felt so relieved.

I said, "I was lying to you, all I heard was she was struck on you, and I had to find out, I couldn't help it, I shouldn't have come out with it like that. And then the way you behaved, running out like you did—I thought you must have gone to *her*."

So he said no, no, of course he hadn't, and I believed him because I wanted to believe him.

We didn't say anything about it for six months or so, and I never heard any more from anybody. But he'd changed, I wouldn't admit it to myself at first, but he was changing; there was something, I don't know, sort of *furtive* about him. Perhaps there had been before but I didn't notice it, because before there'd been no secrets between us. Now I kept wondering, when he was out, where he was, whether he was really where he said he was. Now and then I'd find myself watching him as if I was outside, as if I wasn't married to him—like I was someone else, and he was someone else, as well. I'd watch him talking to people, and the way they'd hang on what he said, when I knew he wasn't being himself; he was so much more than that. And I'd watch him with the children, especially when there were other people there, and he seemed to be playing a part. He'd have Janey on his knee, and read to her and play with the baby, but at other times he'd just play with them for five minutes, and then there'd always be somewhere to dash off.

I *knew* he was going on with other women; nobody needed to tell me. I knew it from what went on between *us*, because it wasn't the same, he didn't want me in the same way, it was always me now that had to give the lead. One night I couldn't stand it any more; I'd felt nothing, and Gerry had just turned away from me, to go to sleep, and I said, "I'm sorry I'm not Jenny."

85

He whipped round again and he said, "What do you mean?"

I said, "You don't want me any more, do you?"

He said, "What's wrong with you? Why do you keep saying things like that? There must be something wrong with you."

I said, "There's nothing wrong with me, Gerry, I'm just the same as I always was. I look the same, I feel the same. Maybe there's something wrong with *you*."

He said, "For God's *sake*, I'm tired tonight, can't you ever make allowances? I was training like hell all morning."

"Oh, yes?" I said. "And what were you doing in the afternoon?" And he kicked the bedclothes off and jumped off the bed, and I said, "Where are you going now? Are you going to run away again, like you did that other time?"

He said, "It's useless talking to you, you're abnormal."

"You're spoiled," I said, "that's what's the trouble with you. They've taken too much notice of you in London."

"Thanks," he said—he'd started putting his clothes on— "it's nice to have a wife that believes in you. It's nice to have one that's always behind you."

"Gerry," I said, "you know I'm always behind you," and I was that fed up with myself I started to cry.

"No," he said, "I don't know it; I've only got your word for it."

I said, "Please don't leave, I didn't mean what I said."

"Oh, yes, you did," he said, "*you* meant it."

I said, "Gerry, you know how I love you, you can't blame me getting upset when I think you don't love *me*."

"Of course I love you," he said, but he didn't even look at me.

I said, "And nobody else? You promise me there's no one else?"

"Christ!" he said. "How many times have I got to tell you? No one else. *Nobody* else. How can anyone convince you?" And he took off his clothes and got back into bed again.

I cuddled up to him and we made love again, and this time

86

I did feel it, but it still wasn't right, I knew that it wasn't right.

Sometimes I thought I'd ring this woman up and say to her, "Look, I know about you and Gerry. Leave him alone, or I'll murder you." Then I'd think, what was the use? I wasn't even sure it was her. It might have *been* her, at some time, but now it might be somebody else.

I'd see her now and then at matches, and sometimes I'd talk to her. She was quite attractive, but a terrible skin; even though she caked her face with make-up, she still couldn't hide it, and she was hard. She had this way of talking, "Oh, darling, this," and, "Darling, that," but it didn't take me in. Sometimes I'd watch her eyes when she was talking and they'd go flicking round, sizing everything up; she was as hard as nails. She'd gush all over Gerry, but you couldn't tell if that meant anything or not, because she'd gush over everybody.

Gerry once said to me, when we'd been talking and she'd asked about the children, and how sweet they must be, and all that soft soap, and wasn't I *lucky* to have such a clever husband, "She's a very warm person."

I said, "Is she?"

He said, "Well, can't you see it?" and I said, "No, to tell you the truth, I can't; I think she's insincere."

I was afraid he might get angry then, because if he did, then I'd *know* there was something between them, but all he said was, "You don't know her," and then he went away to get changed for the match.

I still loved watching him play, especially then, with Chiswick, he was so graceful. I didn't feel frightened for him any more; he was different now, he could control things. Whenever he had the ball, I'd feel this excitement. I'd think, now what? now what? and I'd be so proud of him. I've never seen anyone play football like Gerry played it then. But of course it all came to an end, it was much too good to last.

Gerry came home one night and he said, "They've sacked Lionel." And I said, "What? No!" because I couldn't believe it, it was Lionel and Gerry that *were* United. I said, "You're joking." He said, "I'm not joking," and I could see by his face that he wasn't. He said, "I'm leaving this club. I'll put in for a transfer tomorrow," and when he said that, I suddenly felt this hope—it seemed to come rushing up in me. I thought, if he leaves Chiswick, we can leave London, we can start all over again; but I tried to look very serious and I said, "Where would you go?"

"I don't know," he said, "anywhere. I don't care where I go—back to Jarrow, even—but I'm not staying here. They've victimised him, it's disgusting."

The next night, Lionel Stone came round and I've never seen a man change so. He looked *old*, his whole body seemed to droop, it was like a balloon with the air let out of it. I said, "I'm very sorry, Lionel," and he said, "Thanks, Mary," in this flat little voice; he didn't as much as look at me, where usually he'd be cracking jokes and laughing with you, he had a lovely sense of humour.

He said to Gerry, "Don't leave, boy, what's the point of you leaving? You'll get your knee right, soon, and things'll start clicking again."

Gerry said, "Not without you, Lionel, I wouldn't have the heart; I'll go wherever you go." And Lionel said, "Don't be silly, boy, I may not go anywhere." I said, "Of course you will, Lionel," I hated to see him like that. "Somebody'll snap you up just like that."

He said, "No, they won't; you don't know football." He sat there and he was *wilting*. He said, "When you're on top of the world, everybody wants you, and when you're not, they don't want to stay in the same room."

The next day Gerry did what he'd said, he asked for a trans-fer, and I admired him, because he was standing by what he believed, he was standing by Lionel. He said when he came home, "They won't give it me, but they'll have to give it me —it'll be like Jarrow. I talked to the Chairman—he said, 'It's out of the question, out of the question. I'll discuss it with the Board, but it's out of the question.' And I said, 'I'm sorry, Mr. Rawlinson, but there's only one thing that's out of the question, and that's my ever kicking another ball for Chiswick, after this season's over.' "

Then all the journalists started ringing up and coming round; some of them I liked, and some I didn't. They'd try and worm things out of me on the telephone, they'd say, "Poor old Gerry. It's a shame about Lionel Stone, isn't it? They were working so well together. Of course, you'd want to stay in London, wouldn't you?" I'd say, "I've no idea; we'll have to see first, won't we? They'll have to let him have his transfer, first."

Then they'd say, "Where would you like to go, Mrs. Logan? Back to the North-East again? Have you been feeling homesick?"

I'd say, "No, I'm perfectly happy, thank you," and then they'd say, "Oh, so you *definitely* want to stay in London?"

Then one day this little man suddenly arrived, he came while I was in the middle of giving Duncan his lunch, I could have killed him. I didn't want to let him in at first, he said, "Meeses Loggan?" in this terrible accent, and I stood there holding Duncan's hand and I said, "Yes?" He said, "Meester Loggan's not at home?" and I said, "No, he isn't." I was wondering what he wanted, I could tell from his voice he was an Italian and I was thinking, what does an Italian want with Gerry?

He said, "I'll tell you, Mrs. Loggan, I'm Beppe Valentini, I'm the agent from the Trastevere club from Rome." He was like a little pigeon, very plump, puffing out his feathers, and looking at me with these great, big saucer eyes, like he was pleading with me, "Do something to help me." I wasn't going to let him in, but then I suddenly felt sorry for him, I thought, oh, well, I can't leave him just to wait on the doorstep, and when he came in, he said, "For you, Mrs. Loggan, from the Trastevere club," and he took his little package out of his pocket and I unwrapped it, and it was the most beautiful little gold powder compact, embossed with this shield — it was the Trastevere colours. I was embarrassed, I didn't know what to say to him, because really I'd been so rude to him on the doorstep, then he bent down and started tickling

Duncan under the chin and he said, "He's a beautiful boy, Mrs. Loggan, how old is he?"

I said, "Nearly three," and Duncan started laughing, and Beppe was laughing, too, they were laughing together, and looking at him I thought he was like a big baby, himself. He said, "Let him come to me, Mrs. Loggan, children like me," so I let Duncan go, and Beppe picked him up and started whirling him up in the air and saying, "*Ciào, bimbo, piccolo bambino*, I'm your new uncle, I'm your uncle Beppe!"

Then they started playing on the floor with Duncan's wooden trains, and they were both of them so happy I couldn't help laughing myself, because usually Duncan didn't take to strangers, he was a shy little boy, and he'd come running straight to me.

Beppe said, "I think your son likes me, Mrs. Loggan," and I said, "Yes, you ought to be flattered, he hardly takes to anyone as a rule."

"Oh," he says, "I told you; I always get on well with children, you know? In Italy, everybody love children. If he come to Rome, he have a wonderful time."

I thought, come to Rome? and then the penny dropped. I must have been very slow, but I'd been absorbed in watching him play with Duncan that I hadn't even been thinking of what he'd come for. Besides, this was long before the time of all this Italian business, with this one going to Milan, and the other one going to Turin. And Rome was just a name to me, just something romantic that you saw on the films, I'd never even thought of going there, let alone living there.

I said, "You mean you want Gerry to come and play in Rome?" And he said, "Yes, Mrs. Loggan, Trastevere's very interested. I've seen your husband play many times—I think he's one of the best footballers in the world; I mean it, Mrs. Loggan," and he looked up at me from the floor with those great eyes of his. He was on all fours, and suddenly I thought he was just like a dog, waiting to be patted.

He said, "Mrs. Loggan, you'd love it in Rome; have you ever been to Rome?"

I said, "No, never."

He said, "We'd get you an apartment in Parioli. You know what it is, Parioli? The nicest part of Rome, the newest part. You couldn't live nowhere better. It's like in London, you've got Kensington Gardens—all around there."

I said, "It sounds much too good for me."

"No, no," he says. "In Italy, footballers are very important, the best players earn more than film stars."

Well, I still wasn't taking him seriously; it wasn't that I didn't believe what he said, just that it all seemed too good to be true: us living in Rome, with lots of money, and a big car, and an apartment that was all paid for, and servants.

He said, "You'd have a maid, Mrs. Logan, and someone to look after your children." But the thing that really was going on in my head was, I could get Gerry away from London, I could get him away from all those people that were spoiling him, away from all those dreadful women—not thinking, of course, because at times like that you don't, that Italy could be just as bad and worse, with all those sexy Italian girls.

Beppe said, "You think he'd come, Mrs. Logan? He wants to leave Chiswick, eh? He's not happy there."

"No," I said, "he isn't, not since they got rid of poor Lionel Stone."

"Ah, terrible," he said. "A very good man, Mrs. Logan. A serious man. I met him—you know? In Italy, I think he'd do well. And your husband—he'd do marvellous, Mrs. Logan. He's just what we need at Trastevere, a constructive player, a player of middle field. If he's unhappy here, why he doesn't come to us?"

"But we've never thought of going as far as that," I said. "We've never even talked about it."

Then Duncan started saying, "Play with me, play with me," and for the next half hour he had Beppe down on the floor with him, building with his bricks.

At lunch time, Gerry came back. He stopped in the doorway and I had to laugh, the expression on his face, seeing Beppe down there building bricks for Duncan. But Beppe came springing up, "Ah, Mr. Logan! I'm Beppe Valentini of Trastevere club of Rome!" and he grabbed Gerry's hand and started shaking it and Gerry still looked bewildered, but then he started smiling, with all that charm of his, and he said, "Oh, yes, how do you do?" but rather like he thought Beppe had to be humoured. While he was smiling he was looking at me over Beppe's shoulder, and raising his eyebrows.

But Beppe didn't stop talking, he said, "I've been telling your wife, Mr. Logan, Trastevere's very interested maybe you come to them. You've fans in Italy—yes!"

Gerry said, "Oh, you want me to play in Italy," and Beppe said, "Yes, yes, I told Mrs. Logan; we'd find you an apartment and a car, everything, all from the club! We'd give you a three year contract!"

Gerry said, "Have you spoken to Chiswick United about it?" and Beppe put on this special look of his, so even I knew he'd done something wrong, and he said, "Mr. Logan, what's the use of going to Chiswick when I don't know you're interested? They only say no to me, and that's the end of it. Listen, Mr. Logan; I'm here speaking to you like a friend. Not official; just to find out if you like coming to Rome?"

Gerry said, "It sounds official enough to me."

Beppe said, "Look, Mr. Logan—if first I know you're interested, I go to them. If I know you're not interested, I don't go to them. But if I don't talk to you, how do I even know they tell you Trastevere wants you?"

"Well, you go and talk to them," Gerry said, "and when you've talked to them, then maybe you can talk to me again. If they knew you'd been here, there'd be hell to pay, and you know it."

And I felt so sorry for Beppe then, standing there with this look in his eyes as though he was going to cry, and Duncan was there on the floor, pulling at his trouser leg and saying, "Play, play!" I didn't know then that Italians could turn it on, just like that, and the next moment, when they'd got what they wanted, they could be all happy and smiling again.

So I said, "Well, let's ask him to lunch, anyway, Gerry— he's been so good with Duncan."

Gerry said, "If he wants to, he can, but I'm not discussing any transfers," and Beppe said, "No, no! Of course not! No transfers! It's very kind of you, Mrs. Logan. You're quite right, Mr. Logan! I'll talk about it to the club!"

So I put Duncan to bed—he didn't want to go, he cried and cried, and in the end Beppe had to carry him upstairs—and all through the meal, Beppe kept talking about Italian football. I could see what he was trying to do, he was whetting Gerry's appetite, and eventually Gerry asked, "What sort of players have you got in your team at Trastevere?"

Beppe said, "Very good," and he flung up his little, podgy hand in this way he had, I was fascinated by how he kept using his hands. "I tell you, Mr. Logan—all we need is a player for the middle field. You know? We've got Nils Petersen, from Denmark, he's the centre-forward. We've got Rosario, from Argentine, he's the outside-right. We've got Valdar, from Hungary—he's the inside-left."

Gerry said, "Have you got any Italians in this team?" and Beppe said, "Yes, yes, eight or nine of them Italians: Rosario is an Italian, too, he's played three times in national team, his grandfather came from Genoa."

When Beppe had gone, Gerry said, "You want to go, don't you?"

I said, "I don't know"—and I didn't, really—"why do you say that?"

He said, "You'd never have asked him to lunch, otherwise. Why do you want to go? You want to get me away from London, is that it?"

This was the way he was behaving then, this was why I wanted to get him away. I said, "Who said anything about getting you away? You're the one who keeps talking about leaving Chiswick."

It had been bad enough with this trouble with his knee, because he'd got it in the back of his mind the whole time, even when he was playing, but since Lionel had gone, he'd been ten times worse, I'd never known him so unhappy. He said, "I don't like the way they come sneaking round the back. I don't owe Chiswick anything, the directors are shits, but I don't like all this hole and corner business."

I didn't say anything, because I knew him when he was in this mood; the more you tried to persuade him, the more he went the other way, and besides, when he talked like that, it usually meant he wasn't sure, it meant he was trying to talk himself round.

Next day he came back for lunch, and he said, "Have you heard from that Italian again?"

I said, "No, have you?"

He said, "No, I was just thinking—not that I'd go to his club, because I don't know anything about it, but I've always wanted to play with Continental players; they've got these quick reactions," so I could tell the way his mind was working.

Later on, he said, "If I did go to Italy, that might be one way of getting free from Chiswick. There's two reasons they might let me go there; first of all, they could ask for more money than they'd get here, and secondly they wouldn't have me in England, playing against them." Then, about a half hour after that, the phone went, and he jumped up and rushed over to it, and it was Beppe.

Gerry said, "Yes . . . yes . . . if it was that much, I'd *have* to be interested. I can't promise anything, but there's nothing to stop you seeing them."

So I realised what he was saying was that he *did* want to go, he'd changed his mind, and as soon as he'd changed his mind, he started finding dozens of reasons why he *should* go : that was typical of Gerry. He said, "We owe it to the children, it wouldn't be fair to them to ignore a chance like this. A few years there wouldn't hurt them, they're too young to go to school, and anyway you could have help there, it would be easier for you."

And he started daydreaming about all the things we'd be able to do. He said, "I spoke to Beppe again, and he told me I might make £10,000 a year, that's as much as the Prime Minister gets—and he says he knows ways that I needn't pay any tax on it. You could have a car of your own, and every summer we'd come back to Britain; we'd buy a house somewhere by the sea."

I knew he was letting himself be carried away, because that was Gerry, but I began to get as excited as he was, and I thought it would be wonderful there with servants and a big apartment and all the sunshine. Then Beppe came round again and started talking about the coast, how we could take the children down to the sea, to Ostia. Then he came round looking very sad, and he said, "Your President won't see me."

Gerry said, "Oh, yes, he will, I'll *make* him see you."

Beppe said, "If only you had your old manager, Mr. Stone," but Gerry said, "If we still had Lionel Stone, I'd never leave. But Bill Grogan is despicable, he isn't fit to be assistant manager to Bonnyrigg Rose, let alone to Chiswick." Then Beppe saw Gerry was getting very depressed, so he took him by the arm and said, "It'll be all right; I see to it! If our President comes over, then he has to see him."

But Gerry wasn't sure, and he kept wondering aloud for days, should he let Chiswick know he knew about Beppe, should he refuse to play at all, unless they said they'd let him go? He said, "They don't *know* how bad my knee is. If I say I'm not fit to play, I don't play!"

Then one morning the paper came, and it was all across the back page,

ROMAN CLUB WANT LOGAN
RECORD OFFER TO CHISWICK

Beppe rang up and he said, "Did you see, Mrs. Logan? You see what I did in the *Daily Express*? Now everybody knows!"

I was dreading the whole thing, because I was so afraid we'd have to go through what we'd gone through at Jarrow, all over again, and I think so was Gerry, though he never said so. But then Chiswick suddenly climbed down; I suppose it was the money, really—either that, or else they saw that Gerry was determined to go, and they knew from what had happened at Jarrow, it was no use trying to stop him.

Gerry said it was because they wanted to make a clean sweep; he said, "They don't want any more strong personalities in the club. They've got rid of Lionel and put Grogan in his place, and now they want to get rid of me. That's more important for them than winning championships."

The President of Trastevere came over to arrange the transfer. I didn't like him; he was a great big, pompous man called Molinucci, with a bald head, and this way of standing nodding to himself as though people weren't there. He didn't speak a word of English, and Beppe was buzzing around him all the time, like a little bumble bee, "Si, Presidente, no, Presidente." Not that the President wasn't polite to me, but it was like talking to a sultan or something. He made all sorts of promises to both of us, through Beppe; we'd have this apartment, and a new car, and the club would pay our fares home every summer.

Beppe said, "He's trying to build a great team, the best in Europe. He says with Gerry, we can win the Championship."

He was an industrialist, and he was meant to be rolling in money. I know he brought the most wonderful presents to the house, toys for the children and a crocodile handbag for me. Gerry said, "I like him, he's got a dignity about him. He knows he matters, whereas our directors aren't certain, they're only trying to matter."

I wasn't so sure; I thought that if he really knew he mattered, he wouldn't have to put on all these pompous airs. But I didn't say anything, because when Gerry gets an idea about a person, he hates anybody contradicting him.

We had nothing but reporters, reporters round, all the time. They'd sit out in the front room, waiting for Gerry, and I'd make them tea, then Gerry would come in and he'd give a sort of press conference. He loved it; he'd talk and talk, and they'd lap up every word; all about how badly players were treated in England, and a footballer was an entertainer, like any other entertainer, and ought to be paid as much, and how if *he* left for Italy it might shake the clubs up, because they'd be frightened of losing other players. Sometimes I'd be listening from the kitchen, and all I could hear was just the sound of his voice, going on and on, and it would sound so sincere that I knew if I was in the room as well, looking at him, he'd carry me away, too. But away from it, I'd start thinking; how much of it does he mean; words just carry him away, he means it *now*, but when this is all over, he'll forget, and be on to something else. And I'd want to say to him, "Oh, Gerry, why do you *talk* so well," though I suppose if he hadn't been able to, I'd never have fallen in love with him.

Then at last it was all arranged; he signed an agreement that he'd go to Trastevere at the end of the season, and then he flew over to Rome to meet them all, and have a look at the flat they wanted us to have. Beppe said to me, "You go as well," but I told him I was staying with the children.

Janey was so excited, she kept saying, "When are we leaving, Mummy?" and "Will we go in an aeroplane?" Then Gerry came back and he said, "It's wonderful, Mary, it's the most beautful place I've ever been in; when you get there you'll never want to leave. There's churches and palaces and the Roman ruins; you'd never believe they still existed. And the stadium's this great white bowl, with all the hills all round it, and the turf's like a cushion—you'd think it was never played on."

Everything was marvellous, he said; the apartment was marvellous, as well. It was brand new, in this big, white building, and nobody had lived in it yet. He said, "It's the best part of town, Parioli, where all the film stars live."

I said, "Has it got a garden for the children?" and he said, "No, no, it hasn't got a garden, but there's trees everywhere, and as soon as summer comes, you can take them all day to the beach, the sea's no distance at all."

He made it sound wonderful, but what was more wonderful to me was we were getting away. It was like making a new start, and I think he felt that, too, because things got better beween us, and I really felt he loved me again, and at night I'd lie awake after he'd made love to me and I'd say to myself, "Rome, Rome," and just the very name excited me, I couldn't get used to it all.

I was talking to Campello, the football editor, when Berretti came hurrying into the room, crying, "*Viene Loggan, viene Loggan!*" Campello absently threw a ball of paper into the air and hit it with his right hand; it passed over Berretti's shoulder, and flew out of the door.

"And the Championship's coming to Lazio!" said Campello, impassively.

"*Ma ora è sicuro!*" Berretti cried, his dark face racked with a believer's pain. "It's absolutely sure, it's come over the tapes; he signed this morning!"

"*Bravo Beppe,*" said Campello, with great calm, but Berretti flung an arm round my shoulder and said, "Tell me, Brian, what kind of a player is he? Is he a good player? Tell me honestly : yes or no? And if he's a good player, why do they let him go to us poor devils here in Italy?"

"He's a very good player," I said.

"But they're selling him!" he insisted, and gazed at me with that conniving smile which suggested that every man had his price. "He's been injured, hasn't he? He's got a knee that doesn't function! Tell the truth! *Siete mascalzoni, voi inglesi!* You're rascals, you English; when you know a player's finished, you palm him off on us and make money out of it!"

"He isn't finished."

"We know you," said Berretti, and his arm pressed heavy on my shoulders. "You don't keep promises. You promised to find me an English girl."

"I'm still looking."

"*Non sei serio, non sei onesto.*"

"It was the English who invented seriousness," said Campello, and went bouncing out of the office with his rubber ball walk, his amiable, plump white face—half fox, half bird—provokingly void of expression.

99

"Ah, Brian," said Berretti, grabbing himself by the crotch, "if you knew the satisfactions this has given me!"

And I thought, with confusion, of Gerry coming here, to this strange Constantinople of circus and comic opera, plot and counter-plot, faction and counter-faction. It was as though one's two worlds had been brought with sudden violence together, so that the amalgam was beyond prediction.

The news at once startled and delighted me. I had hoped he'd come, yet it seemed too remote and improbable; a fantasy. And if I was delighted, it was for my own sake; could I have talked to him, I would have told him to keep away from Rome; if he must come to Italy, go to Florence or to Turin or Milan, where football and reality still had some commerce. In Rome, it was surreal, in a surrealist city, part of the mad phantasmagoria of Via Veneto, Via Margutta, Cinecittà. It would fascinate him, but I wondered if it might not also destroy him.

And now, as the news spread round the offices of the *Diario Sportivo*, one man after another came dashing into the room.

"*Uno stronzo di più!*" grunted Franzini, the small and stocky cycling editor, "one turd more. But this time, an English turd. First the English screw us in the war, then back they come again and take our money."

"He's a Scotsman," I said, "not an Englishman."

"Even worse; the Scots are worse than the Genoese; he'll do nothing here, and screw us for a fortune!"

"But *you're* too much of a Fascist!" cried Campello, striding back into the room. "This is a man who knows how to play football! I saw him myself, I saw him in Turin!"

And behind him came the lean Mengalvio, high-domed and blinking owlish in the light, an eternal student, Chekhovian, who had found his way here to the *Diario* by God knew what strange streak of fortune. "Oh, Franzini! How do you feel, now we have an Englishman arriving?"

"*Sempre bene*," said Franzini, "*sempre bene, di vecchio fascista;* always well, like an old Fascist," and he marched out sturdily, with careful, comic dignity.

"They're nice, though, the Scots," Mengalvio said, reminiscently. "John Knox and Robert Burns, and all those Scottish missionaries with their fierce red faces and little pointed knees. *Simpatici.*"

"*Macchè!*" said Campello. "It was the Scots who invented football. They taught it to the world."

"No," said Mengalvio, one finger primly raised, "there I take issue with you. In Italy, it was the English. *Dr. John Kilpin.*" He stressed the words with a certain, narcissistic pleasure. "Of the old Genoa, with his knee breeches, and his little white cap. They wouldn't let the Italians play for them — and they were right! Football *should* be an English game, a game for gentlemen . . . in knee breeches."

"But you're too Anglophile!" Franzini cried, stalking in, again. "Fine, the English invented it, but it was the Latins who developed it, here and in South America. England has never won the World Cup!"

"And that's a good thing," said Mengalvio, more pedagogic still. "That, I find very sympathetic. The greatness of the English is that they already feel superior to everybody; they don't *need* to win the World Cup. The World Cup is for the lesser nations, struggling to assert themselves."

"*Che schiffo!*" Franzini said, and stumped away again.

On the morning that Gerry's 'plane was due to arrive, Mengalvio, a young photographer and I drove to Ciampino Airport to meet him, running the endless, coloured gauntlet of bill-boards; cats-eyes, Chianti bottles, Coca-Cola. Mengalvio talked all the way about Scottish explorers, wearing his small, pleased, pedagogic smile. I had known him for years — through correspondence, an occasional meeting — but it was only when I came to Rome that his formality, the mask of tense punctiliousness, had gradually flaked away. He was a *palermitano*, and was writing a monograph about English families in Palermo.

At the airport, they were there in force; fat Bandini, of *La Sera*, Morande and Castiglione, the clever Neapolitans, vulpine, desiccated Pavlovic. Did Gerry know what was awaiting him, what he was taking on? They surrounded me at once:

"Oh, Glanville! You'll be our interpreter! . . . Cìao, Brian! What sort of person is he?" Then we moved, a great phalanx of us, down on to the white tarmac, where the jet planes screamed, the jeeps buzzed to and fro like tugs at sea; and at last Gerry's plane swooped from the air, came silver and majestic towards us. The steps went down, the inevitable pretty, smiling stewardess appeared, the cameras pointed, and the first man out was Gerry.

How young he looked, I thought, in his neat grey suit, his raincoat over his arm, gazing out, sightless, like a man who has just woken from a dream; questioning, somehow vulnerable. With his bright, fair hair, his fresh, unfurrowed face, he could have been twenty years old, rather than twenty-seven; and indeed, the Italians round me, used to footballers who looked gnarled and middle-aged at twenty-eight, kept up a breathless chorus of, "*Che giovane . . . giovane!*"

As Gerry saw me at the bottom of the steps, he smiled and raised a hand and, descending, he was coming to me, a point of reference in an alien world.

"*Il Presidente!*" I heard, and now the President was among us, cleaving the waves like some splendid and self-conscious galleon, buoyed up by his own, supreme pomposity. As he came up to Gerry, he smiled and extended both arms in a splendid and paternal gesture, while the cameras pointed, clicked, pointed again. I wondered if he would kiss Gerry on both cheeks, and I saw Gerry's eyes move warily, but instead, the President dropped his hands, to grasp Gerry's, smiling still — a second tableau — and again the cameras clicked, recording this wordless moment as the President smiled and smiled, unable to communicate. Uncomfortably, he at last looked round — and there was Beppe by his side, with a fusillade of words, some English, some Italian — smiles, communication. It was Beppe's moment; they depended on him, all of them — he had made it all possible — and as I watched him; the tubby figure, the plump, revolving hands; I reflected on how far he'd come, since I had known him, the rise from Foggia, driven by the relentless need of the *meridionale*. When we'd met, he had still been an interpreter; now he was an agent, buying and selling players, and as an agent, he had had his ups and down; now hero, now scapegoat.

A year ago, he had come to me almost in tears. "*Brian: tu sei un uomo onesto.* You're an honest man, and you understand me. I'm a serious person, I want to do a serious job, but here in Italy, it isn't possible. It's not a sane world, like the English football world."

I didn't say that in the world of our football, there would be no place for him; for the ambiguous figure, half tempter, half trader, that was the Italian football agent.

"Granted his profession," Major Franceschi had said, monklike "Grey Eminence" of Trastevere, austere before the mirror of his austere barracks-room, "Valentini is an honest man."

"*Ciào, Brian!*" Beppe cried now, with urgent, automatic feeling; his eyes did not quite meet mine as he grasped my sleeve, exulting in the drama of himself.

Gerry was borne away from me in the throng of vice-presidents, directors, clamorous hangers-on; among them gleamed the Cyclops monocle of Vice President Guadenzio, Bacchanalian as ever, all things to all men. As they swept him off, Gerry cast a glance at me over his shoulder, in apology and mock-appeal. His whole predicament in Rome, I thought, was summed up by this moment; how little one could do to help him.

"*Ci vediamo, Brian!*" Beppe cried; I was to be excluded. I was irritated, but not surprised. The journalists came clustering round, the procession was brought to a stop, but Beppe waved his arms at them, shouting, "*Dopo, dopo!* There'll be a Press conference this afternoon, at the *sede!*"

"Glanville, ask him something!" the journalists begged, surrounding me, now. "*Quello stronzo Valentini, ci rompe sempre i coglioni!*"

"I'll see you later!" Gerry cried, from among his captors. "I'm at the Quirinale Hotel!" then he was gone.

"Doesn't matter," said Mengalvio, "we shall describe the scene; *opera buffa a Ciampino!* Trastevere always behave like this, they're a small club who try to act like a big one. In any case, you can telephone Logan later, for an interview." As we drove back to town, he talked about the death of Shelley.

Late that afternoon, I found Gerry in his hotel room. He came out pink from the shower, a towel wrapped round his spare body; he looked no heavier than the day I had first met him, at Jarrow.

"Well, it's comic," he said, "all these little men wanting to shake hands with me and be photographed with me, each one full of his own importance, puffed up like bullfrogs, with the President the biggest bullfrog of all : *he* had to croak the loudest. I still like him, though. At least here they're larger than life; at Chiswick, they were smaller."

"You'll find they can be pretty small, here as well."

"They can be childish; I can imagine that—like they were today, all wanting to impress themselves on me; but being small is something different."

"You're definitely coming to Rome?"

"Oh, yes. I think so. The contract's fine, I can't afford to turn it down, and I think I've said to you before, I like this idea of playing with Continental players. I think I can learn something from them, and I think they'll respond to *me*."

"You'll get kicked a lot."

"I got kicked in England," he said, with his young, irresistible laugh. "At least here I'll get well paid for being kicked." And one laughed with him, as one always did.

"Your mind's made up," I said.

"Why? Do you think I ought to change it?"

I shrugged. "I'd never join a Roman club," I said. "It's chaotic."

"But I don't have to stay with a Roman club. The contract's two years, it's a way of escaping from Chiswick. If I don't like it after the first season, maybe I could get them to sell me to a club in Milan."

"You'd be better off, there."

"But I like this city, Brian. It inspires me. I feel I can *play* football here. And anyway, it's a challenge. It's something you've got to respond to; if you don't, you stagnate. And if it's a hard challenge, then you gain all the more by coming through it. That's why I like Hemingway; this was a man who was always looking for a new challenge, even when he was rich and successful. He went to Italy in the first war because it was a challenge; he volunteered; he was a young man but he didn't *have* to go. And then in the Spanish Civil War, he wasn't young at all, he could have stayed there in Havana, catching fish, but he didn't. And in the last war, he did the same thing again, in France. If I was a writer, that's the sort of writer I'd like to be."

"I didn't know you were so keen on him," I said, though as I said it, I recalled a moment of surprise, when I had seen him carrying A *Farewell to Arms*—or perhaps it was *The Old Man and the Sea*.

"Italy meant a lot to Hemingway," he said. "I think it could mean a lot to me, as well."

He went back to London two days later, he "just couldn't wait to be back in Rome." And I, with my ambivalence towards the city and its warm, heartless beauty, trapped, myself, by the suddenly returning Spring, felt impatience with him. I knew, I supposed, what it must be, after the paper-strewn grey streets of Chiswick, Jarrow, Glasgow, to play in the Olympic bowl, beneath the green tumescence of Monte Mario. I knew—who better?—the marvellous, vivid force of the plane trees, bursting into leaf along the Tiber; knew the magic of beautiful women, half glimpsed in evening dusk down some cobbled alley; knew the great, white sweep of the Spanish Steps, throbbing in afternoon heat. But I knew, too, the deadness of it all, the corruption, the vulgarity, the insidious stasis, finding its microcosm in the football world. If he would not be warned, it was his own fault; but thinking this, I felt guilty, and wrote him a letter. He should reconsider; Rome was nothing but a beautiful old whore.

He didn't answer, nor had I expected him to; one might as well try to turn a besotted lover against his mistress. If I had written the letter, it was really to assuage my own conscience.

Soon afterwards, Major Franceschi invited me to dinner, his square, pale face, beneath his cropped, blond hair, loomed heavy above the table. The sight of it made me feel guilty, now, that I had written to Gerry at all. For Franceschi was profoundly in earnest : if he had the ear of the President, it was not through any designs on power for its own sake, but because football was his life and his religion.

The meal finished, he began the endless ceremony of rolls, breadsticks, diagrams. "You're not tired? I'm not boring you? You see, if one team plays *mezzo sistema*, then it's obvious the other team can break through only by counter-attacking, and with numerical superiority." A breadstick was moved. "This is the inside-left. You're sure I'm not boring you? Now, if we had Logan, I believe we should use him *here*. I talked to him, you know, through Valentini : *è un uomo serio*, a real professional. He thinks about the game. We had a most interesting discussion."

I could imagine it; less a discussion than a series of alternate monologues, each face now raptly animated, now blank in the facsimile of listening.

"These tactics I've been showing you require a man like him," Franceschi said. I thought that meeting Franceschi must have been a reassurance to Gerry, at once a point of reference and a guarantee. How could he know that Franceschi was merely a lighthouse, flickering with steady impotence in the centre of a madly boiling sea?

I stayed in Italy that summer, and it was not till August that I saw Gerry again — on his way to join the team in training camp, at Roveta. "I've been learning the language," he said. "Books and records. If you can't speak to them, you're cut off." The smile was more than ever exuberant, radiant with optimism; he clearly felt himself on the verge of a great adventure. "And Ronnie Nelson's here as well," he said. "That'll be two of us : with you to write about us !"

"Do you know him?" I asked.

"No, but you do, don't you?"

"I suppose so. If anybody does."

"Is he here yet? I'd like to see him."

We saw him that evening, in Piazza del Popolo. It was full summer, and the Villa Borghese towered deep green above the square; green, while the stone of the palaces was a warm and marvellous pink, as though it were pregnant with sun, had been storing up the sun each summer, so that if one pierced a wall, it would give out at once an awful, scorching heat, the accumulation of the centuries.

But Nelson came impervious to it all, came jogging compact across the cobbles with his fit man's walk, his pleased enigma of a smile, his smooth-shaved, short-haired neatness, which yet fell always short of elegance, like a chucker-out, wearing a good suit. He had been in Italy for five years, now, managing this club and that. It was the measure of his contemptuous insularity that he still spoke broken Italian, using infinitives for every verb—*lui parlare me lo stesso*—though he could understand everything they said to him.

"Hallo!" he said, and shook hands with Gerry with guarded cordiality. "Welcome to Rome!"

I noticed he'd assumed his "good," defensive accent; the o's very careful and closed, each word a rejection of Sheffield. Characteristically, he wore a lightweight suit, though Gerry and I were in shirtsleeves—and characteristically, the jacket was buttoned up. In winter, he would put on his trench-coat and draw the belt tight; tight against the world.

"I'm sorry you're not with our club," Gerry said.

"Oh, Trastevere's all right, you know," said Nelson. The smile persisted, but his eyes moved privately away, as though he had a thousand reservations. "They wanted me to join them, but I preferred Flaminio; they made me a higher offer."

"That's six good reasons, anyway," said Gerry.

"Cardoni's quite a good trainer, though, you know," said Nelson, damning him with his secret smile.

"I've met him," Gerry said. "He seemed very honest and straightforward."

"Oh, yes," said Nelson, "he's straightforward."

The conversation died a moment, Nelson happy and insulated in the silence.

"And what sort of team have Trastevere got?" Gerry asked.

"Quite good," said Nelson. "There's a good, young right-back called Monicello; you can give him my best wishes, when you see him. He was one of my players at Florence; I'd work with him for hours on his left foot."

"Are they easy to work with, then, Italian players?"

"Oh, yes—if you know how to handle them. You can get anything you want, if you handle them properly. They get jealous of each other; they're like children. They want to feel you're on their side. Once they think that, they'll do anything for you."

They would, indeed, do anything for *him*. That was his secret, the winning of their confidence; he was captain and father to them.

"Do they try hard?" Gerry asked.

"If you keep them up to it. If you can keep them away from women. They're all after women—even the married ones. Half of them only marry for physical. They none of them trust their wives; when we're away from home, they're on the telephone to them the whole time."

"So if the goalkeeper throws in three," said Gerry, "you'll know that his number was engaged."

Nelson did not laugh, he merely continued to smile, and the smile said, "I know more than you do."

"You'll be surprised by some things here," he said. "Don't believe everything they tell you. It isn't England, you know."

"That's why I'm coming," said Gerry.

Afterwards, Nelson left us, for the flat which was his rampart and his refuge; Gerry and I walked up Via Della Croce. It was twilight now, and the dusk had about it the warm, thick, palpability of the Roman summer evening. We walked slowly. Once, a girl brushed by us, like a perfumed miracle, and Gerry's head turned very sharply, then sharply turned back again, without suspending conversation. There was a covertness to it; suddenly he'd told me something which I had not known.

"There's some marvellous women here," I said, casually, but he ignored me, as I'd thought he would, talking on about football, about Nelson.

"He's a very *closed* man," he said.

"Very."

"I'm amazed he's had success here, with that kind of personality."

"He's nobody's fool," I said. "He understands them, on a certain level."

"But how *can* he, when they're uninhibited, and he's so cautious?"

"You'd have to see him," I said.

See him, compact and impervious, still smiling; a rock round whom the players could gather for solace. His calm, which to me seemed too good to be true, to them was an authentic reassurance. "Meester, the directors want to fine me. . . . Meester, I'm having trouble with my knee. . . Meester, I need more money." He stood by them; he was a player's friend; more than a friend, a father.

"How do *you* think I'll do?" asked Gerry.

He stopped suddenly, at the corner of Mario de' Fiori, turning towards me, his face tense and questioning in the darkness.

"Very well," I said.

"Be honest with me. Don't evade it. You still think I've done the wrong thing, don't you?"

"I never thought you wouldn't do well here. You've as much ability as any of them. It's a question of how much one's *allowed* to do."

"Allowed?"

"By the other side, by your own directors and players. By the public and the Press and the manager."

"A good player finds his own level."

"In England, yes," I said, then felt I had gone too far.

"Not just in England. Anywhere."

And we walked on, across Piazza di Spagna, where for the moment he could pass in anonymity.

The season began three weeks later with a friendly; Trastevere and Inter, at the Olympic Stadium; green trees, green seats, white marble, August sunshine and shadow. There must have been sixty thousand spectators there, and they had come to see Gerry, their new Messiah.

It was strange to watch his progress from the tunnel; one was used to him coming loping eagerly on to the field, coltish almost, his sleeves rolled to the elbow, and here he was, constrained to the ambling, ruminative entry of the Italian footballer, conditioned by slow climbs from the shelter of underground dressing-rooms. And instead of the blue Chiswick jersey, with its dashing, open collar, he wore the green, Continental jersey of Trastevere, with its high, hooped neck, its sleeves that reached tightly to the wrists. His head was bent, as though he himself were conscious of the metamorphosis, and when the crowd cheered him, he did not look up.

The game began as an Italian game will, slowly, with little progress, the referee's whistle shrilly, maddeningly intruding. When the ball came to Gerry for the first time, in the centre circle, he stood with it a moment, as if mocking the lethargy of the game, then, as an opponent moved towards him, he bent to the left, moved the ball clear with the outside of his right foot, took it on a pace, then sent it to his winger. The crowd came gleefully to life, loud with surprise, and a moment later, Gerry had the ball again, chipping it perfectly, this time, to his centre-forward, and I felt warm with vicarious pride, sharing the moment.

The match went on in a sustained hubbub of anticipation, the crowd waiting, wanting to cheer as soon as he had the ball, just as they would have been ready to crucify him, I thought, had things gone otherwise. He was lucky to begin in a friendly game, free from the brute pressures of the Championship, in which all was caution and destruction, the one unforgiveable sin, defeat.

He was playing, I noticed, a much more rigorously "deep" game than he had played with Chiswick, always the purveyor rather than the striker, the *giocatore del centro campo*, longed for by every club in the peninsula. Once, towards the end of the first half, as though impatient of forever initiating, never concluding, he suddenly raced forward, shouted for the ball to Petersen, the Danish centre-forward, got it and, instead of passing, tricked a man, another then — inside the area — let fly for goal, with his right foot. The goalkeeper, black jerseyed, flung himself across the goal, a puma leaping from a tree, but the shot was too fast for him, too well placed; he was saved only by its hitting the underside of the crossbar and bouncing down where he, on the ground, was able to clutch it to his breast, like a thankful mother. Again, the crowd thundered for Gerry—"*Bravo Loggan! Bravo Loggan!*" and Franzini, sitting beside me, turned to say, with a wry narrowing of the eye, "*Effettivamente, sa giocare, questo inglese;* he knows how to play, this Englishman."

"Scotsman."

"Englishman, Scotsman, it's all the same."

In the second half, the game, like so many Italian games, faded tediously away. Gerry himself looked tired. Once, when he crossed the touchline on our side of the field, to retrieve the ball for a throw in, I glimpsed his face, red with heat and effort, as I had never seen it in England.

Afterwards, in the tiled dressing-room, there was a dark island of sweat across the chest of his green jersey.

"Hot out there," I said.

"Hot?" he repeated. "It's like running ninety minutes in a Turkish bath."

"What did he say, Glanville?" asked the journalists, clustering round, pencils greedily raised.

"That it's hot," I said, and asked him, "Did you enjoy it?"

"You can't enjoy it, in that heat. It was *interesting*. It's a different type of football."

"Oh, Brian! Ask him who he thought was the best Trastevere player!"

"They were all good," he said, smiling.

"Ask him which is better; English football or Italian football?"

"Say that I'll tell him in six months."

"E *un tipo*," one of them said, "he's a character," and another, "Ask him how much Trastevere are paying him."

"I'll tell him if he'll tell me how much his paper is paying him."

They laughed at this, and went away to talk to other

players as they came out of the bathroom, absently fingering their genitals. What did *they* think of Logan?

In a corner of the dressing-room stood the President, a remote smile of pleasure on his face, his great stomach jutting like a prow. Major Franceschi, his Grey Eminence, stood solid by his side, whispering now and then in his ear, with great intensity, as a Grey Eminence should, but the President barely paid attention to him, such was his euphoria, merely gave him a faint, occasional nod, immersed as he was in his reverie of success, the Championship, the adoring gratitude of the people.

Cardoni, the manager, stood by him, too, mute but restless, as though waiting only to be dismissed the presence; a bald, brown, middle-aged man, with a square, foreshortened chin, a jutting underlip, which gave him a look of rabbit-like uncertainty; it was the face of a demoralised boxer.

At last, the President took his hand, spoke to him, and he moved gratefully away; far away, to the opposite corner of the dressing-room, where the journalists found him, closed round him, and protected him.

The scene, I thought, lacked only Beppe, and then he, too, was with us, erupting through the door like some plump, belated herald. "Oh! *Gerry!* Wonderful! You were wonderful! Eh, Brian? Wasn't he wonderful?" And he took Gerry's hand in both his, stared rapturously into his eyes, holding and prolonging the moment, one more tableau: it was I! I brought him here!

"Thanks," said Gerry. His eyes met mine, glimmered briefly with amusement, then returned to Beppe.

"*Non l'ho detto?*" cried Beppe, to the journalists. "Didn't I tell you? Now you've seen for yourselves! He's a star, *un fuori classe!* With *him*, Trastevere will go for the Championship!"

"Bravo Beppe!" said the fat Bandini, and put his arm, without a shade of irony, around Beppe's shoulders.

"*Un colpo davvero,*" said another journalist, "a coup indeed," and Beppe, now dropping Gerry's hand, strutted like a peacock towards the President. Gerry turned away, making for the bath, pulling the green jersey over his lean, pale back, as he went, but keeping on his shorts until he'd disappeared.

Beppe came scampering towards me; his mien, his sudden air of reverence, implied a new role; faithful liege-man to the President.

"Brian : the Commendatore wants to speak to you."

I followed him. The President received me with an absent handshake, as though he'd forgotten what he wanted me for. Franceschi greeted me more warmly, though he did not smile. One didn't smile in church.

"You're happy, then," I said to him.

He nodded heavily. "*Insomma*, it turned out very well, for the first time. The President was pleased."

The President was staring at the ceiling; his bald head, the angle of his chin, reminded me abruptly of Mussolini. *Molti nemici, molto onore*, said the white paving stones that led up to the Stadium, many enemies, much honour. *Duce, Duce, Duce!* Had he been reading them, too? Was this how he saw himself, a strong man, ringed by enemies?

As though responding to my thought, the door opened, and a man wearing a broad brimmed grey hat came in. "Montico," whispered Franceschi, "one of the Vice Presidents," and he gave him the charged look a Medici retainer might have given a Pazzi or a Pitti. Montico, I remembered, had led an unsuccessful faction at the club's last General Assembly; the President had been applauded back to office.

"The President wants to know if Logan is happy," Franceschi said. "He wants to know if there is anything he needs."

"*Anything*," said Beppe, tensely, as though the implication were that he had left something undone.

"He seems quite happy," I said.

"He's pleased with the apartment? The car's going well?"

"As far as I know."

"*Ottimo, ottimo*," the President rumbled, and trailed his hand towards me like a wind-sock, as though by this very gesture it were momentarily dissociated from him. Then he began drifting, vague and ponderous, towards the door of the dressing-room. He and Montico, I saw, did not salute each other.

The journalists soon followed him, and as they left, Gaudenzio appeared, greeted them with feeling, glanced shortly at Montico's back, then came towards our corner, hands upraised, his head on one side, *"Che giocatore!"*

"Didn't I tell you!" cried Beppe. "Didn't I tell you?"

"Carissimo Valentini, of course you told me, but now I've *seen*! I've seen with my own two eyes!"

"Effettivamente," Franceschi said, and he nodded with immense sagacity, "a fine player."

"But he's a complete player!" Gaudenzio said, and his monocle flashed light. "No joking! He can do anything! Feints, shots, bursts of speed—anything!"

Franceschi nodded again. Gerry came out of the bathroom, and Montico, who had been talking to Bandini, left him abruptly, and hurried forward. The three men beside me stiffended like sails in the wind.

"Let it go," said Franceschi, his hand on Beppe's arm. "Let it go, it's not important."

Gerry and Montico confronted one another in speechless incomprehension, Montico with one hand raised, frozen in mid-air, in the midst of an elaborate, useless compliment.

"*Va*," said Franceschi, "interpret for him," but Beppe hesitated. "I can't," he said. "How can I?" Then Gerry looked at me with resigned appeal, and I went to him.

"*Molto gentile*," said Montico, with curt resentment. Beneath the wide, grey brim, his face was plump and dark and sullen, the face of a man who had always had his own way. "Please tell him he impressed me tremendously. Please tell him I'm Montico, the Vice-President."

I told him; Montico formally shook his hand. Gerry laughed and said, "Tell him there's so many Vice-Presidents I can't tell one from another. Ask him why can't they all wear a badge, and then I'd know."

"What did he say?" asked Montico, and his dark eyes stared at me suspiciously.

"He said he was very glad to meet you."

He relaxed. *"Buonissimo, Tanti auguri per la sua permanenza qui a Roma.* Best wishes for his stay in Rome. Tell him if he has any worries, he can always bring them to me."

A handshake, and he had gone, still ignoring and ignored by the group in the corner.

"Are you going?" Gerry asked me.

He was dressed, now; the white shirt, with its neat, narrow, rounded collars, the green and black silk tie, were Italian. On an impulse, I stole a glance at his shoes and saw that they, too, were Italian; narrow, tapering to a point. He followed my gaze, and laughed. "Well, you know what they say : when in Rome !"

He shook hands with Gaudenzio, Franceschi and Beppe.

"Gerry, if there's anything you want !" Beppe cried. *"Anything!"*

"Nothing, thanks."

"You were *marvellous,* Gerry ! Wasn't he, Brian? *Sinceramente!"*

"Marvellous," I said.

"It's no use being marvellous in friendlies," said Gerry, and we left the dressing-room.

Outside, the sun had grown gentle and mellow, casting a warm, amber light on the trees, the Stadium, the white, hypertrophied Fascist statuary, around the Foro Italico. Gerry laughed aloud with sheer, spontaneous delight. "I'm thinking of Chiswick," he said. "Coming away from *there . . ."*

I thought of it, too, and of so many other English grounds; the dead streets, strewn with dead peanut husks; paper skittering before the wind, with purposeless flurries of haste.

As we reached the green, iron gates, a dozen youths, wearing the Trastevere insignia, were still waiting, and seeing us, they began to cheer, *"Bravo, Loggan! Viva Loggan!"*

"Next week they might be throwing bricks at me," he said, and laughed. It was too near the bone for me to laugh with him.

The car they had given him was a Fiat 1500. He drove out on to the Via Flaminia, turned at the Stadio Torino, where the Roman clubs trained, and went on to Parioli; new, white blocks of flats, exulting in their own expensiveness, the very recency of their own, brash arrival. "Here we are," he said, and stopped outside one of these blocks. "This'll surprise you."

"Splendid," I said, as he unlocked the door of his flat, though it didn't surprise me. I was long since used to such apartments, such evidence of the mad magnanimity of Roman football clubs; felt even that I had been in this very flat before when it belonged to . . . whom? An English manager? A Norwegian outside-left? There was room, light, an aura of chromium costliness.

"Come and look at the bathroom," he said, and I followed him. A towel-rack glinted silver; the smooth, glazed bath was sunk into the floor. "The children will love it," he said. "They'll use it as a swimming bath ! We'll be bringing some of our own furniture out, but I told Mary when she sees this, she won't want it."

The kitchen, too, was large and glittering, though here the motif was white; white walls, white multiplicity of cupboards, white gas stove. "Wait till she sees this !"

We made tea; it seemed a sacrilege. Gerry sat on the plastic-topped table to drink it, boyish, one pointed shoe dangling and swinging.

"What did you think of the game?"

"I thought you had a good one."

"I had to," he said, laughing. "I got the feeling that if I'd played badly, the President would never have got out alive, and that *he* knew it better than I did."

"The President was delighted. He very nearly spoke to me."

"But League games," he said. "They're different, aren't they?"

"Very. You won't be given the time you got today. They'll be breathing down your neck."

"From what they've told me, that'll be the least of it."

"If you're made to play like you played today," I said, "you're going to make it easy for them."

"Brian, I *know* that, I know it better than you do. They've got rigid ideas here, it's like the Trade Union movement; each man does just one job."

"Can you talk them round, do you think?"

"I think I can; the manager's a weak man. He's nice, but he's weak. You saw him there in the dressing-room; the President says jump, and he jumps, and all the President cares about is if we're winning."

"Exactly."

"Well, we won't win if the other side shut me out of the game, and once they see *that's* happening, they'll let me move around more."

It was good logic, but logic did not work in Rome, or rather, the logic that worked had rules of its own. "Argue it out with them now, Gerry," I told him. "In this country, beginnings are everything; you saw that today, for yourself."

"We'll see," he said, euphoric still. "We'll wait and see how it turns out."

One couldn't convince him; it was a world too far-fetched for credibility. He would have to experience it to believe it; he more than anyone, with his passion to see things for himself.

"Let's go out," he said, "let's celebrate," then added, "There's nothing to celebrate, but we'll celebrate!" and we drove into the city, ate in the open, at Otello, in Via della Croce, beneath a trellis of vines, then drove steeply up the Salita del Pincio, into the Villa Borghese.

There, leaning over the balustrade, we looked down on the city he had come to conquer. "There's times I don't believe it," he said. His jacket was hanging open, and again he seemed irresistibly young. "There's times I think, am I really here like *now*. Or am I just dreaming it—in Glasgow, or in Jarrow?"

"It's better than Jarrow."

"And I think to myself, what if the football *is* bad; it's worth it. Not just for the money—though you expect to make sacrifices when it's this much—but simply for the place. That's why I wanted Rome; that's why I wouldn't have gone to Turin, or Milan. The moment I saw this place

I thought, it's my chance; if I don't take it, I'll regret it the rest of my life. It's different for you, Brian ! you come and you go. Italy's another home to you. But when I hang up my boots, that's the day I lose my passport."

We were silent. I felt, somehow, like the serpent in the Garden of Eden. Behind us, in the dark, boys were calling to each other in the loud, coarse sing-song of the Roman back-streets: "Ah, *stronz—o—o!*"

"I know what it meant to Hemingway," he said, at last. "He was always coming back to Italy . . . before he settled down in Cuba."

"Perhaps he got it out of his system," I said.

"Have *you* got it out of *your* system?"

"No."

"What have you got *against* Rome, Brian?"

What, indeed? Disappointment? The illusion, reborn each time one came here, that such physical beauty must have its corresponding spirit; that at last, a key would turn, a cave would open to a password. "Perhaps, I expect too much," I said.

We walked through the paths of the Villa Borghese, be-tween the long, prosaic white rows of busts, ghostly in the dark, obscure men, dully perpetuated; beards, spectacles, flying-caps.

"If we win the Championship," Gerry said, "do they put *me* there?"

"If they win the Championship, they'll make you Pope."

"Then I could sign for Celtic."

And so the Championship began, bringing reality; Traste-vere away to Novara, a goalless draw. I visualised the match as soon as I heard the result over the loudspeakers in the Olympic Stadium; a cruel, sterile game of massed defence, high kicking; the referee's whistle piping in an endless *obbli-gato*; a rich club against a poor, provincial club, struggling for survival.

Gerry rang me up late that night. "We're just back. Is it always like this, Brian? This bastard kicked me twice, and the

118

referee saw him and just gave a free kick, both times; he didn't even caution him."

"He's probably got a wife and children," I said. "You'll get that, in the provinces."

"They're afraid they'll come over the wire at them, are they?"

The Press next day treated him amiably, borne along by the inertia of his first game. "But is it really worth the trouble of bringing celebrated players here at great sacrifice when, once they're in Italy, they are not allowed to play?" asked *Momento Sera*.

On Tuesday morning, I went to the Stadio Torino, where the Trastevere players were training; a hundred or so *tifosi* had somehow found time to come and watch them. Gerry, I noticed, was limping a little as he ran and afterwards, in the small dressing-room, he showed me his left leg, mottled with bruises.

"Red, white and blue like the flag," he said. "The second time he kicked me, honestly, Brian, it was the nearest I've ever been on a football field to retaliating."

"But that is what they want!" said Petersen, the handsome Dane, looming above us, with his chiseled face, like some huge, friendly dog. "They *want* that you retaliate, and then—off you go! *Espulso!* The referee send you off the field! Oh, yes; I know; I have been playing here five years."

"And the little things make you madder," Gerry said. "The shoves, and the times they grab you by the jersey."

"Yes, yes!" said Petersen. "When I go up to head the ball —a little push! Only a little push, *that* is not a foul; just that I am put completely off my balance!"

He stood there, a fine light in his eye, the embodiment of moral outrage.

"It'll be better playing at home," I said.

"At home, too!" he cried. "Yes! Against Spal last season, I am going through and bang! they bring me down, they trip me—and nothing! Not a penalty, oh, no! We play on : Spal win the match."

I looked at Gerry; his expression was merely one of resignation. I wanted a word to console him, but could think of none; these were the realities of football, here.

Trastevere were at home to Genoa, the following Sunday, and I was tempted not to go. He was on trial, they wanted too much from him, and if they did not get it, then they'd subject him to a small Calvary of abuse.

And indeed, for the first hour he played like a dejected man, deep in midfield again, followed step by step by a Genoa forward who was really a defender, laying the ball off as soon as he got it, as though he disliked the very sight of it.

The crowd began, like children, by responding to everything he did, exploding, "*Bravo, Loggan!*" every time he touched the ball, each cheer an act of faith, an incantation. Thus it was some time before, in their euphoria, they realised that he wasn't playing well. There was a transitional period in which it blamed everyone but him, whistled his colleagues when they gave him a poor pass, whistled the Genoa players if they fouled him. At half-time, they applauded him off the field, but five minutes after the interval, when he passed inaccurately behind his winger, there was silence, and two minutes later, when he failed to trap a ball, a storm of accumulated disappointment.

The whistling seemed to have physical body, it beat against the ears like hailstones. I saw Gerry look up once, as though the noise bewildered him, but this was his solitary reaction. In front of me, a man jumped to his feet and shouted, "Ah, *Loggan, sei stronzo come gli altri!* You're a turd just like the rest of them!" and everyone around him laughed.

"Ah, *Loggan, guadagni troppo!*" another shouted. "*Vieni qui per rubarci!* You're earning too much, you've come here to rob us!"

"*Scozzese davvero!*" a third cried, "he's a proper Scotsman!" but I knew it could get worse than this; when their passion was at the flood, they'd no time for competitive badinage.

I was longing for him to score, to do something to silence them; to defy his manager, as he'd done two weeks before, by deserting his post, and going up for a shot. And with two minutes left, this was what he did, bringing the ball upfield, staying there when he had passed it, though Cardoni leaped from his bench by the touchline and began to gesticulate, like an outraged general defied by his troops.

Gerry ignored him; it was as though he had a private vendetta to attend to, in which Cardoni had no part. Cardoni sat down again, but he moved restlessly on the bench, and within five minutes he was on his feet once more gesturing now at Rosario, the outside-right, to drop back instead of Gerry. Goals were secondary; it was the gap in midfield which was anathema, obsessional.

Gerry's "shadow" was still with him, but following him less certainly now, as he moved widely about the field, now on the right wing, now cheek by jowl with Petersen—a second centre-forward—now as far away from his own position as the left touchline. And it was here that his shadow faltered, uncertain whether to be pulled so far afield so that Gerry had room to collect the ball, control it, take it past him and, with his right foot, curl it, in a beautiful exact parabola, across the face of the goal. As it began to descend, there was Petersen, his tall, heavy body flying inexorably through the air like that of some marvellous Viking, head meeting the ball like a hammer, to send it rocketing through the goalkeeper's upstretched, beseeching hands. The goal roar rose from the crowd, tentative at first—goals had seemed unthinkable—then growing in crescendo of delight. Petersen was surrounded; his colleagues hugged him, kissed him, swarmed over him as over some green rock. And when they had finished with him, they ran to Gerry, unaffected by his calm detachment, which in England had spared him such attentions. But there, emotion ran in rivulets; here, it was a flood-tide. I could not see his face as they bore down on him, but his whole posture was one of frozen amazement. Then they were upon him and he, swaying a moment in the chaos of green shirts, was down on the ground. And here, too, they followed him, crowding round on hands and knees, pummeling and embracing, till the referee pulled them off one by one, shoving them in turn towards the centre circle, and Gerry was left there, prostrate, arms outspread, like the victim of a riot.

The fat masseur jogged on to the field with his box of medicaments, knelt beside him, finally revived him, while Cardoni, who had followed unhurriedly behind, leaned supervising over them. Gerry stood up, turned towards Cardoni and the masseur, half raised his left hand, palm upwards, in a gesture of bewilderment, then limped back to his position. Hardly had Genoa kicked off than the whistle went, the game was over, Trastevere had won, I wondered how long he could continue with these eleventh hour redemptions.

Nelson, when I met him a few days later, smiled his knowing smile and said, "I hear Gerry Logan's not finding it as easy as he thought."

"It's never easy, here."

"Ah, but he wouldn't listen, would he?" Nelson said, and his smile widened. "They come here, and they think there's going to be no difference."

"He made a lovely goal for Petersen."

"But what else did he do? I heard that was all he did in the whole match."

It was almost true, but I couldn't allow him his triumph. "I wouldn't say that," I said.

"Well, I can only go by what I hear. That's what people told me who were there."

At the *Diario Sportivo*, the climate was uncertain.

"*Oh!*" said Berretti, confronting me as though I were responsible for everything. "*Ma questi scozzesi!* He plays like a real Scotsman, your friend; doesn't spend a thing until he has to, then the crowd goes away and says, 'Bravo, Logan!' because we Italians are ingenuous and you English know it."

The season was a month old when Gerry's family arrived from London. "Oh, it's lovely, isn't it?" said his wife, when I visited their flat. "I mean, it's marvellous; I've never had a kitchen like this! I'm afraid to cook on that stove!"

"Everything you want, Mrs. Logan," said Beppe Valentini, who was with us. "You only have to ask the club: everything!"

"She'll think of something," said Gerry, coming in. "You'd better not ask her."

"A garden, that's all I want," she said. "Then it would be perfect. I could plonk the children out there, and that'd be that!"

"A villa," said Beppe. "You prefer a villa? It's difficult in Rome, but maybe I talk to the President. . . ."

"Don't listen to her," Gerry said. "If she had her way, we'd be moving house every day of the week."

"We *would* not," said Mrs. Logan, with feigned resentment. But the role didn't suit her, even in jest. She seemed to me neither frivolous nor capricious; there was a seriousness about her, a maturity, which lightness of manner could not disguise.

"But you *like* Rome, Mrs. Logan?" Beppe appealed to her.

"Oh, I love it, it's beautiful, it's bowled me over."

"You'll never get her away now," Gerry said. "I'll be in Rome forever. When I've packed up playing, I'll sell postcards to the tourists. "

We laughed, and Beppe laughed with us, but briefly, in mere token of solidarity; it was not a joke to amuse him. "I think, Mrs. Logan, everyone here in Rome is very pleased with your husband," he said. "You know? They're glad he's come to Trastevere."

"Is that what they do when they're glad?" asked Gerry. "Whistle?"

"No, no, you must understand, Gerry; the public here is very different. Eh, Brian? *Non è serio, come in Inghilterra.* In England, people are more serious."

"It seems to get pretty serious here, at times," said Gerry.

Beppe's plump face grew taut with dismay, with the anguished need to convince. "*Gerry; ti giuro! Ti vogliono bene tutti!* Tell him, Glanville; all the Trastevere fans. They all wish him well!"

"All the fans like you," I said.

"Then the ones that whistle must come with the away teams," Gerry said, and Beppe, seizing this at once, cried, "Exactly! They are jealous! They come just to whistle—

nothing else; Lazio and Flaminio supporters, too. They wish that you were playing for *their* club!" He turned to me again, to be borne out, and as he did so, I saw Gerry and his wife exchange a smile, behind him, a smile in which there was more than shared amusement; an intimacy, a confidence that what amused one would amuse the other. I thought I could see, then, how important she was to him.

She brought tea into the sitting-room, and Gerry played the gramophone; Frank Sinatra, George Shearing, Dave Brubeck. When he'd exhausted the records, he turned on the radio; it was late enough to get an English station: *In A Monastery Garden*, violins sobbing in their sugary death throes, while a crooner whistled like an aviary of birds.

"*Bella musica, eh, Glanville?*" Beppe cried. "*Bella musica!*"

"Then, there's a substantial fact," said Bulgarelli, and he laid his brown finger by the side of his brown nose, and slowly winked. "It was the President who brought Logan here, therefore it's in the interests of the Vice-President that he should be a failure."

"We're in Rome," I said.

"Precisely; *siamo a Roma.*"

We sat at lunch in a restaurant in Via dei Condotti. Nearby us, at a longer table, a group of sleek, contented, preening men in white shirtsleeves were loudly disagreeing about Flaminio's last match: "*Ma è stronzo, quell'ala destra!*"

"So he'll try to create a climate," said Bulgarelli, "in which Logan *can't* succeed. Through the *consiglio direttiva*, through the other players, above all through the newspapers. Warn Logan to be careful."

"Careful in what way?"

"Just to stay awake—off the field even more than on it; especially when he's in any public place. You know what this Roman journalism can be. Scandal journalism."

"They won't find any scandal there."

"They don't need to," he said. "If you give them the chance, they can invent it." His round, droll face wore its usual smile, knowing yet tolerant, like an amiable policeman; a smile of shrewd simplicity, peasant acumen. No one could be more Roman than he, yet by some dispensation he had lived in this world, stayed part of it, without surrendering his detachment—or his hope of better things. When I'd known him first, he was a junior coach with Flaminio; now, he was the manager of a minor Roman club, a semi-professional team of derelicts and aspirants. But his job was secondary; he was a figure and a character in Roman football, known to everybody, blandly indestructible, at once lampooned and respected.

"He's very ambitious, Montico," he said, now. "His family's in textiles; he has a great deal of money. He doesn't mind what he spends. *Sta attento!*"

"Can he influence Cardoni?" I asked, remembering the cameo in the dressing-room, Cardoni a faithful if unhappy hound at the President's side.

"*Be'!* It remains to be seen," said Bulgarelli. "Cardoni was a compromise choice; the President's group wanted Monzeglio, from Naples, Montico wanted Bernardini, from Fiorentina, Cardoni is a good man, a serious man. . . ."

"Yes, he's a good man!" cried a rakish fellow with a moustache and a roguish look in his eye, from the next table. "He doesn't do pee-pee in the street, he doesn't beat his father and mother. *Insomma*, he's a manager like you are!"

Bulgarelli grinned, as he always did when he was teased—the grin of a large, delighted dog—and he said, "Aoh! What do Flaminio supporters know about football?"

"Enough to get rid of a lousy trainer like you!"

"That was a happy day," Bulgarelli replied, continuing to grin. "That was the happiest day of my life, the day I left Flaminio."

"The day we chucked you out, you mean!" shouted another man, with the wiry black hair, the irascible good looks, of some Italian film star.

"*Chi se ne frega?*" Bulgarelli asked. "Who gives a damn? It was enough to get away from people like you!"

"*Che porcheria!*" they shouted, and returned to their meal.

"Then what do you think will happen?" I asked.

"It remains to be seen," said Bulgarelli. "At the moment, the results are so-so, neither good nor bad. If they improve, then Montico can do nothing. If they deteriorate, that's when he will get his chance."

"Like Mussolini."

"*Ecco!*" he said, and beamed.

And the hard times came; a defeat away by Sampdoria, a defeat at home by Juventus; the Trastevere team whistled off the field. In the dressing-room afterwards, the President wasn't to be seen. Instead Montico in his broad grey hat, stormed to and fro continuously, like an avenger; a Savonarola of the football stadiums.

"*Abbia la cortesia di non scrivere!*" he cried, tapping my open notebook as he passed me. "Our goalkeeper played well, and that's enough! No interviews!"

"Take no notice of him," Gerry said, and laughed. "I never do."

This time, there had been no late, redeeming moment, no saving piece of virtuosity. He had subsided into greyness, with the rest of his grey team, though as always, he could rise above disappointment, as cordial now as though he'd scored five goals.

"He and the President," he said. "You know those little models they make, those little houses that tell you the weather? They're like one of those. When it's good weather, when we've won, the President comes out, and when we've lost, *he* pops back, and out comes the other one."

Montico hastened past us again, his grey eyes, hostile in the swarthy face, darting us a look of suspicion. For a moment I thought he would take issue with me, but he seemed to change his mind and he went on, Cardoni now his quarry.

"Terrible, wasn't it?" Gerry said. "When it's bad here, it's bloody diabolical. You'd think that at least Juventus, with all the players they've got. . . ." I shrugged. "I know," he said, "you told me so!"

"They didn't give you much room."

"You told me that, as well! It seems to me the only way

126

you can get room here is by getting out there before the other team arrive!"

He had, indeed, been followed from pillar to post, and all his peregrinations—upfield, deep, out to the left wing and the right—had been futile. When an Italian League team marked a man, it marked him.

"Nothing vicious, though," he said. "A couple of pushes and a kick; you can get worse in a friendly game at home. The only thing is, we could all the three of us just as well sat here in the dressing-rooms, and let the other nineteen get on with the game."

"Five years!"—and Petersen was upon us—"I have had this for five years!"

In the corridor outside the dressing-room, the plump Bandini of *Roma Sera*, turned peevishly away from me, as I passed; the knives were out, this was as good a barometer as Montico.

"Enough of these British confidence tricks," wrote Bandini, next day. "They play well, these Englishmen, when it doesn't matter. But Trastevere still have time to cut their losses; give this phlegmatic Scotsman to a provincial club, as soon as the transfer lists reopen in November, and start looking now for a foreign star to take his place. But please, not another Scotsman."

Nor did Beppe Valentini escape. That Tuesday, he was pilloried in *Calcione*, a weekly Roman broadsheet of polemics, scandal gossip. The cartoon on its front page showed Beppe; *a meridionale*, in a beret and a shabby suit, standing on the British Isles, one arm round the bony shoulders of an ancient man in football kit, while Molinucci, the President, stood on the Italian boot. "*Ah, Presidé!*" Beppe was calling. "I've found you a new British player!"

Beppe rang me up; he sounded tearful. "Have you seen *Calcione*! Have you seen what they've done to me? I shall sue them! I shall have them in court! It's not fair of them to go for me like that! Is it my fault if I bring them a great player and he can't do anything because Italian football's a *casino*, a whore-house? Yes or no?"

"Of course it's not your fault!"

"But this is the end. I'm not going on. Why should I sacrifice myself? Listen, Brian, you know me. *Sono una persona per bene. Una persona che non scherza.* A person who doesn't joke around. If I take them to court, they'll pay me fifty million lire! A hundred million! I'm not joking, *sai!*"

"Of course you're not."

"But I'm giving up now. *Basta!* This isn't a world for honest people. When you bring off a coup, and nobody appreciates it...."

"Yes, they do."

"Thank you, *carissimo*, thank you. *You* do because you're an Englishman. *Sei una persona onesta.* But the others! In a world like this, you don't find honest people. I'm going to get out of Rome. I'm going to start a business. I'm finished with football; finished!"

He had been finished with it before, and would finish again, up one moment, down the next, with all the volatility of the Italian—finally irrepressible.

"Take no notice of them, Beppe," I said.

"Grazie, caro, grazie."

At *Il Diario Sportivo*, that evening, I found Mengalvio coaxing Campello, the football editor : "Show them, Gianni, show them! Show them how you can shoot!" And when he saw me, "Show Glanville!" This was the other side of his eternal studentship; high jinks, when the books were put away.

Campello lowered his eyes and shrugged, like a modest virtuoso. In his fawn jersey, with its long sleeves, he looked curiously child-like, a chubby boy dressed for a party.

"Please!" Mengalvio urged him. "Glanville's never seen it!" and Campello shrugged again, capitulating—ready, after all, to recite in front of the visitors.

"Watch, watch!" cried Mengalvio, rolling up a ball of paper Then, with great diligence, he lobbed it slowly to Campello who, raising a plump hand, smacked it through the open doorway, where it bounced off Berretti's head, and on to the floor.

"*Stronzo!*" Berretti cried.

"*Macchè stronzo!*" Mengalvio retorted. "*Era un capola-voro!* It was a masterpiece!"

Campello gave a third shrug, amiably self-deprecating, then he shouted, without looking at me, "*Eh, allora!* What about this Loggan?"

"What about him?" I replied.

"He did precious little on Sunday."

"So did everyone else."

"But that's not the point," he muttered, entering a new mood; this, too, familiar to me; unemphatic, world-wise, his comments thrown whimsically away, with weary scepticism. "When you've paid so much money for a player, you're entitled to expect something extra from him. The public was very disappointed."

"*Il pubblico romano è stronzo*," said Franzini, shuffling in. "Turds, all of them."

"*Eh!*" said Campello. "To you, everyone's a *stronzo*."

"The Roman public more than anyone. When he's allowed to play, anybody can see that he's a good player."

"I was talking to Montico at lunch. He's less convinced than you are."

"*Montico è stronzo*."

Campello shrugged yet again.

"*Oh!*" said Berretti, coming in, wearing his scoundrel's smile, and laying his hand on my shoulder. "Is it true that Valentini's going back to England, to look for another British player?"

"I'll ring up Montico," Campello said, with a mischievous air, "I'll ask him," and he picked up the telephone, the others crowding round his desk.

"*Commendator Montico? Sono Campello.*" He paused, and held the receiver a little way from his ear, so that we could hear Montico's voice, loud, distorted, manifestly agitated.

"Glanville here," Campello said, into the phone—he wore an expression of bland innocence—and at once, Montico's voice grew louder and more strident still, while Campello's eyes widened, and he gave me a slow, wondering nod.

"But Vice President," he said, "the thing is this. Glanville's heard you want to get rid of Logan . . . that you're looking for another Englishman. . . ."

Now Montico's voice rose so loud that one could hear him as clearly as though he were in the room : "*E bougiardo! Non è vero! Niente inglesi! Mai un altro inglese al Trastevere!* Liar ! No more Englishmen at Trastevere !"

Campello pulled a comic face into the mouthpiece of the telephone : "No more Englishmen, he says," and then, "*Va bene, commendatore, grazie, commendatore, tutto chiaro! Buona notte!*"

"*Cos'ha detto, cos'ha detto?*" they all cried.

"*Ma!* That Logan's a disaster, that they needed a spearhead player, and they've bought a midfield player."

"Gerry can do both," I said.

"Eh, *va bene, va bene,* but he's primarily an organizer, isn't he? You can see it clearly."

It was my turn to shrug; such arguments would go round and round in circles.

"He's a good player," said Campello, "but whether he's right for the Italian Championship remains to be seen. *Pazienza.*"

"Which Montico hasn't got," said Franzini. "*Di calcio, capisce un bel cazzo.* He knows fuck all about football."

"Eh, *eh!*" Berretti cried, thrusting his large, brown face towards Franzini, his hands outstretched in taut appeal. "Does the President know? Does the other Vice-President know? Show me a director who does !"

"Montico knows less than any of them," Franzini said, and stumped away, the epitome of disgust—for football, for Montico, for a decadent, post-Fascist era.

"Of course they're disappointed," Gerry said. "They're all like children, they expect too much, and they want it all at once. A new player's a magician; he waves his wand, and he wins you the Championship. If they signed another forward in November, I'd be happy, because it would be *him* they'd be on to then, not me."

"Would you like to go back," I asked.

"No, no, I'd never go back, not unless they sent me back. That's running away from things; you've got to accept the challenge." The challenge, the challenge. "It's harder than I thought it would be, but that's just something you've got to accept."

"And not as enjoyable?"

"Well, I'm disappointed, I admit it. I don't enjoy playing with all these good players as much as I expected to, but that's not *their* fault, it's the fault of the system. This forward-line of ours could be a great forward-line, Nils Petersen's the best centre-forward I've ever played with; he knows what you're going to do before you know it yourself. I can't get used to it; at Chiswick, Dave Brent just put his head down and kept running, and if he found the ball in front of him, he'd be going so fast a brick wall couldn't stop him. Then there's this fellow Valdar. He's a temperamental bugger, and he's lazy, but have you seen the way he pulls a ball down? He's got more brains in just his left foot than most people have got in their whole heads. I think I can play here, Brian; it's just a question of time."

But time, here, was gold dust, water in the desert; to ask for it was to be met by a face of stone.

"Like children," Mrs. Logan said, in her turn, and shook her head, astonished. "First Gerry was the hero, now he's the villain. When I went out shopping to begin with, people were all over me when they knew who I was, it was embarrassing. Now, when I go into a shop, they pretend they don't know me. I'd rather that, honestly—but they're children."

"I'm seeing Italy, anyway," Gerry said. "Florence last week, Palermo next week: that's *one* thing. All I'm waiting for now is us to be relegated or Venice to be promoted, and then I can go on the Grand Canal."

"Gondolas, Gerry!" said his wife, "oh, I'd *love* to go there!" and her face was raised, her eyes closed, in a moment of rapturous fantasy. "He never takes me to all these places."

GERRY LOGAN

I THINK in those early months I'd have gone home, if it wasn't for the travelling. I had to keep saying to myself, with the football going like it was, you came to Italy for two reasons. So it was the away games I looked forward to, even though in most ways they were the hardest games of all, because they could kick you from here to Sicily and the referees wouldn't bat an eyelid. They were nearly every one of them cowards, they'd give the home team everything and the away team nothing, but I sometimes wondered, would British referees be any better? After all, we used to complain about them as well, and they'd nothing like the same to put up with.

These Italian crowds could be really vicious, it was a matter of life and death to them, and I heard stories of what they'd done to referees. There was one they'd followed all the way back to his home, a hundred miles, and when he got out of his car they'd beaten him up outside his own front door. This violence was something I couldn't get used to, because you got it on the field, as well, and from players who you'd never expect it from. Off the field, they could be very well mannered, even gentle, in the way Italians are, then they'd get out there and the first thing they'd do would be they'd kick someone up in the air.

Our left-back was like that, Meneghini. He had this soft face and this quiet voice and he always wore a religious medal round his neck, and yet I've seen him take a flying kick at a winger who'd gone past him, and stop another one by sticking his elbow in his face. In England, it's very rare you get a man sent off, but here, it was all part of the game. One of the first matches I played, there was three sent off, two from our side and one from the other. That was because it was an away game; if we'd been playing at home, it would have been the other way around.

Playing at home was bad as well, though, because you'd

get this partisan Roman crowd, and they were the worst crowd I've ever known. The first match I played there, I was lucky, because it was a friendly, and there was plenty of opportunity to play football. The next one I was luckier still, because I made the winning goal just on time, and then I was a hero, they all wanted to cheer me, whereas up to then I'd got the feeling they wanted to tear me apart. There was just no in-between.

Then there was this whistling of theirs; if you shot wide, if you even put a pass wrong, they'd whistle you, and it was unsettling at first, it was like being caught in a cloudburst, you'd feel it coming at you from all sides, and you couldn't escape. I'd heard it before, I'd played on the Continent a lot of times, but somehow it never seemed so hard before; at Rome, you felt that it was directed at *you*. There was something vicious about it and for the first few weeks I was conscious of it; then I just didn't notice it any more. It was a pity about it, because that was a beautiful stadium, the pitch was a pleasure to play on. It never churned up, no matter how hard it rained; there was none of this business you get in Britain of ploughing through mud, with the ball as heavy as a cannonball.

So there were good things and bad things, but as far as the football itself was concerned, they were mostly bad things. There was one game against Atalanta, up at Bergamo, an early game, when it turned into a free fight—this is the one I was talking about, when three players got sent off. One of our men knocked one of theirs flat with his elbow, after he'd been kicked, then one of theirs knocked *our* player flat, then two or three more joined in, and before you knew where you were, there must have been ten or twelve of them at it, kicking and punching; the referee had to call the police on, those little fellows in grey with the guns. In the end he sent three off, and we had to play with nine against ten.

And the football itself was very bad, that was what surprised me. They were good players, but they all had this fear about them, they'd never take a risk, there was too much at stake if they lost. The fear went right through every club; it started with the President, *he* was afraid of the supporters and of the other directors, then went down to the manager, *he* was afraid of losing his job—they'd get through two or three managers a season—and from the manager it was passed on to the players; *they* were afraid of being dropped, or of being fined.

This fining was something I couldn't get used to, especially when it came from the club; to me, it was like an act of revenge. A team would lose a match and its directors would say, "Who can we blame? Who can we punish?" and they'd pick out the player they'd expected most from and fine him for not trying, for *non rendimento*, they called it. It happened to Valdar, this Hungarian inside-left of ours. I came in one day for training and there he was on his own, in a corner of the dressing-room, looking down at the ground and not talking to anyone. I said, "What's the matter with him?" and Nils Petersen said, "He's been fined. Two hundred thousand lire: *non rendimento*."

That was more than a hundred pounds, and I felt sorry for the fellow, although I didn't like him; because if you were going to fine him for not trying, you could fine him every week. And of course, what happened was he played even worse; for the next three weeks, you might as well have not had him on the field at all. Then we went up and played Torina, they had eighty per cent of the game, but ten minutes from the end we broke away and Valdar equalised; it was the only thing he did in the match.

The President came into the dressing-room and he said, "A bonus for everyone, a hundred thousand lire each," then he went up to Valdar, he threw his arms round his shoulders and whispered something in his ear and Valdar started to smile, and I knew what had happened, he'd got his money back.

That was the one thing I liked about Ronnie Nelson, that he'd never fine his players. He was a difficult man to make out, a *closed* man. When I arrived in Rome it was as if he resented me, as if he was the only Englishman who had a right to be there, and I was taking something away from him. He'd done well in Italy, but you couldn't tell whether he really liked it or not, I don't think *he* knew. You'd meet him one day and he'd tell you how terrible everything was, how it was all corrupt and you couldn't keep the players fit because they were screwing the whole time. Next time he'd be on about how well he got on with them, and how he understood them and what respect they had for him.

I was walking with him once, we were going past the Pantheon, and I said to him, "It's marvellous, isn't it, living here? Wherever you go, you see something beautiful," and he said, "I don't know, to tell you the truth, I never notice," and I looked at him, I couldn't believe it.

Because to me, this was what *made* Italy, this wonderful thing that wherever you went, wherever you looked, there was something to excite you. For instance, when we played Naples, we took the boat to Capri, and I was wandering about on my own, looking at all these marvellous views there, and looking down on those great rocks, whatever their name is, standing up there like sentries, you felt there was something alive about them; they *looked* so intelligent—I don't know quite how to explain it; and going into the Blue Grotto in a rowing boat.

And Florence was fabulous, too. I'd like to have stayed there a month; the square where they've got the Palazzo Vecchio and the statues of David and Perseus, and the other little square with David, where you can look down over the city and see the river and the Ponte Vecchio and the cathedral. They were things I'd read about, but I'd never thought I'd see them; the other players couldn't understand me. I said, "You're Italians, you live with this, it's part of you. You can come here any time, I may never get here again."

Another thing that made up for the football was the people and their way of living. I liked them, I felt I had a lot in common with them temperamentally, even if I couldn't understand what they were saying. In fact I felt much more at home in Rome than I ever had in Glasgow, or even London, because there the people were closed, whereas here they had this exuberance about them, they came out to meet you. You hadn't got this snobbery about football, either. In Britain, soccer was something for the peasants; playing cricket for money was just about all right, but if it was football you played, people turned their noses up at you. Whereas in Italy, a footballer was a sort of hero to everybody, not just the working classes—everybody. Trastevere had supporters who were princes and millionaires and actors and writers, and when you met them, it was very stimulating. You weren't sealed off from them, like you were at home; they *wanted* to meet you, so that when you were talking to them, even the most intellectual ones, you felt you were giving them something, at the same time they were giving something to you.

That was how I met Gino Rossi, because he was a fan of Trastevere. He was a fascinating man, he was an actor and a writer and a director, he wrote his own films, and he acted in them, too. We'd talk for hours not just about football but about books and films and about life, generally. His English was very good, and I think it intrigued him to meet a footballer who could talk to him about the things *he* did, just as it was interesting for me to meet a man like him who was crazy about football.

He was like me, he was a tremendous fan of Hemingway's, he'd say, "If only Hemingway had been a European, he'd have written about football as well as boxing and bullfighting. Football needs a poet, but it's never had one."

And we had this idea for a film, we were going to write it together and he was going to play the lead; he wanted me to be in it as well, he was all for using actors who weren't professionals. He used to say, "For my sake, Gerry, I'm glad you came to Trastevere, but for your sake, I don't know if it's a good thing. Trastevere won't win anything, none of the Roman clubs ever will. Rome is chaos, and football is organisation."

I said, "Yes, but it's imagination as well, your footballers have got imagination, but they're not allowed to use it."

"That's Italy," he said, "we squander everything we've got—and it's typical of Rome. Have you ever tried to get anything done here, get a licence for something, or a *permesso di soggiorno*? If you have, you know what it's like; crazy bureaucracy, one little clerk after another. We're the most spontaneous people in the world, and the most regimented. A people of paradoxes."

He didn't come from Rome himself, he was from somewhere down in the South; Calabria, I think. He said, "You're a provincial and I'm a provincial, but in England, being a provincial's just a joke, in Italy it can be a tragedy. It's like a scar; we never lose our provincialism, however long we've been away."

I said, "Maybe that makes you what you are. Maybe that's what gives you your ambition."

He said, "Yes, probably you're right. That's our curse, our ambition; that terrible ambition of the provinces. We can never escape from it, however far we go."

"I wouldn't want to escape from it," I said. "When you've no ambition left, you stop growing, you've nothing left to live for."

He said, "What are your ambitions?" and I said, "I don't know, ambitions change. You fulfil one, and then you find another. When I was a boy in Glasgow, I wanted to be a professional footballer, then when I'd become that, I wanted to play for Scotland; then, when I'd played for Scotland, I wanted to be in an English team that won the Cup and the League; and now, I want to make a success of things in Italy, and that's the most difficult one of all."

He said, "And this is all you want to do—football?"

"No," I said, "football's just a means to an end, football's a way of doing what I want to do, of finding out what I want to do, of being able to do what I want to do for my children. Football's allowed me to see the world, and when I'm too old for football, that's something they won't be able to take away from me."

He said, "I envy you. If I had your gift, I'd never have become a writer. I'd have expressed myself on the football field, and afterwards, I'd have settled down in the South. I'd have been satisfied."

"But you wouldn't," I said. "When you've got that, you want something else. What use is it fulfilling all your ambitions by the time you're thirty-five? You've only got to find new ones."

But he couldn't see that. He said, "An athlete's life is complete in itself. I only became a writer because I failed as a footballer. It was a compensation. If I could only change places with you, I'd be a very happy man."

I said, "Not unless you *enjoy* being kicked !"

Because the football itself wasn't getting any better. We'd had some bad results, and this was terrible, because with Italians, it's everything or nothing. You only had to look at their faces in the dressing-room, before a game, to realise that the only thing that could give them confidence was an early goal—but with the manager so defence minded how *could* we get an early goal? I was still having this battle with him. He said, we bought you as a midfield player, all right, you *play* as a midfield player, and I was trying to tell him, if the other side always know where they can find me, I might as well take the day off. I think he *saw* my point of view, even though we always had to speak through an interpreter, through Beppe or through Nils Petersen, but he was afraid for his job, and he couldn't afford to give way. And so there was deadlock. I just had to go ahead and do what I thought best *without* his permission, and sometimes, when it came off, he'd be all smiles, and others, when it didn't, I'd come off the field, and he'd have a face like thunder.

One advantage I'd got was I couldn't read the papers yet, because from all I heard they were vicious, and looking at some of the reporters, I'd have expected them to be vicious. There was this big, fat fellow on *Roma Sera*, he was introduced to me as "a very good friend of the club," and the minute I heard that, I was suspicious, because a good journalist shouldn't be a friend of any club, otherwise you're back again in Jarrow, or somewhere like that, with these local men who blow hot one day and blow cold the next.

Anyway, this big fellow was all over me when I came, as far as he could make himself understood, and he was all over me again after the friendly game, and the match against

Genoa when I made this goal. Then things started to go wrong, and he wasn't speaking to me any more.

Well, I wasn't going to let him get away with it, and one day in the dressing-room I got hold of Beppe and I said, "Ask him why he doesn't speak to me now." Beppe didn't want to at first, but I persuaded him and in the end he went up to the chap, and when he asked the question, you'd have thought he'd stuck a gun in his ribs. The fellow jumped three feet in the air then shot away and was out of the door. I said, "What did he say?" and Beppe told me, "He said it wasn't a polite question."

Every week they'd mess around with the team; they'd try youngsters from the reserves and sling them out after one game, they'd put Nils Petersen at inside-left, or Valdar on the wing—and once for a fortnight they left him out altogether. I turned up at the stadium one morning and found I was down for outside-right; I couldn't remember playing there since I was a schoolboy. I said to Beppe, "Who picks the teams? Whose ideas are these?"

He said, "The directors meet every week and they argue, and the manager does what they tell him. Every director wants a different team. They've all got their favourites."

I'd got my own ideas on what we ought to do, because I could see we had the talent if it was only used properly, but trying to put them forward was useless; it always had to be through Beppe or Nils, and while they were explaining, Cardoni wouldn't be listening. His eyes would be moving all over the place, and as soon as they'd finished, he'd dash away.

The third time we lost a match at home, we were stoned. The coach was going out of the Stadium when there was this bang! against the window, then another bang, and everyone was shouting, "Giù! Giù! Get down!" Claudio, the masseur, was going crazy, he wanted to get out of the coach and fight them, and we had to hold him back. He was Trastevere mad, the club was his life. If he'd got hold of them he would have killed them.

So it was a strange situation; I'd gone there to play football and I was enjoying everything but the football. I did a lot of thinking about it, and in the end I came to the conclusion I'd have to change my rhythm of play, because here, the rhythm was completely different. In England, you'd train so you could keep going for ninety minutes, moving the whole time. There were some players took rests, but most of them kept running. Here, it was the opposite. Nobody was fit, and if you played in a game that was good before half-time, you knew that in the second half it would be terrible. It was all stop-go, stop-go, and if you *did* keep running, you'd be running on your own.

I didn't train any less hard, but now when I went out to play I'd be husbanding myself, I'd do a lot less chasing. Then, when I thought I saw a chance, I'd suddenly stop coasting and go like the clappers, and I found this was the way to get a response from the others. It suited their temperaments, these nervous bursts of energy, whereas a British team would just keep pegging away at the same pace till something turned out right.

In a way, I realised the Italians were right, because if you're up against a massed defence, you're never going to get through it just by plugging away, all you'll do is strengthen it and give it confidence, while at the same time you're exposing yourself to a breakaway.

Nils and I would work a few moves out together, he was an extremely intelligent player. One of them was, I'd go right with the ball, taking the defence away from him, and he'd go left; then suddenly I'd curl this long ball nearly from the touchline, over to the far post, and he'd go belting in to meet it with his head. It brought us a marvellous goal away to Lanerossi.

Valdar it was harder to work with, because you couldn't tell him anything, he was a sullen little devil most of the time, and I was told he did a lot of hanging round newspaper offices, which was another thing I didn't like. But the real nigger in the woodpile was this Montico, the Vice-President. What he knew about football you could have written on your thumbnail and still had room; yet he was interfering the whole time. More than anything else he wanted *me* out of the team, because that would be one in the eye for the President, who'd bought me.

To tell the truth, I was a bit disappointed in the President; he wasn't as big a man as I'd thought he'd be. Now that things were going wrong, he tended to disappear into the background. But Beppe said, "Don't worry, he's only biding his time."

I said, "Till when? Till we've been relegated? If you ask me, he's leaving things a bit late."

In the end, Montico got his way, and I was out of the team, not because I was dropped, though, but because I was injured. I wondered who they'd put in my place; we were away to Spal, one of the little teams—and what they did was put in a full-back, and play him with a number eight on his jersey; *catenaccio.* As soon as the ball was kicked off, back he went to be a second centre-half.

Naturally *they* couldn't score, and naturally *we* didn't score, so we came away with a point. I didn't go up for the game, but I was told it was terrible, practically the whole of it played around the centre circle.

What happened then was that Montico whipped up this campaign in the Press; the team mustn't be changed, Logan's a luxury, safety first until we're clear of relegation. Gino Rossi talked to me about it, he said, "I wouldn't worry too much if I were you, this is Rome and everything's a nine days wonder."

"I'm not worrying," I said. "If you don't score goals, you can't win matches, and they'll never score a goal with that forward-line."

Then I had a telephone call from Beppe, very secretive; I always got the impression that they enjoyed being secretive, and it amused me the way they'd whisper over the phone, as though someone might be listening outside the door. He said, "Major Franceschi wants to see you." I said, "Okay, bring him along." He said, "No, no, we can't come along, if we come to your apartment we'll be spotted, and it'll be all over Rome, there'll be terrible trouble. There's already a Press campaign against Major Franceschi; they say the President does everything he tells him, and that's why things go badly for Trastevere."

This Franceschi was an Army officer and he lived for football. He was a big, heavy man and he was full of these big, heavy theories. Some of them held water and some of them were absurd, but at least he was sincere about them.

I said, "Where shall we meet, then?" and Beppe said, "At the old Caffè Greco, it's near the Spanish Steps. That's a place nobody in football ever comes."

Well, when I got there, I could understand why, because it was one of the gloomiest places I'd ever been in; full of red plush and these little marble tables and old yellow newspapers and posters of Buffalo Bill hanging on the walls. It was ten o'clock at night and I must have been the only person there, except the waiters. Beppe had said quarter to ten, so of course he turned up at quarter past. I could see him from where I was sitting when he came in, but he couldn't see me, and he was looking around him with this anxious expression on his face, as if he was ready to go rushing out again at the drop of a hat. Then he came a little farther in and saw me, and he turned round and beckoned, and Franceschi came in, and by this time I was nearly killing myself.

Beppe said, "The major wants to know why you're laughing," and I said, "All this cloak and dagger stuff, I think it's very funny," and Beppe told Franceschi, then he turned back to me and said, "The major says he doesn't think it's funny."

Then Franceschi started apologising to me, through Beppe, for what had happened. He said it wasn't the President's fault, the President was in a very difficult position. He still had just as much faith in me, but he was trying to give Montico enough rope to hang himself; in a few weeks things would get better. I didn't say anything, but I was thinking that as far as I could see, Montico had enough rope to hang the lot of us, the President as well.

Then he started in with his diagnosis again; how if we'd done this, Fiorentina would have to do that, and if we did *that*, the next Sunday, then Milan would have to do the other. I said, "That's all very well, but I may not even be

142

playing on Sunday," but he said, "Yes, yes, you will be," he seemed very certain about it. "Montico daren't overplay his hand," he said, "the people still like you in Rome," and he was right—I *was* in.

It was quite a good game, too, because Milan were a footballing side, and they allowed *us* to play some football: and this was the sort of game that suited us. It was the first time I'd played against Liedholm, and I thought what a great player he was, never in a hurry, always in the right position, and using every ball. He had this calm about him, he steadied the whole team, and he used the long ball beautifully.

We scored first; we started off with a lot of enthusiasm, because nothing was expected of us, and Milan were cautious, because they knew they were on a hiding to nothing. After about ten minutes, Rosario, this Argentinian outside-right of ours, who could be a good player when he wanted to, beat the back, took the ball down to the bye-line, pulled it across, and Valdar leaped in the air and hit it in on the volley; it went in like a bomb, and he went mad, he went dancing all over the field. I'd seen him do this volley in training, but it had looked the sort of thing you can bring *off* in training—never in a game.

Anyway, that gave us confidence, and for a time we were playing really well, but even though we were a goal up, I still wasn't sure, because this confidence of ours was very artificial, it wasn't *based* on anything, we kept it going from moment to moment, like a juggler with a lot of rubber balls: so if *they* broke away and got a goal, I knew that would be the end of it.

Instead of which we held them till ten minutes from the end, and by this time the game had slowed up, and neither side was playing well. Then Milan got a free kick out on the right, Liedholm took it, and Gunnar Nordahl, the big Swedish centre-forward, got up above the whole of our defence and headed a goal. It was the only thing he'd done in the game, he was heavy now, but you could see just from that what a player he must have been a few years back. If the goal had come twenty minutes earlier, it might have demoralised us, but coming when it did, it just irritated the team, it gave us a new incentive, as though everyone was saying to themselves, you got that goal unfairly, we'd *proved* we were better than you, and now we're going to prove it again.

I could see Milan were happy with a point—they hadn't really expected to get one—and this helped us, because they went back on defence and let *us* have the initiative. There couldn't have been more than a minute to go when Nils Petersen pushed me the ball and went belting through, calling for a quick return. I let him have it back first time, what the coaches call a wall pass—they've a name for everything—and he went after it like a tank with these three Milan men with him, and it was obvious what was going to happen: they'd all go down in a heap, and they did. The referee blew up right away and pointed for a penalty. He must have been at least twenty yards off and I was only ten yards off and I couldn't tell what had happened; but we were playing in Rome and not Milan and he wanted to get home alive, so it was a penalty.

The Milan players came round him and I thought they were going to tear him apart; he was flailing around with his arms and he had his little book out and his pencil, and by the time he finished taking names, he must have filled up every page. Taking the penalties was my job, just like it had been with Chiswick. I got hold of the ball and put it on the spot, and somebody kicked it off. Then the referee put it on the spot and it was kicked off again, so he sent off the player who'd done it, and this time they left it there.

There was all the usual whistling and commotion, but I was resigned to it. I looked at the goalkeeper and thought, he's worse off than I am, they *want* me to score; so I jogged up to the ball, like I did in England, feinted one way, then rolled it in the other, and it went in along the ground, just nicking the far post.

With the noise then, you'd have thought an atom bomb had gone off in the Stadium, but the only thing that worried me was getting pulled to pieces by the other boys.

It was bonuses again that day, the President came in with

a great, big smile on his face and congratulated me, and Montico was there in a corner, pretending to smile, and looking like someone had told him his house was on fire. The man from the Italian radio came round with his microphone, they were mad about these interviews, and he stuck it under Nils Petersen's nose and Nils said, "It was a marvellous win, and I'm particularly glad for Gerry Logan, because it showed his importance to the team."

I said to him, "You'd better be careful, Nils. If Montico hears that, the next game we lose he'll have you thrown to the lions in the Colosseum."

He said, "I don't care about Montico, I say what I believe." But when Mary and I were round at his flat that night and turned on the radio, that part of the interview had gone, cut right out! Just Nils saying he was glad, and that it was a marvellous win.

From then on, I realised how serious Montico was, and it amazed me. By comparison, Pyke and Dawson at Chiswick had been amateurs. I lay awake that night trying to think how I could get the better of him, but in the end I decided it was no use trying to beat him at his own game, the only way to fight him was out on the field. Mary was awake, too, and she said, "You're worrying about that broadcast, aren't you? That's what he wants you to do." And I saw she was right, she could be very shrewd at times; what he was trying to do was undermine me, and I had to stop brooding on it, because the more you brooded, the more you thought everybody was against you, and I kept telling myself it wasn't true.

There was the President, for one, even if he did fade away as soon as there was any trouble. There was Major Franceschi —though he was trying to make himself invisible—there was Cardoni, the manager—he wasn't against me, even if he he wasn't for me—and there was Beppe. After all, he'd brought me here, and his reputation depended on my being a success.

There was this fellow Bulgarelli, too, I'd been introduced to him. He was a small team trainer and he spoke a little English, and as far as I could tell, he was an honest man. The trouble out here was that the honest men were with the small clubs, they were all on the outside of things. Bulgarelli was very intelligent about the game, he asked a lot of questions. He was a great practical joker, too; he told me he was always taking rises out of the journalists who were working for Montico. He'd ring up the fat one, Bandini, in the night and put on a voice and say, "This is Logan, I'm coming round to get you." Another time, he turned up at Bandini's office and gave his name as mine, then whipped round to the back entrance, and stopped Bandini as he was sneaking down the stairs. I got the impression, though, that he didn't dislike Bandini, in fact they seemed to be quite friendly, and this was the funny thing about Rome, everybody was somehow tied up together with everybody else, even when they were fighting.

One day Beppe said to me, "Be careful of Gaudenzio, he's changing sides." Gaudenzio was the other Vice-President, the one with the monocle, and I'd been careful of him anyway, because if anybody looked a villain, it was him. I was always expecting him to come up to me and ask me to smuggle dope for him, or offer to line me up a girl. If you were ever at a nightclub or eating at a posh restaurant, he would always be there, and he was always the life and soul of everything, jogging around with this monocle of his — and whenever he met me, he'd give me this terrific welcome, as though he hadn't seen me for a year, so that I'd always wonder, what's he covering up?

The other players told me he was great at fixing them up; they said, you want to go to some of his parties, the women are marvellous, but I'd been told to watch my step in Rome, that the Press would blow up the tiniest thing, and I steered away. Soon after Beppe warned me about him, I ran into him one evening in Via Veneto and wondered, will he speak to me, but he was just as friendly, which to me meant that he hadn't written me off yet, he wanted to keep in with both sides.

Via Veneto fascinated me, I could sit there for hours at one of these tables on the pavement, and just watch the people going by. Sometimes I'd go with Mary, and sometimes I'd be sitting there with Gino, and he'd tell me this one was an actress, and this one took drugs, and that one was a Russian painter; sometimes they'd stop and join us at our table. It was like one long, endless river going by, and I'd think of London or Glasgow, and how dead they'd be by this time, while here there was all the bustle and the light and the noise; I never got tired of it.

The only snag was when I'd get recognised, and then you'd get a little group of people on the pavement, gathering round and staring, as though I was some sort of animal, till in the end we'd have to get up and go away.

It was Mary who didn't like Rome, and I couldn't understand it. I told her, "You ought to be enjoying it, you've got help with the children, you haven't got the worries I've got, it's *me* that ought to be feeling homesick, not you."

She said, "At least you've got things to distract you; what have I got? I just feel cut off here, it's worse than London. At least in London I could understand what everybody said."

I asked her, "Why don't you learn the language, then? That's something you can be doing. We've got the records here, we've got the books."

She said, "It's no good trying to send me back to school, Gerry, that's no solution."

I said, "What *is* the solution, then? You've got Nils Petersen's wife you can see, *she* speaks English; you've got Mrs. Nelson."

She said, "Mrs. Nelson's like a dog they keep chained up all day on a lead. Whenever we make an appointment, *he* gets to hear of it, and there's always a phone call at the last moment to say she's got a headache or she's got to go to the dentist. If she goes on telling me how marvellous he is, maybe one of these days she'll believe it herself. He's frightened of people, if you ask me."

"Well, what do you want me to *do*?" I said. "Send you all home again? I don't understand what you want out of life," and she gave me this curious look and she said, "*You* know what I want out of life, Gerry?"

"No I don't," I said, "you just bewilder me. You've got this flat, and people working for you, helping you with the children; you can use the car whenever you like, we've more money to spend than we've ever had. If you want to meet more people, why don't you join one of the clubs, or something? Rome's full of English people."

She said, "They're not *my* people, Gerry."

I said, "How do you know they're not your people, if you don't attempt to find out? There's bound to be a settling-in period, it can't be easy for either of us, but it's more difficult for me than for you."

She said, "Of course it is."

I said, "There's no of course about it. But if I've got this worry about you on top of everything else, if I'm going to have that in the back of my mind the whole time, then it's going to be twice as difficult."

"All right," she said, "I won't say anything. Just tell me when *you've* got no more worries, and then I'll let you know what mine are."

When she got in a mood like that, it was useless talking to her.

After that Milan game, things really started getting better. As I said before, Italians are peculiar people, there's no happy medium; they're either walking on air and they could knock over a house, or they're down in the depths and anyone can walk on them. You could tell now they all thought luck was on their side, just from how they'd sing in the coach on the way to matches—the radio was always on, full blast—and from the way everybody wanted the ball now, in training games. It made the most difference in defence, because the defence were all Italian players, whereas in the forwards, there were four of us were foreigners.

Previously they'd been covering badly; standing square and blaming one another, but now they were going in like lions, and Mario Caldini, the goalkeeper, was throwing himself around like a madman, whereas before, if he thought he'd been let down, he'd stood still and he wouldn't try. He was a real old soldier, he was thirty-one now, and in Italy, that was old. He'd been capped quite a few times and he was always playing this part, the great goalkeeper, very temperamental —stand over there when I tell you to, or how can yo.. expect me to save? I used to call him Toscanini, and I think he liked that.

He was a great grumbler, too; there was always something wrong. One of the Italian journalists that spoke English said to me one day, "That's how Caldini tries to get people to like him, by grumbling." But when he wanted to play, he could play, and it was like he once said to me, a good goalkeeper can inspire his own team, and at the same time he can demoralise the other team.

It was Mario, really, who won the game against Flaminio, though I got most of the credit for it, just because I'd scored the goal; which was typical of Italian football. It was just after Christmas, Flaminio were doing well then, they were top of the League, and we were still struggling, so everyone expected them to eat us alive.

I said to Nils Petersen, "This is a good game for us; if we can get an early goal, they'll panic, and *our* boys will get their tails up. Don't say anything to Cardoni, but for the first ten minutes, I'll play upfield, and we'll see if we can get one. If we don't then I'll drop back."

We had to keep it dark from Cardoni, because if he'd known, he'd have blown his top. Taking risks in a local derby; that was a terrible thing, unforgivable; it could lose him his job.

But as it turned out, the plan worked, because we took them by surprise, as I'd hoped we would. They expected us to come out all cautious, with eight men in defence, and instead of that we went straight down to their goal and started bombarding them. After five minutes, Valdar crossed the ball, Nils went up with the keeper and headed it clear, and I came running in and belted it into the net on the volley. As we came back for the kick-off, I said to Nils, "I'm not dropping back yet, why throw away the initiative?" and I ignored Cardoni, he was yelling at me from his bench, and for the next half-hour or so we were still on top, and playing really well. Flaminio were dazed.

At half-time, Cardoni came storming into the dressing-room and started shouting at me, I could tell it was because he was frightened. He was yelling, "*In profondità, capisci? In profondità!*" meaning you'll play deep this half, or else; I could understand quite well, now.

I said to Nils, "Tell him if I play deep we'll let them come back into the game," but he kept on shouting that he didn't care, if I didn't obey him, he'd suspend me.

So I played deep, and of course they *did* come back into the game, they started hammering us, and if it wasn't for Mario, they could have had two or three in the first twenty minutes. He stopped one, when the centre-forward was through on his own, and I've never seen a goalkeeper come out quicker; he was on him when he'd barely crossed the eighteen yard line.

In the last minute, I thought they'd equalised; their inside-right ran on to a cross, and he couldn't have been more than five yards out when he headed it, but Mario came flying across and he got a finger to it; he turned the ball on to a post, and when it came back, our centre-half cleared off the line. When the whistle went, several of the players were crying, they were so happy, and I don't think I've ever been so pleased to win a match. Some of them got hold of Mario and some of them got hold of me and they carried us both off the field. The crowd was singing—*our* supporters, anyway—and they were throwing these little fireworks that exploded on the running track.

Ronnie Nelson came into our dressing-room, I will say that for him, and he said, "Congratulations, Gerry"—he was very calm, like he always was—"that was a good goal. It ran a bit for you in the second half, though."

I said, "Our goalkeeper did! You're welcome to the moral victory, as long as you let *us* keep the points, because we need them more than you do."

So he smiled this tight smile of his and he said, "Well, these things happen in football," and he shook hands with Cardoni and went out.

We never set eyes on Montico that day, but Franceschi turned up in the dressing-room again, with the President, it was the first time for weeks, and there was a two hundred thousand lire bonus for everybody.

I thought that would be the last of Montico, but I'd underrated him or rather, I'd underrated the lengths he was prepared to go. You couldn't take anything for granted—not in Rome.

WE all went out to dinner that night, after the victory; to a restaurant in Trastevere. We were Beppe's guests, Gerry, Mary Logan and myself, and Beppe's ebullience was that of a condemned man who has suddenly been vindicated. He sat at the head of the table, exploding now and then with small detonations of delight, leaning forward to clasp my hand, to clutch Gerry by the shoulder.

"Oh! Ma che gol! Che capolavoro! Eh, Glanville? Gerry : it was a marvellous goal ! Eh, Mrs. Logan?"

"Oh, yes, marvellous," she replied, without looking at him, and I noticed Gerry glance sharply at her, across the table, while Beppe raised his glass, undeterred.

"To Gerry, eh? To all the Logan family, and to Trastevere's victory against Flaminio !"

"Thank you," Gerry said, without enthusiasm, while his wife raised her glass with an expression of long-suffering, as though she were resigned to joining in such tiresome cele-brations. I saw Gerry glance up at her suddenly, taking in her ironic pose, and his own face go taut and resentful. I won-dered if they had been quarrelling, that day.

"Now I think everything will be different !" Beppe cried. "After today, everything will be better. Eh, Mrs. Logan?"

"What?" she said. "Oh, yes, I'm sure it will be better." She drank off her glass and thrust it towards him; she seemed to me, in that moment, like a defiantly naughty child. Again, Gerry looked angrily at her, but she took no notice, though I was sure she was aware of the effect she'd caused.

The proprietor beamed over us, a huge man with the Tras-tevere badge in the broad lapel of his blue suit; gold fillings gleamed bonhomously in his teeth. "Desiderano signori?"

"Una bella bistecca per tutti," Beppe said. "That's good, eh, Gerry? That's nice, Mrs. Logan? A lovely steak !"

'Oh, yes, that'd be marvellous," Mrs. Logan said, with a

parody of enthusiasm, as if she were reading lines which had been written for someone else. But Beppe took it at face value, smiling, smiling at her.

"*Che allegria eh?*" said the proprietor. What happiness, indeed!

Mary Logan picked up her glass again. "But we must have spaghetti first!" she said. "We must make it a proper Italian celebration!"

"Oh, yes! Of course!" cried Beppe, his arms a windmill of agitation, as though he were ashamed of his forgetfulness. "Of course we have spaghetti!"

"*Al sugo?*" asked the proprietor, inclining his great, imperial head. "*Al pomadoro?*"

"What's that—*pomadoro*?" she said.

"Tomato," said Beppe, "it's tomato."

"All right—I'll have pomadoro, then."

Her colour was very high. As the meal went on, she continued steadily to drink. Once, as she refilled her glass, Gerry said quietly, "Mary!" but she answered, "I'm all right. Don't spoil the celebration! We hardly ever go out; don't spoil it now!" and it seemed to me that in some strange way, she was punishing him. Certainly he looked like a man who was being punished, as he grew more and more silent, drawing into himself—physically, too, I thought—like a tortoise.

Even Beppe, now, had realised there were undercurrents, and his exuberance was muted, replaced by a certain quiet dismay, an excessive punctilio. "*Ancora vino, Brian? Gerry:* will you have some fruit?"

We were saved by the sudden, flamboyant arrival of Vice-President Gaudenzio and his troupe; elegant young men in blazers, hair *en brosse*, three slender, gorgeous women. "*Ma guarda chi c'è!*" he cried, one arm upraised in statuesque surprise. "*Guarda! Il nostro carissimo scozzese! Quello che ci ha dato la vittoria!* The man who won the match for us! *E anche la signora!*"

With sweeping gallantry, he bowed over the table, took Mary's hand, and kissed it, while she lowered her eyelids with a complaisant smile.

"Ciào, Beppe! Buona sera, Glanville."

"Ingegnere, join us !" Beppe said.

"Ma no, ma no, you're all my guests !" Gaudenzio cried, and he reigned, like some Lord of Misrule, over a small pandemonium, as waiters scurried, the proprietor clapped his huge, plump hands, tables were brought, cloths flung over them, and our table grew and grew like a telescope.

I noticed how quickly Gerry revived, now he was on public show. As for his wife, she was high, but not too high to be beyond control. Once, he looked at her again, but she flapped a hand at him—"I'm all right, I'm all right"—and he quickly turned away.

"He's happy now," she said to me. "He's in the middle of everything, the little hero; he's got all the girls listening to him. I won't disgrace him, so he needn't worry, he needn't worry about me."

"Of course not."

"You've not seen me like this, have you?" she said. "It doesn't happen often, in fact I don't remember it happening for years, so don't think too badly of me. Don't think, poor Gerry, fancy having a cow like that to put up with."

"I won't."

"Won't you?" she said. "You're very nice," and she pressed my hand. Her voice was louder than usual, but Guadenzio's was louder still, a megaphone.

"*I'm* the one that puts up with things," she said. "You don't believe that, do you? Other women say, we envy you. . . They say your *brill-*iant husband." She looked across the table at him, unmasked; knowing and sardonic. He was talking to one of the Italian girls; her pretty face was turned towards him, the mouth slightly open, the eyes intent on his, in what or may not have been fascination, while his own face was mobile and alive. "How nice to *share* him, they mean," Mary said. "I *share* him with other women."

"Mrs. Logan," Beppe said, leaning towards her, "will you have coffee?"

"Yes," she said, "I'd better have a strong one, hadn't I? Nero, is that it? Oh, I'm learning." She put a hand on his sleeve. "Beppe brought us here, you know that, don't you? If it wasn't for Beppe, we'd never have come to Rome. We'd never have had this lovely flat, we'd never have had all this money."

Beppe watched her, transfixed, his large, dark eyes pleading and alarmed.

"Do you know where we'd be now?" she said. "We might be back in Jarrow! What a terrible thought—Jarrow! You've never been there, have you, Beppe?"

"No, no, I never been there."

"I don't think you'd like it. Do *you* think he would, Brian? There's no sun there, none at all, and there's these terrible, cold winds coming blowing in off the sea. But I'll tell you one thing—they do speak English."

"Yes, yes," he said, groping for a stepping-stone, "of course they do."

"*You* speak English, Beppe," she said, clutching his forearm again, " so I can talk to you. But the others—I can't say a word."

"Yes, Mrs. Logan."

"Not Mrs. Logan—Mary."

"Yes, Mary."

"A toast!" shouted Gaudenzio, springing from his chair, and one seemed to see round his head a wreath of merry vine leaves. "*Al bel gol di Gerr-ree Loggan!*" and then, in English, "to the *beau*tiful goal of Gerry Logan!"

We raised our glasses; Mary's was half-way up when it tilted in her hand, splashing wine on the tablecloth, where it left a small, red archipelago.

"*Evviva!*" shouted one of the elegant young men.

"*Al bellissimo gol!*" cried Beppe, and he, too, stood up.

Gerry bowed his head, gave a brief, restrained smile of modest pleasure, then looked up, suddenly remembering, at his wife; Banquo's ghost of his Macbeth. She met his eye very coolly, her chin resting on her hand, regarding him with silent defiance, till once again he turned away.

Beppe was fretting anxiously in his chair. Once, his eyes met mine in bewildered appeal, and I gave him a grimace of reassurance. Gaudenzio and the young men had started a noisy and elaborate game with toothpicks, and the girls were encouraging them with little cries of shock and admiration.

"Excuse me," Gerry said, "I'm very tired." He rose to his feet; the apologetic smile was impeccable.

"*Sì, sì!*" Gaudenzio said, at once all solicitude. "Take him home, Beppe, take good care of him. *Un giocatore come questo, sai.* . . . A player like this one . . ."

"*Certo, ingegnere,*" Beppe said, "*va bene, ingegnere,*" and for once, his solemnity seemed genuine to me.

"*Must* we go, Gerry?" Mary said.

"Yes, we must," he replied, with quiet intensity, and I felt sorry for him, where before I had been feeling sorry for her; sorry, without taking sides.

"All right, all right," she said, and rose from her chair, then foundered, head and shoulders drooping, and I caught her by the arm. There was a moment's sudden silence; the eyes of the girls, of the young men, Gaudenzio's monocle, all turned towards her, but almost at once she said, "I'm all right—some fresh air, that's all I need," and she walked slowly out of the restaurant, clinging to my arm.

The night was cold, the smell of rain hung in the air, and she stood very still on the cobbles, her head raised, diligently breathing. "That's better," she said, at length, and walked at the same, slow pace to Beppe's car, while Gerry followed her, hands in the pockets of his raincoat, head bent, as though he were alone.

They were quiet in the back of the car as Beppe drove us home with his usual tyre-screeching panache. When they got out, in Via Archimede, Gerry's smile, his thanks, as he looked in at Beppe's window, were calm and unexceptionable. As for his wife, she stood waiting for him on the pavement. She made no sign until we drove off, then raised an arm : "Goodbye! Goodbye!"

"*Povero Gerry,*" Beppe said.

I did not answer; it was not as simple as that. There was too much I did not know, too much to be digested and unravelled. It wasn't Mary who had surprised me, but the new prospect of Gerry she had given me, with which I must now come to terms.

"*Con una moglie simile. . . .*" said Beppe, righteously. "*Non sono cose de fare.* She shouldn't behave like that. *Poverino;* and after he'd scored that goal . . ."

The photograph appeared a week later, on the front page of *Roma Sera.* Berretti brandished it in my face as I came into the offices of *Il Diario Sportivo.*

"*Ecco il tuo Loggan!* Now we can see what he is! *Un donnaiolo!* A womaniser! *Un bel pezzo di mascalzone!*" and from every corner they came crowding; Mengalvio, in shirt-sleeves, Franzini, the little Fascist, Campello, strutting like a peacock; the boxing editor, the Third Division football correspondent, the military sport correspondent, flocking round me to savour the moment of truth, the recognition, the unmasking of a charlatan, grinning, eager to confront me with his perfidy.

"He dances well, though," someone said, and they roared with laughter.

I recognised the girl at once; she had come in with Gaudenzio, the girl who'd sat next to Gerry in the restaurant, gazing at him with such rapt attention, and at once the thought came wildly into my head, had Gaudenzio contrived it all? Had he followed us, put the girl next to him, arranged the very photograph? They were dancing cheek to cheek. The reproduction was a huge one; you could clearly see the expression on his face. He seemed to be talking to her, breathing something charged and intimate in her ear, to which she was listening with a pleased, piquant smile.

"*Allora, cosa dici?*" demanded Berretti. "What are you going to tell us about this Logan?"

"Nothing," I said.

"*Ma come, niente?*"

"I've no idea of the circumstances."

"But look, look, it tells you there!" and he jabbed his long, brown finger at the caption. "Taken at 3 a.m. this morning at La Colombina night club, in Via Veneto. The Trastevere footballer Gerry Logan dancing with Anna Rubini, a cinema actress. *Oh! Ma non è mica la moglie!* It's certainly not his wife!"

"There's probably an explanation," I said, flatly.

"Oh, yes, a fine explanation. The explanation is that he's going round screwing little actresses!" They laughed again.

"*Ma insomma*," said Mengalvio, "he's certainly not the first to do that."

"How many children has he, Glanville?" someone asked.

"Two," I said.

"Two, eh?" They were making the most of it. "And this is how he goes on?"

"*Ma non esaggeriamo*," Mengalvio appealed, his hands cupped and extended before his chest, like those of a pleading monk. "At least he plays! At least he scores goals! When the others play around, they come on to the field half finished."

"*Oh! Ma tu sei scemo!*" roared Berretti. "That's not the point. The point is, it's expected of us Latins, but this one's a Scotsman; people who're always preaching morality at us!"

"*Be'!*" said Campello. "A Scotsman's a man as well," and the argument took fire like petroleum; gesturing hands, contorted faces, a chaos of shouting voices, so that anyone listening outside would think that violence must be done. Instead, as I well knew, it would blow over in five minutes, when the group would disperse with no more than a few, explosive grunts—"*Oh! Oh!*"—each wound magically healing

I slipped away from them, down the ancient, tenebrous, broad stone staircase, out into the evening street. I wasn't surprised. The other night had prepared me, just as, I realised, that earlier glance in twilight had prepared me for the other night. Or rather, I *was* surprised, but only to find myself so disappointed in him, as if I had been proved right when I was still hoping to be proved wrong; as if something still remained of schoolboy hero-worship; the footballer-hero who didn't smoke, didn't drink, and was happily, sexlessly, married.

I bought the paper for myself and looked at the photograph again. It was well taken and cunningly selected; the whole pose, the very tone of it, mocked the possibility of innocence. I wondered whether Gerry had seen it, whether *she* had seen it; whether one should warn him and prepare him. But I decided not to, remembering the impregnable wall of privacy he built around himself; the inner citadel, right at the centre of his easy outwardness. So I did nothing, heard nothing, merely wondered — and kept away from *Il Diario Sportivo*.

Trastevere were away from home that week, playing in Catania, and I went to Flaminio's match in the Olympic Stadium, where they beat Bologna.

"Your friend's been stupid, hasn't he?" Nelson said, smiling in the dressing-room.

"I suppose he has."

"Ah," he said, "they come to Rome, you see, and they don't keep their eyes open. I mean, they suddenly find themselves with a lot of money, when they're not used to it, and then they come across temptations."

I nodded, without answering him; it annoyed me to hear Gerry tagged and categorised, stripped of all his individuality, buried among a dull regiment of simple Scandinavians, provincial British bumpkins. Whatever the explanation, it went deeper than that.

Nelson gave me his quizzical, knowing look. "You're a friend of his, aren't you?" he said. "Well, I've got nothing against him. I'm sorry for him. I'm sorry for his wife, as well. But he's been silly."

When I got back to my apartment, after dinner, the telephone was ringing. It was Mary Logan. "You don't mind my phoning you?" she asked, in a drained, dejected voice. "I just want some advice."

"If I can help. . . ." I said, then stopped. The words sounded too pat, as soon as I had said them; the words of a marriage guidance counsellor.

"You saw the photo?"

"Yes, I did."

There was a silence, then she said, "Can you come over here? I won't keep you very long. Gerry's not here. He's not back till tomorrow."

Her face, when she opened the door of the apartment to me, was very pale, devoid of make-up. She did not attempt to smile, but turned and led the way solemnly through the hall, negotiating an obstacle race of children's toys—two dolls, a model railway train, a red, rubber ball—and into the living-room.

"I suppose everybody in Rome is laughing at me," she said. She sat down in the corner of a white, leather sofa, and lit a cigarette with weary automatism, as though she'd long ago realised its futility as a source of comfort.

"No, they're not," I said, as automatically.

"You *say* that, but they must be. It's a good joke, isn't it? The great footballer leaves his dreary English wife for a little Italian film starlet."

"They're not laughing," I said. "To tell you the truth, I think they're a little bit shocked."

"They shouldn't be shocked," she said, and drew on the cigarette, giving her momentarily a tough, abstracted expression. "If they knew anything about our marriage, they wouldn't be shocked. And they needn't think it's just Italian girls."

There was nothing to say. She didn't want help from me, I realised—what help could I give?—but merely someone to listen.

"I'm not staying here," she said. "Not to be a laughing stock. Just crammed into a corner, like Ronnie Nelson does, with *his* wife, except as far as I know, he doesn't carry on with Italian girls. Or maybe he does. I don't know : does he?" and she suddenly looked at me, as though she disliked me, as though all of us were aligned against her.

"I don't think so," I said.

"You see, Gerry's used to getting anything he wants," she said. "There's no rules for Gerry; he makes his own rules, only *you're* expected to keep them, too. I said to him, 'The rules are that everything you do is right, and anyone who objects to it is wrong. Well, I'm tired of keeping your rules.'"

There was an hiatus, till at last I said, for want of anything better, "And what did *he* say?"

"Oh, the same sort of thing as he always says. You can't get a straight answer out of Gerry. That I was being unreasonable. Do you think I'm being unreasonable?"

"No," I said.

"He said, 'You see a photograph, and right away you jump to conclusions.'" She laughed. "'Well, Gerry,' I said, 'I'd have to be pretty daft not to, wouldn't I?' He's like a little child, at times."

Another silence. At last I asked, "What did he do then?"

"Oh, walked out, of course. As usual. That's Gerry's way, when there's something he doesn't want to face."

"But he was out at three o'clock . . ." I found myself saying.

"You mean I must have *known* what was going on. Well, I suppose I did, really. He'd told me he was going over to see Nils Petersen. If I'd wanted to, I could have phoned there, but even if I had, he'd have had some story—you don't trust me, what do you mean by spying on me, I went to the club house first and got caught up there; something like that. Oh, you *know* all the time, you know and you don't know. As long as you're not quite sure, you can kid yourself it isn't happening. I'm very good at that; I've had a bit of practice."

"There may be nothing in it," I said, still casting round for comfort.

"Oh, very likely, but that won't be *his* fault. And if there's nothing in this one, there will be in the next one, or maybe in the one after that. He's so vulnerable; I could tell she was making a play for him, there at the restaurant, I wasn't *that* far gone; she was obviously a little tramp. Looking into his eyes and flattering him; he laps that up. All she probably wants is some publicity, but Gerry wouldn't see that; he's so *naïve*. I've said to him, 'You really surprise me, Gerry, the intellectual way you can talk, and yet anyone can take you in; people would never believe it, the ones that admire you so much.' Oh, he gets furious when I say that. I don't understand him, I'm trying to undermine him. 'The trouble is, Gerry,' I say, 'I *do* understand you. You're not looking for someone who understands you; you're looking for someone who sees you the way you see yourself.'

"He won't find them here, not with Italian girls. They're sly, if you ask me: I've watched them. I've met some of the players' wives. Oh, they know how to butter a man up all right—that's just where Gerry's so vulnerable. You can see them turning it on and turning it off, it makes me sick. I said to Gerry, 'This one listens to you, doesn't she? I saw her listening to you at the restaurant; that's why you like her, and she knows it's why. *She'll* listen to you, *she'll* tell you how wonderful you are, until she's got whatever it is she wants out of you—then it's goodbye.'"

Poor Gerry, I found myself thinking, poor Gerry, with his clever paradoxes, his supple fluency; it seemed so brittle, now. There was a penetration here which he couldn't aspire to, with all his dragonfly intelligence.

"Did he answer you?" I asked.

"Oh, no, he just walked out again. I told you: when he hasn't got an answer, that's what he does. He said, 'You're making me lose my temper, I'm going before I say something I don't want to say.' 'Go on, then,' I said. 'One of these days you can get out and you can *stay*.'"

"Did you mean that?"

She considered this for a moment, then said, "I meant it *then*."

"But not now?"

"I *suppose* not," she said, with slow reluctance.

"But I'm sure there's nothing in it," I told her, though I wasn't sure. "It's probably been engineered."

"What do you mean?" she asked, sharply. "By who?"

"By people who wanted something of the sort to happen."

"Who?"

"Gaudenzio, perhaps. People connected with Montico."

"But that's a *filthy* thing to do."

"There's worse things done in Rome. It's just a theory, though. Gaudenzio may have nothing at all to do with it."

"*He* could have something to do with it, the oily old devil. I've not trusted him from the moment I set eyes on him; all that slobbering over my hand. Well, you give him a message from *me*; you tell him he'd better stop what he's started. . . ."

"*If* he started it," I said.

The rage went out of her, as though she had been deflated. "Quite right, you're quite right," she said. "It's no use blaming him; he didn't *have* to get hooked, did he? And if it wasn't that one, it would be another. You know the only thing that's really worrying him? Whether that picture gets in the English papers. He says 'I'll sue them if they publish it, it would finish me, it would finish my career.' He's been rushing out and buying every paper. The *Sunday Pictorial* rang up; he doesn't know that."

"What did you say to them?"

"Oh, I told them there was nothing to discuss, it was just a mountain being made out of a molehill.

"What do I do?" she asked me, suddenly. "Stay here? I'm stifling here. I've only got the children, otherwise there's nobody, I might be living on a desert island. And *they* don't mean anything to him, don't think they do! Only when he *feels* like it, when he feels like being the father. Then he'll play with them for half-an-hour, or read to them for twenty minutes, and think he's done his duty. Oh, and if anybody *comes*, of course, then he'll take notice of them. He's on show, then. And Janey gets taken in, she'll do anything for him, but he can't take Duncan in. It would serve him right if they did publish that photograph."

I had nothing to say at all, now, silenced alike by her bitterness and by the image of this new, smaller Gerry Logan she had shown to me, which bitterness alone could not account for. Would she stay? Would she go? If all she said were true, it would make no difference.

As I sat there, it wasn't Gerry the adulterer in whom I was deceived, so much as Gerry the spoiled child, who must always be right in all he did; Gerry the ingenuous, who felt he could go dancing with a girl in Via Veneto, in the small hours of the morning, and if necessary, explain it all away. He was trapped by his own tongue, I thought, the dupe of his own, endless fluency.

"Have I shocked you?" she asked me, with a narrow look. "I shouldn't have said so much, you probably had your illusions about him; everybody has, that's the trouble. I've still got illusions myself. I tell myself things will get better."

"Maybe they will."

"No," she said, in a weary voice, "I don't think they ever will. Not now, I don't, when I'm looking at things without blinkers. He's made like he is: I can't change him. No one ever will. Only, like I've told him, 'It's a bit late, now. There's not just you and me; there's Janey and Duncan as well.'"

"*Sono deluso*," Major Franceschi told me, and in disappointment, the great, white cliff of his face looked heavier than ever. "*Lo credevo una persona seria.* I thought he was a serious person."

"As far as football's concerned. . . ." I said, a little weakly.

"Excuse me, one can't divorce the private life from the footballing life. One reflects on the other. That's why football is in decline in Italy; there's no more discipline. An athlete must practise himself."

Bulgarelli was more tolerant. "*Una cosa che capita a tutti*," he said, "the sort of thing that happens to everyone. I asked Bandini, 'Oh! But why did you publish that photograph? Why do you want to ruin Trastevere?' And he was offended. He said to me 'Me? I don't want to ruin Trastevere. *Sono affezionato al Trastevere*; I'm very fond of them. You know I am.' 'Well,' I said, 'It doesn't look like it.' '*Ma come, non lo sembra?*' 'Because you're trying to embroil their best man,' I said, 'you're trying to demoralise Logan, and once you've demoralised Logan, you've demoralised the team.' Well, then he was *very* offended. He said, "But *you're* not fair, Bulgarelli! Logan's a rascal. He takes the club's money, then he goes out on the town.'

"'*When* does he go out on the town?' I asked. '*Ma!*' he said. 'You *know* when he goes out on the town ! He was out on the town the other night, when we published the photograph.' 'Oh! And last year, when *you* were a little drunk at the Trastevere banquet?' 'But that's got nothing to do with it !' 'Certainly it's got something to do with it. According to you, if I wanted to, I could say, Bandini's a drunk. *Oh*: how

164

do you know? Because I saw him drunk once last year, at the Trastevere banquet!' And then, I said, 'You're forgetting a substantial fact. *Dimentichi un fatto sostanziale.*' 'What's that?' he said. 'That he scores goals!'"

The photograph had appeared in England. That night, when I left Mary Logan, I had gone to Via Veneto, and there, amidst the pop-eyes and the garish chaos, had bought the *Sunday Pictorial*. The picture was there, on an inside page, "Scottish international footballer Gerry Logan, now with Roman club Trastevere, dances with Italian film starlet Anna Rubini. Picture was taken last week in the small hours, in a Rome night club. Miss Rubini said, 'There's no romance, Gerry and I are just very good friends, and I think he's a marvellous footballer.' His wife, Mrs. Mary Logan, said, 'The whole thing is nonsense.'"

Was Montico behind it all, I asked Bulgarelli.

"I've the impression that he is. She's quite well known, this Rubini; *tipo puttana cinematografica.* A sort of cinematic whore. They say she was once the mistress of Gaudenzio, the one who's Vice-President of Trastevere, now; then she made progress!"

"Gaudenzio brought her into the restaurant, the night Gerry met her," I said.

"Then everything's explained!"

But to explain it did not cure it. Gerry, when I saw him now, was just as courteous and cordial. It was merely that one saw him less; he seemed always to be hurrying out of dressing-rooms, disappearing into cars. So far as Rome was concerned—as I would have told him, if he had let me—one good goal would settle everything—and he scored it in their next home match. He went through on his own, from Nils Petersen's pass, beautifully side-stepping the Udinese goal-keeper, and put the ball into the deserted net.

"Ah, *Logan!*" shouted a supporter, "*puoi ballare anche 'sta sera!* You can go dancing this evening, too!"

Later in the game, he scored again: he was back on his pedestal.

I hoped he would give the girl up, now; that his wife would

165

tell him in turn what I had told her—that she was probably sponsored by Montico and Gaudenzio. I wished I could make sure of this, by telling him myself, but it was he who must first raise the subject, and he never did; the whole affair might never have happened.

"*Ma!*" said Campello, at *Il Diario dello Sport*, "*può darsi che ballano, gli scozzesi, ma non chiavano*. Maybe the Scots dance, but don't screw."

MARY LOGAN

I THOUGHT in Rome we were really finished, I just couldn't see any future. If it hadn't been for the children, I wouldn't even have given it one thought, I'd have caught the next plane back to England.

It was Phyllis Nelson who showed me the photograph, she'd kept it for me, it was very kind of her. I'd heard all about it, of course, but I hadn't seen it. And when I saw it, I just burst out crying, I couldn't help it; the look on Gerry's face, and the way he was whispering to this stupid little girl. What made it worse was Phyllis stood there watching me with this *smug* expression, and I just knew what was going through her head: Ronnie and I, Ron and I, it would never happen to *us*. I nearly yelled at her, "You and your bloody Ronnie, don't think that *you're* any better off, the way he keeps you locked up all day." "Never mind, dear," she said, "he's not *worth* crying about. If I were you, I'd just give him an ultimatum: behave yourself properly, or I'm leaving you, and I'm taking the children with me. You'd have everyone on your side."

"I don't want them on my side," I said. "Not you, not them, not anyone else. I can manage these things on my own." "Oh," she said, "I'm quite *sure* you can," in this bitchy voice, and then she went out saying she'd make me some tea. But I didn't stay for that, I couldn't bear any more of it; I couldn't bear her, and I couldn't bear to be in the same room with that photograph. All I thought about now was the children. Duncan would be all right, I knew that, you could dump him down anywhere and it wouldn't worry him, he'd come up smiling, but Janey was different, I knew Janey would suffer, and if there was any way of stopping that, I was going to.

Gerry was staying out most of the time, and when he was in, he hardly spoke to me. One evening, I'd put the children

167

to bed and I was sitting there doing some sewing when he suddenly let himself into the flat, came rushing through the room without a word to me, got something from the bedroom, and then came rushing back. As he went past, I said, "It can't go on, Gerry."

He stopped then, and looked at me in this terrible, cold way, as if he didn't know me, then he said, "What can't go on?" And when he said that, I felt so weary; I felt, oh dear, oh *dear*, we've got to go through the whole thing *all* over again.

"Gerry," I said, "why can't you ever face things? You're living in this flat like a lodger, you're no good to me and you're no good to the children. If you want to live with your little whatever her name is, I'll clear out, and take Janey and Duncan back to England."

As soon as I said that, he got frightened, like I knew he would, because if there's one thing Gerry hates it's being made to face facts, he wants you to leave him alone in his little dream world. "You're mad!" he said. "You don't know what you're saying!"

"*I* know what I'm saying," I said, "and I'm perfectly serious. You don't believe me, do you? Well, you just say the word, and we'll go."

"You can't go," he said.

"*Oh*, yes, I can," I told him. "I'm not going to stay here as your housekeeper, Gerry."

He said, "The children are mine as much as yours."

"Well, it's a pity you don't take any notice of them, isn't it?" I said. "They've hardly seen you for a week, now."

"You're trying to destroy my career!" he said.

"You're destroying your own career!" I told him. "You're doing just what Montico and Gaudenzio want you to."

"*What* do you mean?" he said.

"You've walked into their trap. You're like a fish with its mouth open. They throw in a little bit of bait, and you're hooked."

"*Who* told you all that?" he said. "That's bloody nonsense!"

"Who told me?" I said. "I can't remember—everybody

168

seems to know about it. I should have thought you'd have cottoned on yourself. She came in with Gaudenzio, didn't she?"

"You don't know what you're talking about!" he said.

"Go and ask *her*, then," I said, and I just went on sewing, I knew it maddened him. "Go and ask your little mistress."

"She's *not* my mistress!"

"Oh, no," I said, "of course she's not; I read it in the paper, I forgot. She said you're just good friends."

"She said nothing of the sort! I'm suing them!"

"I shouldn't sue them, if I were you," I said, "I'd leave well alone, I'd let it blow over."

He didn't answer for a minute, so that in the end I looked up, and the expression on his face was terrible, I'd never seen him like that before; he looked completely lost. I was afraid he was going to cry, and I couldn't stand it; I got up and I went to him and put my arms round him, and he said, "Mary, for God's sake, I don't know what I'm doing, I don't know what's happening to me. Don't leave me; you know I need you!" and suddenly I knew he did need me, I knew for the first time that, whatever he'd done, he needed me more than I needed him.

"You've got a funny idea of showing it," I said.

"I'm made like that, Mary," he said, "I can't help myself."

"You'll have to change, Gerry," I told him, "you'll just have to change."

I suppose I knew deep down that he never would, but I fooled myself he might, because I did still love him. But I loved him in a different way, now. To begin with, I'd loved him for what he was, or for what I thought he was; I loved everything about him. Now, I loved him *despite* what he was; there were things about him I knew I'd despise, if I didn't love him. I can see now that he needed me because he needed comforting, he needed *mothering*, and that was something I don't think his mother had ever given him. I can't imagine anyone running to *that* hard face, when something had gone wrong. He wanted me to say, "There, there, everything will be all right, no one will think worse of you in England, just because one photograph's been published; by the time we get back there, it'll all be forgotten."

Then he began to talk about leaving Rome, he said, "Not to go home, I want to stay in Italy, but I want to make a fresh start. People are right: you *can't* play football in Rome, I should have listened to them. This is a dangerous city." I remembered how he'd raved about it at first, how it was the only place where he could live, but I didn't say anything.

I wanted to get out of Rome, too, I hated it; I didn't like the place and I couldn't stand the people. Even the flat wasn't as wonderful as it looked, which was typical of Rome. Things kept going wrong; the plumbing was terrible, we had a man in and he said we'd have to have some of the pipes completely replaced. When I told Beppe, he said, "That's all right, Mrs. Logan, you have it done, Trastevere will pay," but when the bill came, it was us that had to pay it, and whenever Gerry wanted to see the treasurer, he was always out. Then when winter came, it was a rotten winter, worse than England; at least in England you knew what you were in for, even in Jarrow, at least you knew that, but here, where you expected sunshine, it could pelt with rain for days—and then turn freezing cold. The worst thing about it was the humidity. The children had colds all the time.

Gerry said, "I wish I had as much time as you've got, I could go round seeing things. I don't understand you, you're wasting your chance," but I'm not a great one for paintings and that, and anyway, you soon get sick of going to places on your own. In any case, whenever it came to the point and there was a chance of going together, Gerry always had some excuse why he couldn't come with me.

There were some Italian families in our building that I tried to be friendly with, but it wasn't easy, partly through the language, and partly because they seemed to want to keep themselves to themselves. I'd always heard everyone say how unfriendly we were in England, but compared to most of the Italians I came across, we're hospitality itself, honestly.

The lazy life they had, Italian women—that was something else I couldn't get used to. This one that lived opposite us, her husband was a lawyer; she never got up till twelve o'clock, and the maids did all the housework and the shopping—I know, because my maid used to talk to them, and tell me.

As for the men, they made me sick, it was their conceit that really got me, they seemed to think they'd only got to look at any woman—even the ugliest of them—and she'd fall into bed with them, she'd be so flattered. And I didn't even care for the good-looking ones, because they *knew* they were good-looking, they were almost as bad as women, the way they held their heads and the way they turned their profiles, they'd *preen* themselves. And when you went out in the street, they'd never let you alone, following you and calling after you. One English girl I met said she liked it, she said, "At least they take notice of you, at least they make you feel you're a woman."

I said, "Yes, *any* woman, anything in skirts."

Gerry had this friend, Gino, he was a writer and a film star, and now and again he'd bring him to the flat. He was good-looking, I'll give him that, very distinguished, with this grey hair and a little moustache, and always wearing very expensive clothes—but oh, didn't he know it! Even he had this conceit about him. He'd pay you compliments, but there was an undertone to them, I felt he was thinking, poor Gerry, fancing being tied down to somebody as dull as *her*. I thought he was a bad influence on Gerry, not in the same way Sam Cowan had been, though I had an idea that *he* might be introducing him to girls, as well, but in a more direct way.

He made Gerry think too much of himself, he encouraged all these daydreams that I knew he had of not being just a footballer, but being a great writer and a great intellectual as well. I knew Gerry was very intelligent and clever, but because he was so eloquent, he could make people think he was cleverer than he was. But he couldn't keep up with them, he hadn't the education, and I was afraid he'd overreach himself.

It was great fun for Gino of, course; Gerry was a novelty to him, he was entertained by him. He could sit there with this smile on his face, listening to Gerry for hours, as if he was at some kind of performance, but Gerry couldn't see this, he thought they were talking on level terms. I was afraid Gino might try and persuade Gerry to stay in Rome, but he said to me one day, he spoke very good English, "Mrs. Logan, for me it would be a terrible thing if your husband left Trastevere. I would lose the pleasure of seeing him play, and my favourite club would lose its best player. But for *his* sake, I think it's good if he leaves Rome, I've told him so."

Gerry said he'd like to go to one of the Milan clubs, he said, "They're obviously the best run, and they've got the most money. The Roman clubs all seem to live from hand to mouth; when things get desperate, one of the directors puts his hand in his pocket and pays the bills, and when *he* drops out, another one comes in."

He told Beppe he wanted to leave. Beppe said, "Leave it to me, I'll find you a club, I've finished with Trastevere. But don't say a word to anyone." But it got round, of course, like everything always did in Rome; it was all over the papers about Gerry wanting to go, with all sorts of hints that it was my fault, that I'd insisted on him leaving, because of this girl. I didn't care, I didn't care what they thought, it just made me all the more pleased we'd be getting out of Rome.

This Major Franceschi came along and tried to persuade Gerry to stop. He brought Beppe with him to interpret for him, and I thought this was very funny, seeing Beppe had promised Gerry he'd help him to get away. Franceschi wasn't anything to do with the club, really, he was just a friend of the President that the President was meant to listen to. He was so intense I found him a terrible strain, and I think Gerry did too, but he used to say he was the only one of the whole bunch that he trusted.

Major Franceschi said, through Beppe, that the President was terribly upset; the club were doing so much better now, and it was mostly thanks to Gerry. He knew there'd been some difficulties, but they'd only been made by a certain group, and after the next assembly meeting in the summer, he'd probably be able to get rid of them. Then he looked at me in an embarrassed way so I knew what was on his mind, and he said the President was satisfied with **Gerry** in *every* way, the President still had complete faith in him. He knew Gerry was a real professional and he tried hard and gave the club everything he had. The President didn't take any notice of the newspapers, and what they published and what they didn't publish. He said if Gerry would stay, Trastevere would be very generous; he could name his own salary, if he liked. When Beppe translated that, I was worried for a minute; as far as I was concerned, staying in Rome wasn't worth it at *any* price, not even a thousand pounds a week; then Gerry turned round to me, and he must have seen from my expression, because he turned back to the others and said no, he appreciated it very much, but there were a lot of reasons why he couldn't play in Rome, and he hoped the club would let him go. Then Major Franceschi looked glummer than ever—he always looked glum—and he said, very well, he knew the President didn't want to keep anyone against his will, but maybe Gerry would give it to the end of the season, and perhaps then he'd have changed his mind. Gerry said he wouldn't change his mind, but to tell the President he was grateful for what he'd said.

As Beppe was following the major through the door, he turned round, and whispered to Gerry, "Don't worry, everything will be all right."

And so Gerry played out the rest of the season, and Trastevere finished five or six places from the bottom, and stayed in the top division. I didn't go to many games. I just found them boring, the way they played there, all defence and stopping and starting and booting the ball up in the air, and fouls the whole time, and players every time they got hurt going into such a performance about it and rolling about on the ground as if they were at their last gasp.

Gerry came home, a couple of weeks from the end of the season, and he said, "I've bloody well had enough. They want to sell the game." They were playing against a team which looked as though it might go down. He said, "I'll have nothing to do with it. Nils won't, either. The others were saying, 'We don't need the points, what does it matter?' It's Mario

Caldini, the goalkeeper; he's behind it. I always knew he was a villain. Nils said it's always going on, at the end of every season, you can't do anything about it. He said if we'd been in trouble we'd probably be doing it ourselves. He said the only thing we can do is to see if we can talk some of the younger players into trying, and maybe the rest of them won't be able to lose the match: but what hope is there of that, when your goalkeeper's one of them?"

They did lose it, and I don't think I've ever seen Gerry in such a rage as he was when he got back that Sunday night. He said, "We could have beat them easily; as fast as Nils and I were scoring goals down one end, our own defence was throwing them in up the other. Nothing would make me stay here now—nothing."

So the end of the season came at long last, and Trastevere agreed to let him go. Beppe came round and told us, "Ambrosiana want you"—that was one of the Milan clubs—"they've offered a hundred million lire, but I still think they'll go higher if Trastevere say it isn't enough."

The funny thing was that now the sun had come out again and all the greenery, I was beginning to come round to Rome again. The season didn't end till June, and I'd drive the children down to the sea at Ostia, and they'd love it on the beach there.

We went home for the summer; we went to Jarrow and stayed with my parents, then we all of us went to Whitby, for a holiday. We didn't stay in London, we'd given up the house—it was a club house—and I managed to talk Gerry out of going up to Glasgow, to stop with his mother, because I couldn't stand that again. Then it was Milan, and this time the children and I came straight out with him, and stopped at a hotel.

There was nothing beautiful about Milan, not like Rome, of course, just a big, bustling city, with all those great white cubes going up on the outskirts; but in a way I didn't mind that, it didn't seem so *foreign*. The people seemed to work much harder, there wasn't this same feeling you'd had in Rome that everyone had all the time in the world. If you wanted something done, you could get it done, you didn't get all this stuff about *domani* and *dopodomani*. Gerry said he'd rather have gone to Milan than to Ambrosiana, because he'd like to have played with Liedholm, the Swedish player, but it seemed a much better club than Trastevere, the team was much stronger, it didn't all depend just on Gerry, and the President didn't put on airs, the way he did in Rome.

We were there for two years, the children went to the international school, and Gerry was making even more money than before; it used to frighten me at times, when I thought about it. I'd think to myself, you'd better not get too used to it, you won't always be able to go into a butcher's shop or a greengrocer and order whatever you want, you won't always be able to buy a new hat when you feel like it; don't take it for granted. At other times, I'd use it to cheer myself up, I'd tell myself, what are *you* being so soft about, saying you're homesick? You've got everything you could ask for, you've never had all this in England.

But it didn't work long, because you do get used to things. You get used to anything.

GERRY LOGAN

ITALY changed me. Not just in my attitude to football—I was disappointed in the football: in my attitude to life. When I got back to England, I found I was seeing things in a new way. I don't say I was seeing them like an Italian, but I had a detachment from them. Everything in Italy's so different from what you've been brought up to that at first—even though you like *them*—it's like a head-on collision, and you reject a lot of it; Mary went on rejecting it right to the end, because she's more conservative than I am, and she had less to do with Italians. But gradually as time goes on, you find there's some things you still reject, but there's a lot of things that you accept. Temperamentally, as I've said before, the people were a lot closer to me in many ways than British people.

One thing we had in common was the way we could both get excited about things, but at the bottom we were very realistic. You'd think, looking at an Italian, when he got worked up, during a football match or even just having a discussion, that he had no sense of proportion, that he was controlled by his emotions—but the fact was, he could always cut his losses. You'd see it with the players, at Trastevere and then at Ambrosiana; they'd get thrown over by a girl, or the club would fine them for not trying, and you'd find them in tears, it was the end of the world; they'd never be the same again, they'd never kick another football. Then, in a week or maybe less, you'd see them with a new girl friend, better looking than the last, or they'd come out on the field and they'd play a blinder.

They had a very practical attitude to marriage, too; the married men went after other women as a matter of course, and their wives seemed to take it for granted, too. They were all Catholics, and there was no question of a marriage breaking up, there wasn't any divorce, but there was this unspoken

176

understanding, a man was a man, and it was no use trying to alter him. I don't say I admired the way a lot of them behaved, because there's a happy medium, and besides, you can't be a ram at the same time you're trying to be a professional footballer—but in *principle* I was in sympathy with them.

I came home in the end for various reasons. First of all I was over thirty, and I was taking too much out of myself in Italy. Every season there was like two seasons in England, and I wanted to go on playing at least till I was thirty-five. Then I wanted to try out in England some of the things I'd learned in Italy; they were tactical things, mostly, and I thought they'd work well at home; also, I knew that I was a better player than when I left home. I could pace myself better, and I'd been up against much more tightly organized defences. Mary was very keen to go home, too, she'd never settled down like I had, and she wanted the children to go to English schools.

Ambrosiana wanted me to stay, they told me, "You'll never earn what we're paying you, in England." I said, "Money isn't everything," and they laughed at me, but besides that, I thought there was a lot of opportunity for me in England, outside football—in journalism, for example. I'd got a lot to tell people about the game, after these three seasons in Italy, I wanted to go back and change things; this was a new challenge for me.

And finally, there was this chance to go to Borough. I'd always had a secret ambition to play for them, ever since I was a boy in Glasgow. They were a great name then, even in Scotland, with this terrific forward-line of theirs, and they used to win everything. They'd come to Ibrox once a year to play the Rangers, and every time they came they'd pack the ground out. I remember once being taken to see them by my father; they came out on to the field like giants. It always seemed to me they had something special, even after the war, when things started going badly for them; even after I'd come to England, and started playing against them myself. You'd see their players arrive before a match in these smart blazers, at a time when they were the only club that had them, and there'd be this confidence about them, they seemed to be saying, "We're Borough; you can take us or leave us, we don't care." They were like the aristocrats of football, even if they'd fallen on bad times, like a lot of aristocrats had, and had to show people round their homes.

I think if Borough had wanted me, I might even have turned down going to Italy, but at that time they were in this, "We won't pay inflated transfer fees" period—even though before the war, they'd been the biggest spenders of anyone.

I wasn't all that impressed by their football, what I'd seen of it over the last few years. It was too static, their own tradition seemed to be a burden on them, yet at the same time I liked the idea of the tradition being there. It seemed to me you could use it positively or you could use it negatively, but at least you had it, and it was something none of the other clubs had, except perhaps Arsenal and the Villa. I thought maybe with the ideas I'd bring back with me from Italy, I could be the one to renew the tradition, and get things working again.

Manchester United were keen to get me, too, Matt Busby flew over to see me, and I'd always had a great respect for him; but I was finished with the provinces; if I was coming back, it was London or it was nowhere.

Borough's manager was Jack Westborn, he'd been their centre-half before the war, and that was part of the tradition; a manager had to be one of their ex-players, all in a long, straight line going back to nineteen-twenty-something when they'd had this manager Wilfrid Cunliffe, who'd made them into what they were. I wasn't quite sure about having a manager who'd been a centre-half; it was one stage better than having a manager who'd been a goalkeeper, but that was all. I think you can judge a footballer by the position he fills: a goalkeeper will always be a little crazy, and a centre-half will never have much imagination. If he had he wouldn't be content with playing centre-half, just destroying all the time.

Jack Westborn seemed quite pleasant, though. He hadn't

178

been at Borough when I was with Chiswick, he'd been the Exeter City manager, then, and after that, he'd had a spell with Derby. He came from one of those little Lancashire towns and there was something very unpretentious about him; I thought we'd get on. He said, "I want you to come and help me, Gerry; I want to make Borough into a great club again. You and Lionel did it at Chiswick, you and I can do it here." He wasn't in Lionel Stone's class, I knew that, but Lionel was managing a non-League club, so there was no hope of joining up with him again.

I'd always go and see him when I came home for the summer, and the change in him was terrible, his confidence had gone, I'd never have believed it. Even his voice had changed; it used to be so lively, he'd keep everybody going with his jokes, but now it was tired, as though he had to make an effort just to speak. I tried to persuade him to let me find him an Italian club, but he wouldn't let me try, he'd say, "They'd never have me, Gerry; they'd never have heard of me." I felt if I could get him there, into a different atmosphere, he'd come to life again, it was only a question of finding a stimulus.

He was trying to use our Chiswick methods with this club, in the Southern League, but of course he hadn't the players to do it. He said, "They're a lot of camels, honestly, Gerry; their League clubs knew what they were doing when they put *them* on the list. There's one or two good little local boys I've got, but when they *are* good you can't keep 'em, it wouldn't be fair to them."

I'd say, "Lionel, there must be a place for you here, there *must* be, after all you've achieved."

"They wanted me in Newcastle," he said, "but I said no. I didn't feel up to it, Gerry; besides, I didn't fancy it up there, it's a foreign country, the North-East."

I took Mary down to see him, the second summer we were back, and when she came away, she cried. He didn't even seem to have the heart to talk about tactics. I was excited when I first came back, I wanted to discuss with him what I'd found in Italy, but he didn't respond—only out of politeness.

He'd say, "Go on?" and "Do they?" but he wasn't really listening, you could tell that.

Borough got us a house in Barnet, and I liked it out there; it had a big garden, and it was almost out in the country.

It was very strange being back at first, it was strange to hear people talking English all round me, and another thing I missed was the smells. There weren't as many in Milan as in Rome, in all those little alleys, but you'd still get them there. I used to enjoy myself picking out which was which, cooking oil and pasta and sometimes just drains—I decided that you couldn't have one without the other, that was the price you had to pay; you either cut out all the smells, or none of them.

On paper, the team they had at Borough looked a mediocre one, but then so were Chiswick, when I first went to them. They had one very good player, Ronnie Scott, the centre-forward; he was a little fair-haired London boy who was in the England team, he was only nineteen, but he'd scored a phenomenal amount of goals, and the idea was that I'd make some more for him.

Ronnie was what I'd call an instinctive player, he'd do the intelligent thing, but he wouldn't do it because he'd thought it out, he'd do it by instinct. I suppose that's true to some extent of all goal poachers, they glide into the right position at the right time, though they don't know why they do it, themselves. Ronnie *had* this. You'd shoot against the cross-bar, for example, and he'd be there to put in the rebound— it *looked* a goal anybody could have scored, but they had to be there first to score it. He had a marvellous burst of speed, too, he'd be off the mark like a greyhound. A lot of people said he wasn't in the game enough, they said he didn't con-tribute anything except score goals, but to me, that was non-sense, it was like saying a pilot can't do anything but fly an aeroplane. In any case, I'd learned in Italy that his sort of player was the most effective kind, the player that *explodes*. You can forget about him for maybe twenty minutes, and then *bang*! he pops up and he's won the game.

You couldn't talk to him about football. He wasn't stupid,

he had this London shrewdness, but he wasn't interested in plans or tactics. Sometimes I'd get frustrated, and then I'd realise that this was *part* of Ronnie. If you tried to force him to take an interest in these things, you were trying to change his whole personality as a player, and you were as bad as all those qualified coaches who would have written Puskas off, because he hadn't got a right foot ! You could give an ordinary player *three* feet, and he wouldn't be able to do with all three of them what Puskas does just with the one.

Jack Westborn was keen for me to try and play the way I'd played with Chiswick United; he was still thinking in terms of the nineteen-thirties, really, when every club had copied Arsenal and tried to find an Alex James, someone who could do it for them in midfield. In a way, it was like being back with Trastevere. But I told him I thought all this had run its course. For one thing, at Chiswick I'd had Charlie Barker, who was a constructive player, too, like I was, so we could take the weight off one another, especially if I was being tightly marked. At Borough, we hadn't got anyone like Charlie, but on the other hand, at Chiswick we'd had nobody like Ronnie Scott, the centre-forward there was just a chaser.

Another thing was, I didn't want to turn the clock back, Chiswick was in the past, other clubs had time to study all that; I was keen to try something new.

It seemed to me that I should play two parts—in a way, the exact reverse of what I'd been at Chiswick. First of all, I should be making the openings for Ronnie, and secondly, by playing upfield a lot myself, I should be drawing the defence away from him—just in the same way Charlie Barker had, for me, by dropping *back*. I thought we could get a lot of goals like that, because compared with Italian defences, English defences are wide open. Against an Italian team, Ronnie would have found two men on him all through the game, and where he'd go, they'd go. Between us, I felt we could make a lot of scoring chances, and I was encouraged in this because we had a very good right-half behind us, Cliff Evans, the Welsh international. He was a *complete* half-back, and if you went upfield and left him on his own, you knew he could look after himself. To me, going upfield was necessary; you could make *more* chances from there; it was a fallacy that a constructive inside-forward had to lie deep the whole time. Obviously the nearer he works to goal, the more damage he's in a position to do.

Cliff could give you a ball just where you wanted it, too, he had a perfect touch. Off the field he was a bit of a wild boy, when he wasn't looking for a drink he was looking for a woman, and when he'd found one, he usually wanted the other. It was a bit surprising to find him there at Borough, because they'd always maintained they'd never have a player, however good he was, unless he was what they called the Borough Type; so I thought to myself maybe the Borough Type had changed.

Another thing was, they were very hot against illegal payments, no money under the counter, and I knew very well Cliff would never have left his last club if he couldn't put something in his pocket. Afterwards I found out the way they got round it was to sell him a club house for the same price they'd paid for it in 1936—so that kept everybody happy. As far as I was concerned, I was entitled to twelve per cent of my transfer fee anyway, under Italian regulations, so I was happy.

When I explained these ideas I had to Jack Westborn, he was very enthusiastic, he said, "*That's* it, that's what we need," but later on I found out that was how he responded to almost any new idea. He was very impulsive, and he could be just as violent in turning against something as he was in being for it, at the beginning.

I liked working with British players again, it was much more restful. They didn't have the brilliance the best of the European players had, but at least they were predictable. You knew more or less where you stood with them from one morning to the next, and you knew more or less what sort of game you could expect them to play, on the Saturday. It may not have been as exciting, but it wasn't as exhausting, either.

The Borough Stadium was the best I'd ever played on in Britain; the best appointed. You couldn't compare it with the

Olympic Stadium, of course, not for modernity, and even less for its surroundings; no trees or hills or blue skies, or anything like that, just the usual rows and rows of shabby little houses. But in a way, this made the stadium even more impressive. You'd think you were lost in this miserable desert, then suddenly you'd come across these great stands, all glass and metal, with the flags flying on the top.

There was cover all round the ground, too, which was something there hadn't been at the Olympic Stadium, because they'd kidded themselves they didn't need it in Rome —and inside, the dressing-rooms were wonderful, all tiled and heated, and the treatment-room had all the new electrical gadgets, diathermy heat and everything. It was a great club for players—I'd always heard people say that nobody ever wanted to leave Borough, and when I got there, I could understand why. In some ways it was a bit insidious, though, because you'd get these players who'd been there since they were boys, and suddenly they were men, and they'd realise they'd missed their chance. They'd have been through the third team, then stuck in the second team, with just an occasional game in the League side, if they were lucky, and they'd be content with that, because the club looked after them so well. Until the day came when they woke up and found they'd played their best days away in the reserves, and there was nothing left for them but to drift out of football with a Third Division club or a non-League club. I could understand it, though, because whereas an Italian club would treat a star player well and make a hero out of him—until another star player came along—you really felt that Borough looked after everybody.

One of the expressions you'd often hear was, "That's not Borough," or, "He isn't Borough," and I didn't really like it, there was a smugness about it. Sometimes I opposed it; I'd say, "Why isn't it Borough? Maybe it's right, and Borough's wrong." The great oracle of what was and what wasn't Borough was the old Assistant Secretary, Peter Graves. At least, they *called* him Assistant Secretary; I don't think he did anything else, just sit there in his office and let people come and consult him. He'd been with the club nearly forty years, he was a player when Wilfrid Cunliffe arrived as manager, and they seemed to think he was in touch with Wilfrid's ghost. Even Jack Westborn seemed to be a bit afraid of him, I suppose it dated back to when he was a player there himself, and he'd had this great respect for Peter.

I'd got nothing against Peter myself; he was a nice, harmless old man. The first day I was at Borough I was brought up to his office and introduced to him and he shook hands and said, "Welcome to Borough," as though it was some sort of holy place and he was the priest. I managed to say, "Thank you," then he said, "Do your best for *us*, son, and you'll find Borough will always do its best for you," and that was that —I'd been initiated.

I found it wasn't so easy at first getting back to the rhythm of English football, and after the first couple of games, some of the papers were saying I'd slowed up. I knew I wasn't slower; what they couldn't realise was what I've explained before, about the different tempos, and when you tried explaining it to *them*, they thought you were trying to excuse yourself. It didn't worry me, though, because I knew it was going to be a lot easier than adjusting to Italy, and anyway, after the Italian Press, the British Press was almost harmless.

In the third game of the season, we really came off for the first time, and funnily enough it was at Chiswick, of all places; in a Wednesday evening. It was a strange feeling going back there, with another club—four or five of the old team were playing, though Charlie Barker had gone, and they were just a mediocre side now. We beat them 4-0; I put Ronnie through for two goals in the first ten minutes, and it seemed to knock the fight out of them; it never would have done in my days there, I was very disappointed in them. Later on, Ronnie got his hat-trick, and I got a goal as well, so all the papers immediately started talking about was this a Borough Revival.

I felt a bit disgusted by them, though I suppose I shouldn't have been, there was no reason why they should have got any better since I'd been abroad. The only thing was, I felt the

Italian papers had an excuse for being what they were, they were the sort of papers you'd expect Italy to have, if you'd lived there; very emotional, saying one thing today, and another thing tomorrow. But with our papers, you felt they *could* help it, if they wrote what they did, it was because this was how they thought they'd get the biggest sales.

I could hit back, though, because I had a column of my own now, in the *Daily Gazette*, and I wrote every word of it myself, too; that was something I'd always insisted on, whatever newspaper I wrote for—no ghosting. So when journalists misquoted me, or when they wrote something I thought was rubbish, I could hit back at them on the Tuesday, and that made them more cautious.

I'd got two ambitions in football now; to play in the World Cup and to play in the European Cup; I hadn't done either. To play in the European Cup, your club had to win its League Championship, and when Chiswick had won it, the competition hadn't been started. The previous season, with Ambrosiana, Juventus had beaten us by a point, and if we'd won, I think I would have stayed with them another season—just for that, the European Cup. I wanted to pit myself against Di Stefano, and Real Madrid. They were the greatest team I'd ever seen, but I'd only played against them once, and that was just in a friendly, in Milan. We held them to a draw, 2-2, but I had the impression that they weren't really trying, they were playing with us.

We got two in the lead, and I thought we had them, but in the last fifteen minutes, *bang, bang*! just like that. I admired Di Stefano, because he was doing exactly what I wanted to do, only of course he had far more support than I'd ever had. He was a great technical player, he had marvellous ball control, but at the same time he wasn't just a technical player, he wasn't static like, say, Boniperti; he worked harder and he covered more ground than any player I've ever known, I don't know where he got his stamina.

And yet I thought I could see ways in which they could be beaten, if you had the men to do it; their defence was very vulnerable at times, because they obviously reckoned they'd always score more goals than the other side. It was a philosophy I liked very much, but I thought it could be dangerous to them; and I got through twice that day, myself.

As for the World Cup, Scotland hadn't qualified the last time, and it was more than a year since I'd played for them, anyway. In the beginning, they'd argued the toss with Trastevere and they'd flown me back a few times for matches at Hampden, though Trastevere didn't like letting me go. But after that, this was a good excuse for not picking me; they'd still got this mania about speed and power. Now I was back, though, if I played well enough, I thought they couldn't ignore me, they'd have to give me another chance, even if it was only in the hope I'd play badly, so they didn't have to pick me again, but if I played well, then I'd stay in.

Television was something else I enjoyed, as well as writing. I found it very easy, I enjoyed it. Some people said it made them feel nervous, but I always felt very relaxed. It had come on a lot in the last three years, there was commercial, as well, and now if you went on it, everybody you met the next day seemed to have seen you, you'd even get people coming up to you in the street. I realised from this that it was a power, probably more of a power than the newspapers, because television requires less effort; you turn on a switch and you look and you listen, and I thought maybe this was *why* the Press was getting more and more sensational, because subconsciously they realised they were being left behind.

I got a lot of letters through being on the television, and I had an impression I was building up a following, which was something I liked, because when I made these appearances, I didn't feel I was just standing for myself, I was representing all the *other* professional footballers. I wanted to show the public we weren't just morons, with our brains in our boots, because if you could change public opinion, public opinion could change the people who *ran* football, and sweep away all this prehistoric shambles of one-sided contracts and limited wages.

Now and again people would ask me, "Don't you get bored, mixing with professional footballers, the whole time?" and

I'd say, "If you mean, do *they* bore me, no, they don't, we're in the same game together, and if you mean do I *only* mix with footballers, no, I don't."

Of course, it wasn't as flexible as in Italy—especially Rome, where everybody mixes with everybody else—and it frustrated me, coming back into this world where a footballer was somebody who was inferior. Often I used to wish that Gino was here, because I missed our conversations. I'd always seen him whenever Ambrosiana played in Rome, and he also came quite a lot to Milan. We'd never had time to get down to the film, what with me going off to Milan, but we still had it in mind, and one day I was sure we could do it.

So I fretted a bit in London at first, I wasn't getting the right stimulation, though there *were* one or two of the sportswriters, especially Dudley Welsh.

Dudley worked on one of the highbrow Sunday papers, the *Sunday News,* and I'd been friendly with him when I was with Chiswick. I found him very strange when I met him to begin with, because I wasn't used to that sort of person, especially in connection with football; he was an eccentric. I thought, "Who's this fat little man, with his hair all over the place, and a button off his coat? What's *he* doing at a football match?" Then I began to read his articles, and they impressed me. His style was very elaborate, like the way he talked, and he wasn't very interested in tactics, but what he could get was the *atmosphere* of a game; you felt you could respect a man who wrote like this. The other Press boys laughed at him a bit, but they seemed to admire him, they seemed to feel *justified* by him; he'd got the education and the eloquence *they* hadn't got.

He had a flat in Chelsea, off the King's Road, one of those little service flats—and he lived there all by himself; I think he'd been married, but his wife died. He was quite a drinker even when I first knew him, but by the time I got back from Italy, he was a lot worse. There were times when I'd see him at a match and his eyes would be red, and I'd wonder how he'd manage to write his report; but he always did, and it was always just as good.

Before I got to know him, I couldn't believe he was really interested in football, even though he wrote about it, but I realised in time that football was as much a part of his life as it was of mine. He was a romantic, and football was a great romance to him; he'd go on and on about games he'd seen and players he'd admired; Hughie Gallagher, and the Arsenal forward-line of the thirties, and Stanley Matthews' Cup Final in 1953. He'd get up from his chair, this tubby little fellow, with his big stomach hanging over the top of his trousers, and he was Matthews. He'd say, "He beat Banks like this, and Hassall like that, and then he went past Barrass," swaying and sidestepping, and he was so intense about it that you couldn't laugh at him.

He was very excited when I told him I was going to Italy, he said, "Rome: my dear Gerry, how I envy you! I haven't been to Rome since 1938. I stayed in a little hotel near the Pincio. God, those sunsets, I can still remember them! And the little men with guitars, coming into the restaurants to play, while you were eating. Go, go: don't let anything stop you! How I wish that I could go, too!"

"Well, come and stay with us there," I said.

"Can I?" he said. "Can I really? I should love that, Gerry, if you're sure I wouldn't be in the way. I should adore it."

"Okay, fine," I said, "we'll expect you," knowing very well he'd never come. He was always planning things, but they'd stay plans, he never really meant to do anything about them.

Now I was back in London, I'd go to his flat, and I'd drink orange juice while he drank port, or more often, whisky, and played Italian opera on the gramophone; that, and Dixieland jazz. He'd say, "Did you ever hear *Aïda*, in the baths of Caracalla?" and I'd say, "Dudley, I was too busy playing football," and he'd say, "Tell me about it!" then, when I told him, he'd say, "*God*, how Italian! How *typically* Italian!" He'd usually be smoking a cigar, and the ash would fall over his lapels, but it didn't worry him, he'd let it stay there.

His whole flat was packed with books; there were only these two small rooms, but there must have been bookshelves

188

round every wall; I'd often borrow a book from him. He'd been to Oxford and before that, I think, at Harrow; he said he'd hated it because they didn't play soccer, he used to sneak away on Saturdays to watch the Arsenal.

We'd talk about football, then about writing, and about music; he was a great talker, and we'd lose all track of time, but when I had to go, when I left him alone there, I'd feel like I was deserting him. He'd say, "Stay and have another lemonade! Let me make some coffee!" or, "Let's just hear one more record," he was a lonely man. Sometimes we'd go out in the King's Road to a pub—I still drank lemonade—or maybe to a café, to meet some of his friends, but even then, when the party broke up, he'd always try and get me to go back with him.

I found it wasn't all that long before I started meeting the sort of people who really interested me; partly through Dudley—he knew a lot of writers and painters round Chelsea—partly through the television I was doing, and partly because a new sort of person seemed to be getting interested in the game, a more intellectual kind. The trouble was, it wasn't too easy to bring them home. I'd often be kept out late, and Mary would resent it, she'd say, "You've got a perfectly good home of your own, what's wrong with bringing them here. You're not ashamed of me, are you?" and I'd say, "No, of course I'm not ashamed of you."

But the truth was that I'd developed, and in certain ways I'd gone beyond her; it was something neither of us could help.

I was captain of Borough; Jack Westborn made me captain, before the start of the season. I said, "I'll do it, but on two conditions; first of all, that it doesn't upset anyone, and secondly, that I *am* captain; I don't just lead the team out and toss the coin."

"No, no!" he said, "you *will* be captain, I promise you. I want someone on the field I can trust to take decisions. That's been part of the trouble in the past, nobody's *wanted* to be captain, they're all afraid of the responsibility."

But of course there were bound to be clashes; Jack and I

didn't think alike in the way that Lionel Stone and I did, and I never had the same respect for him. One day, after we'd lost a match at Bolton, he came storming into the dressing-room and said, "You'd no right to take chances after we'd equalised, you should have gone back in defence."

I said, "For Heaven's sake, there was still a quarter-of-an-hour to go, and we were hammering them; with any luck we would have got the winner—*their* goal was just a jammy one."

"Yes," he said, "but they got the winner, *we* didn't. You won't see anything in the records about us hammering them; you'll see Bolton Wanderers 2, Borough 1."

I said, "That's a defeatist mentality, that's the mentality of a team that's fighting relegation. I'd *rather* lose a game and know we've played the better football, than draw one, because we've played negative football."

"Then you'd better find a club that isn't interested in getting League points," he said. "You're no bloody good to us, if that's the way you think."

I'd got an answer for that, all right, but all the boys were listening to us, and I thought I didn't want it to go too far.

In the train back, he was sulking, he never said a word to me, and on the Monday morning, he sent for me to his office. He said, "You may be the captain of this club but I'm the manager."

I said, "You've made a mistake, I *was* the captain. Now you can find somebody else, who's content to be your yes-man."

"I *will* find someone else," he said, "and if you want to stay with this club, you can get some of these Italian ideas out of your head. I'm the manager, and don't you forget it."

I said, "I can't possibly forget it, and as for staying with this club, I don't care if I leave tomorrow. You told me when I agreed to be captain I could make decisions on the field for myself. You should have explained yourself, you should have said, as long as they always turn out right."

That put him in a corner, so he started blustering all the more. He said I'd lost us the match on Saturday with my stupidity, and I'd insulted him in front of his own players.

190

I said, "*You* insulted *me* in front of the players; that's another reason why I'm finished with the captaincy—what authority would I have, now?"

He said, "You've no authority here, I have the authority."

"Well," I said, "you'd better use your authority to put me on the transfer list, because I'm not prepared to respect it any longer," and I walked out.

Ronnie Scott was in the dressing-room, getting stripped, and I must have been red in the face, because he said, "What's the matter, Gerry, Jack done his nut?" I said, "We've both done our nuts." He said, "You don't want to take no notice of him, he's a nut case, in half-an-hour he'll have forgotten all about it."

"*He* may," I said, "but *I* won't."

Jack and I didn't speak for the rest of the week; he never said a word to me, even at the team conference on Thursday, but I was surprised, because he didn't say anything about a new captain, either. When the team went up on the board next day, there I was, still captain, and I realised this was his way of admitting he was wrong. Later on, he came past me in one of the corridors and he said, "Don't forget it's young Reggie Miller's first game, Gerry, you'll have to nurse him a bit," and I could see he was anxious, waiting to hear what answer I'd make, but I'd decided to go along with it for the moment, so I just said, "Okay, Jack, I'll keep an eye on him."

We won that game, and there was peace for the next few weeks. On the whole, though, the boys hadn't much respect for Jack. Footballers are shrewd, and they know when a manager's got real ability and when he's really bluffing. If they'd got any problems about what they should do on the field— or even off it—they started bringing them to me, and Jack knew this, and he resented it. But he wouldn't have a showdown now, we were both very careful of each other; if he was upset, he wouldn't come out with it, he just wouldn't speak to me. I think he was a little afraid of me, as well as being jealous; he was afraid of my ideas, because he hadn't got any ideas, himself, he'd just jump at them when they were put up by other people. Then, I was appearing more and more on television, and people were reading my column, and I think this made him feel all the more insecure.

He didn't have an easy job, because from what I could make out, the Chairman was a pig. He wasn't a small businessman, like the directors had all been at Chiswick, he was a very *big* businessman, a property owner, and he'd made his own way —I believe originally he came from Liverpool. He knew nothing about football, but *he* was very big, so anything he was associated with had to be big, as well. Sometimes he'd come into the dressing-room before a match, and he'd say, "Pass to a man, boys, pass to a man," as though he was giving us some very valuable advice.

I'd made up my mind that I never wanted to be a manager —I'd decided that when I saw what happened to Lionel Stone, because it was obvious to me that the ones who got on were just the yes-men and the lucky ones, and the yes-men got on only as long as they were lucky. A strong manager with new ideas made directors feel inferior, because most of them were small men. They'd put up with him, as long as their team was successful—like they had done with Lionel—but as soon as it stopped winning, he'd be out.

So I put up with Jack Westborn, because I knew that wherever I went, I'd never find another manager like Lionel. Borough were a good club to be with, they were a London club, they treated their players well on the whole, we had a good team, we were winning matches—and if I did leave them, where would I go? As for later on, I had ambitions *outside* football, I wanted to use football as a springboard—I wasn't sure to what, yet; something in writing and entertainment; but there was plenty of time to find out.

I was enjoying playing for Borough; what made us effective was this three-sided combination between Ronnie Scott, Cliff Evans and myself. We'd got no set tactics, in the way we had at Chiswick; nothing laid down, that is, though we had various plans we worked at free-kicks and corners and throw-ins, and one or two simple basic moves which Ronnie could easily join in. Generally speaking, though, we worked things out on the field; Cliff and I were always looking for new ways we could use Ronnie's acceleration.

There was one move Cliff and I had from a free-kick which brought us some very good goals; one of them won the game for us, at Chelsea. What would happen was, we'd get this free-kick on the edge of the penalty-box, on the right, say—so Ronnie would move left, to distract the defence. Then Cliff and I would both run at the ball, with me a little behind him, so the defence wouldn't be sure which of us was going to take it—they'd think, if anything, we were working the old dodge, with Cliff jumping over the ball, and me shooting. But instead of that, Cliff would jump over the ball and keep on running, and I wouldn't shoot at all, I'd just slide it through the defence, into his path, for him to move on to. Nine times out of ten, we'd surprise the defence; it would just depend on his catching the ball right, and not scooping it over the bar. At Stamford Bridge, we timed it perfectly, and the ball was in the roof of the net before they realised what was happening.

Ronnie was getting goal after goal; he was wonderful to play with, because he seemed to know exactly when you were going to give him the ball, so that he was moving as soon as you'd kicked it. His anticipation was so quick that often he was given offside when he wasn't offside, because he was too fast for most referees.

We had this other Derby match at Christmas, at White Hart Lane, and Cliff put him through at the halfway line; it was perfect, he ran half the length of the field with nobody near him, went round the goalkeeper, and just rolled the ball into the net. If we'd been a little stronger in defence, we'd have walked away with the League, but we had a bad centre-half, Joe Finch, he took too many chances, and this was very expensive, particularly when Cliff was playing well upfield. The goalkeeper, Don Watts, was good on the line, but very slow at coming out to a high cross. So after Christmas, we were tucked in a point behind the Wolves, and I was sure we could overtake them, even if we *were* getting on to the heavy

193

grounds, which are the only grounds Wolves' type of football can look good on.

We had to play them in the middle of February at Molineux—three days after a Cup replay with Sunderland. It was raining when we left Paddington, and all the way up we were praying it would clear. But instead, it got worse, and by the time we reached Wolverhampton, it was belting down. There were puddles all over the pitch when we had a look at it, and I knew what kind of game it was going to be; Wolves' wing-halves ploughing through like battleships, and the only way you could move the ball at all would be by thumping it as hard as you could. I said to the boys, "I bet Stan Cullis is smiling."

I'd been thinking a lot about it in the train, it was obvious to me if we tried to play our normal game they'd go over us like a steamroller; they were a much *stronger* side than us, physically, and they based their game on strength. If we stood any chance at all, it was only by pacing the match, let them do most of the attacking, and every now and then, turn it on; in other words, play it like an Italian team would play it. But an Italian team played it naturally, we *didn't* play it naturally, we were geared for going on at the same speed for ninety minutes.

So I realised it depended on me. If I played deep, that meant Cliff would have to play deep, and we'd naturally give Wolves the initiative—which was a very different thing from letting them *take* the initiative. As long as they were forcing the pace and doing the attacking, they'd be using energy, and we'd be conserving it. Then, just for short periods, I'd move upfield, supporting Ronnie, which would leave Cliff room to come up and support *me*. I told Jack about this, and he thought it was a wonderful idea, as I knew he would; anything cautious was always a wonderful idea. I explained it to the others, as well, though it was mostly for Cliff's benefit, he was the key man—and so that Ronnie shouldn't think we'd abandoned him, because he was a temperamental little fellow.

For the first ten minutes, though, before the pitch really

194

churned up, I wanted to try and play some football—and we very nearly got a goal. We had this quick one, two, three move; Cliff to Ronnie, Ronnie a side-flick to me, me back-heeling it and Cliff running on to it and hitting it. Malcolm Finlayson got a hand to the ball and he turned it over the bar, but it was more of a reflex action than a save.

When I saw the ground was turning into a swamp, I dropped back, and we let them come at us, but they weren't making much progress, because our defence was controlled defence, we were funnelling back and packing the goalmouth, so most of their shooting was from outside the box. It got the crowd excited, but there was no danger to it.

Just before half-time, we came out of our shell again, and I put Ronnie through. In ordinary conditions it was bound to be a goal, but the ball just stopped dead in the mud, and he was slide-tackled. He said, "Don't give it me down the middle, Gerry, it's like a fucking water splash," and I couldn't blame him.

In the second half, we let them attack again, but they still couldn't score, and they were getting desperate. There was only Peter Broadbent in that forward-line who was capable of making an opening, anyway, and Johnny Briggs, our left-half, was sticking to him like a postage-stamp—the Italian expression. It was really frustrating me, the gaps Wolves were leaving, because on a normal pitch we could have ex-ploited them, but here it was an effort to kick the ball twenty yards. Then, after half-an-hour, we turned it on again. We'd got this big, strong outside-left, Doug Jenkins, he could move like a tank and go past everybody, though when he'd passed them, he didn't know what to do with the ball. I'd told him at half-time to move into the middle more and look for the ball, because he was strong enough to get through this mud, and when I came clear with it after we'd broken up an attack, I saw him standing square with Ronnie, in an inside-left position. Ronnie instinctively moved right, to make himself more room, taking the centre-half with him, and I sent the ball through the gap for Doug to run on to. He shook off the right-back, the centre-half was out on a limb watching

Ronnie, and there was only the left-back could possibly stop him, if he got across in time—unless Doug made a balls-up of his shot.

But he hit the ball as soon as he was over the eighteen-yard line; he'd got tremendous power, and of course the great thing was that he was running straight. Finlayson hurled himself across, and he got a hand to it, but the shot was too strong for him, it finished in the left hand corner like a bomb, and we held out for the rest of the match.

It was around this time that I first met Professor Hodgkinson, when I was on a television programme, at Lime Grove. I'd seen him many times, on the Brains Trust, and on this archaeology programme of his, and I had a great respect for him, he seemed to have a very unusual mind, a very *fresh* mind. I got a great surprise, because he suddenly came up to me in the bar there, where the producer had taken me, and he said, "Mr. Logan, excuse my intruding on you, but I've always wanted to meet you, I'm a great admirer of yours."

He was a very tall, thin, bald man, and he had this nervous way of talking, his head would keep bobbing all the time. He said, "I've been a Borough supporter for thirty years, I never miss a home match. I was delighted when you joined them, you'd always been such a menace when you played against us for Chiswick and Jarrow."

I said to him, "Well, I'm very flattered, because I'm an admirer of *yours*, but I never thought someone like you would be interested in football."

"Oh, yes," he said, "indeed I am. I played at school, I wasn't much good. I never could abide that dreadful other game, though; sheer hooliganism, and all this ridiculous snobbery about it."

He'd been on a programme in one of the other studios, and he asked me would I go back to his house when mine was over, and have a drink with him.

Well, I did go; he had a marvellous house up near Regent's Park, one of those ones that are painted cream, and inside it was more like a museum, paintings and statues and old cups and vases he'd dug up. I wanted to keep looking round, but all he wanted was to talk to me about football, he was fascinated. He wanted to know how the Borough team was picked, and how we worked out our tactics, and what sort of thing players said to one another on the field, and what did I think of this player and that player.

His wife came in while we were talking; she was a very distinguished looking woman, tall, with a very straight backed way of moving, and talking in this formal way I didn't think anybody used any more, "Will you have this, Mr. Logan? Will you have that, Mr. Logan?" and he said to her. "We're talking about football, dear, you know you're not interested in football. Mr. Logan's a very famous player." And she said, "I suppose you mean *you're* talking about football, and Mr. Logan's listening to you. Never mind, I shan't disturb you." He was a dominating personality, but I could see she'd give him as good as she got.

When he talked about football, though, he was almost like a little boy, it was hard to believe, I said to him, "Why don't you come down to the dressing-rooms after one of our home games, and meet the boys?" and that really gave him a thrill. He said, "Are you sure I could? That would be wonderful!" and he made me feel it wasn't him that had done the favour by inviting me to his house, but me, by coming.

I must have been there till two in the morning.

IT was the night he appeared on the Brains Trust that his progress seemed finally out of control, to have taken on a mad momentum of its own, leaving one dizzy in its wake, plagued by hints of paranoia. Could one really be right while everyone else was wrong, crying the Emperor's Clothes? And if one *was* right, was this any consolation? For it meant one was living in a world still more meretricious than one had suspected, a world so bored with itself, so void of standards, that it rejoiced in its own deception.

The pompous music played, the question master smiled with toothy expertise from the screen, the camera focused in turn on Dr. Rothenberg, the swarthy scientist, smiling complaisant from his chair; on Professor Hodgkinson, with his thin, clever, arrogant head—and finally on Gerry himself, terribly youthful, trading on youth, smiling a modest, boyish smile, wearing a good, grey suit, a clean white collar; at ease, but not too flagrantly at ease; inoffensive, perfect.

I thought, as I had thought before, of the legion of slick American books and films about those monsters created by mass communications; yodelling hillbillies, barefoot boys with cheek, who'd won the pulpy hearts of a nation. Germany, after all, had followed a house painter.

The first question concerned a united Europe; did the members of the Brains Trust think it possible or desirable? Professor Hodgkinson answered first, all historical allusion, quick qualification, fingertips poised together in a small steeple, his voice high, rapid and precise, his smile faint, self-communing, narcissistic. He was, one gathered, sceptical; but then he was sceptical of everything.

Dr. Rothenberg, by contrast, was optimistic, as a scientist should be. "Yes, of course it must come, it is historically necessary. A hundred years ago, there was no united Germany, there was no united Italy."

198

"Two rather unhappy analogies," the professor said. His face, tilted to one side, retained its smile.

But Rothenberg smiled happily back at him. "We are not talking of analogies. We are talking of inevitabilities."

"How sad!" said the professor.

And at last it was Gerry's turn. He looked demurely down at his feet, raised his head, then said, "Well, politics is something I don't know much about, but I have had some practical experience of what a united Europe might mean. When I was playing football for a club in Rome, our forward-line consisted of one Dane, one Hungarian, one Italian, one Argentinian, and a Scotsman."

"And how did they get on?" asked the professor; but now there was a new, benevolent look in his eye; a father, contemplating a favourite child. "Did it work?"

"Oh, yes, it worked," said Gerry. "There were complications, but it worked, all right."

The camera focused on all four of them; Dr. Rothenberg and the chairman were smiling at him, too.

"There were temperamental difficulties," he went on. "There were some days the Hungarian wouldn't be speaking to the Danish player, other days the Italian wouldn't speak to the Argentinian, and others when the Argentinian wasn't speaking to anybody. But we all understood each other. Nils, that was the Dane, talked English and Italian, the Hungarian and the Argentinian talked Italian, too, and when the others started shouting at me on the field, I could always ask Nils what it was they were calling me."

"But did you win your matches?" Dr. Rothenberg asked.

"Oh, we won some of them. We weren't a very good team, but that was nothing to do with our having so many nationalities. The team that won the Championship had two Swedes, one Uruguayan and a naturalised Brazilian."

How winning he was! They laughed, and he deserved their laughter.

"So you think European union is both possible and desirable, Mr. Logan?"

"It's possible, yes, and I think it is desirable. I think different countries have something to teach one another. I think we're too insular here. We're an island, we've got an island mentality; foreigners are wrong just because they *are* foreigners. I thought in a lot of ways, the Italians were right and *we* were wrong, but I had to go there before I found it out."

He had survived *that* question splendidly, but then, it had been made for him; would he be able to turn the others as skilfully?

But the next question, too, fell into his lap. "Does the Brains Trust believe that there is an unhealthy concentration on violence, in contemporary literature? Mr. Logan?"

"Well, *no*, I don't. I think a writer writes about what he sees, and if he writes about violence, that's because he sees violence around him. For example, Hemingway. . . ."

Yes, yes: Hemingway; who else?

"Hemingway wrote *mostly* about violence; about war and boxing and bullfighting. These are things that exist. He wrote about war because he's been in three wars."

The challenge; when were we coming to the challenge?

"But why did he write about bullfighting?" asked the professor, ducking his bald head, addressing this question to himself. "I accept *war* as a central fact of our time; one can't really avoid war, though Hemingway did seem to me to make a special effort to involve himself—but one *can* avoid bullfighting; bullfighting seems to me, I must say, a gratuitous form of violence."

"A ceremonial form of violence," smiled Dr. Rothenberg.

"But what appeals to Hemingway about bullfighting is *not* the violence!" Gerry cried. "It's the challenge! A bullfighter goes into the ring, and he knows every time he's facing death, and everyone who's watching knows he's risking death, so by risking it, he's not only proving something to himself, he's proving something to *them*, as well."

"But in a violent way," smiled Dr. Rothenberg. "Mountaineers also risk death. Why does he not write of mountaineering?"

"You're arguing *round* it," Gerry said, and for a moment,

Dr. Rothenberg's smile flickered and dissolved, his eyes lowered in surprise. "Climbing a mountain is a challenge, too, but it's a different challenge. A mountaineer knows the mountain isn't trying to kill him; it's *there*, and it will stay there, whether he tries to climb it or not."

For a second, despite myself, I felt afraid for him; the gap in logic was so wide, the blade of Professor Hodgkinson's intelligence so swift and sharp, but the professor said merely, "I'm afraid I don't share Mr. Logan's admiration for Hemingway; I've always found his bulls so very boring."

He had been spared, had got away with it, had ridden his two hobby horses round the ring with all the competence of endless practice.

When the programme was done, I switched off the television, wondering if I had been too hard on him. If I had never known him, wouldn't I, too, have been impressed, astonished? And, knowing him, how much of my antipathy mere jealousy, a feeling that I, not he, should have been on that screen?

My telephone rang at that moment; it was Mary Logan. "Did you see it?" she asked.

"Yes."

"Did you think it was good?" The question was heavy with contempt.

"I thought he was very facile."

"Oh, he's always that. Gerry can talk until the cows come home, whether he knows what he's on about or whether he doesn't. I just thought *they'd* see through him, I thought *they* might put him in his place."

"Not Professor Hodgkinson. He's a Borough fan, isn't he?"

"Oh, it was Professor Hodgkinson got him on the programme. We've had Professor Hodgkinson in this house for months—when he's been home. Professor Hodgkinson says this, Professor Hodgkinson says that, I'm going round to Professor Hodgkinson's tonight."

"He didn't get much chance to say anything, this evening."

"Oh, I wouldn't expect him to. You know what Gerry's

like once he's got an audience; no one else in the world exists."

"I think you and I are going to be in a minority."

"Yes, but *why*? Can you tell me *why*? Why can't people see these things, when they're so obvious? I just dread going out tomorrow: 'Oh, Mrs. Logan, isn't your husband marvellous, didn't he look handsome last night, wasn't he wonderful on television? We saw him!' One of these days I shall just blow up, and I'll tell them. You know we had another row, this morning?"

"No."

"I gave him an ultimatum. I said, 'Gerry, I mean this. I'm giving you a month; if things don't change by then, either you can get out or I will, and I'll take the children with me.' He said, 'You're jealous of me, you want to ruin my whole career.' I said, 'I only want to see that you don't ruin the *children's* lives. You've already done for mine.' And of course, that started him off again; I'd trapped him into marrying me, I'd only got myself to blame, I was an impossible woman to live with. I'd always tried to restrict him in every way.

"I said, 'Gerry, I've told you before, you're like a little child talking. Anyone who won't let you have your own way in everything is restricting you. When are you going to grow up? When are you going to realise you've got responsibilities, as well? You've got two children. They're not pets, Gerry, they're children; you can't just give them a pat on the head when you feel in the mood to. Luckily you can't upset Duncan, he can do without you, but Janey can't, she needs you, and if she's never going to get anything from you, then she's better off away from you where she won't be hurt and she may forget you."

"And what did he say to that?" I asked helplessly; help-less, because the pattern was fixed beyond appeal; could be broken, now, but never changed.

"He just stormed out of the house, of course; what would you expect? I don't suppose I'll see him tonight; he'll go round to his Jenny Cunningham, so she can tell him how brilliant he was. I've said to him, 'It's easy for *her*; all she's got to do is listen to you and admire you and say, 'Poor Gerry, yes, Gerry, no, Gerry.' Wait until she has to put up with you as a husband; *she'll* get a few surprises!' But he won't believe I'm serious, he lives his life in two halves. Outside the house, everything's perfect, everybody thinks he's wonderful, all the little boys want his autograph, people recognise him in the street—so he keeps out of the house as much as possible, because then he can pretend what happens here isn't real. Oh! I know Gerry!"

Oh, yes, she knew him, and there were moments when I wished she had never shared her knowledge with me, moments when—however unjustly—I even resented her for it. For the Gerry she knew was still a Gerry who was scarcely known to me. What business of mine was his private life? It was his public image which concerned me; above all, his image on the football field. Whenever I met him, he was so consistently affable that I felt I had betrayed him. That charm, I had to remind myself each time, that damned charm. I believed in the other Gerry, but it was an intellectual belief, which his presence could destroy; why couldn't we be left with our heroes?

"Did you know about his brother?" she asked me, now. "His brother Ian, the one who wanted to become a footballer? He had an accident at the power plant, he's in hospital now, they think he may be crippled for life. You'd have thought Gerry would go up and see him, but *oh*, no. I'd like to have him down here to stay with us when he's a little better, we've plenty of room in the house and he's such a nice lad; he could sit out and rest in the garden. But Gerry won't have that: 'It isn't necessary, he'll be perfectly well taken care of at home. Why do you want to meddle with my family?' But I know what it is; he's jealous of Ian."

"Why should he be?"

"Because he can't *bear* any sort of competition, he's always got to be the centre of everything, and now he can't be, at least in the family, because Ian's been hurt, he's become a rival to him."

Stop, stop, stop.

And she did stop. "What can I do? I'll have to leave him. What point is there in going on? Can't *he* see there isn't any point?"

Yet he was playing more brilliantly than ever, mocking the old belief that a troubled player must be a bad one. Italy had toughened and tempered him; he played more economically now, more cunningly. He had never been a hasty footballer, but now he had the contemptuous calm of Schiaffino, Liedholm, Gren. When he had the ball, he moved with a serenity which denied the existence of all opposition, the very possibility of a tackle. He was the absolute general, but a general in the manner of Montgomery, not Haig, ready at any moment to move into the front line.

And in Ronnie Scott and Cliff Evans he had his perfect *aides de camp*, Evans to assist his strategies, Scott to execute them. Perhaps the football Borough played was not as immediately rewarding to the eye as Chiswick's; it was more staccato, hadn't the same sustained effervescence, was more of an acquired taste. But then, in terms of spectacle, Chiswick had had nothing to match Ronnie Scott, with his marvellous, darting runs, his motor-bike acceleration, his sudden manifestation in the goalmouth, his executioner's right foot.

By New Year, it was plain that Borough would win the League, if only they were spared by injury. A few days after Gerry's appearance on the Brains Trust, they were due to play Aston Villa, away, in the Fifth Round of the Cup, and I travelled up to Birmingham on the perennial 11-10, from Paddington; the football train.

Dudley Welsh, of the *Sunday News*, was on it, too, and roaring Rigby, of the *Daily Post*, and Ted Colville, of the *Daily Graphic*. We shared a table together, in the diner.

"Wasn't Gerry brilliant?" Dudley asked. "Did you see him on the Brains Trust? Wasn't he quite superb?"

"I thought he showed them all up," said Rigby. "That's what they've always needed on these programmes; somebody who'll talk a bit of sense and bring them down from the bloody clouds."

"But didn't you *love* the way he turned their flank on Hemingway, over the bullfighting and mountaineering? And that glorious anecdote about the Italian forward-line—where one player could tell him what the others were shouting at him!"

"Bloody good," said Rigby, "bloody good."

"Yeah, I enjoyed it," Colville said. "You've got to give it to him, haven't you?"

"That marvellous sense of humour," Dudley said, "the quickness of it, the lightness; so unusual in the Scots. *That's* what made such a difference to the programme." He reached out slowly for his gin-and-tonic. His fat, white hand, shaking, made the journey with enormous caution, closing at last around the glass, and bringing it back in careful triumph. His grey, cloth tie was tied in a fat, untidy knot—a miniature Dudley, it suddenly occurred to me—and the point of his shirt collar was turned up at a reckless angle. "Did *you* see him, Brian?"

"Yes," I said.

"Didn't you enjoy it?" It was almost a plea.

"I was fascinated."

"Brian, you're too sophisticated. Why can't you be simple, like the rest of us, just lean back, and accept things for what they are? It's so much easier."

"He kept reminding me of something Dr. Johnson said," I answered—though I hadn't intended to. "The old chestnut about a woman preaching. Like a dog walking on its hind legs: it is not well done, but it is strange to see it done at all."

"Very cruel, Brian, very cruel."

"Well, I thought it was damned well done," said Rigby, and he lowered his head, as though stubbornly prepared to charge and gore any opposition.

Dudley looked at me over his glass; he would not let it alone. His smile was half-amused, half-hostile. He felt threatened by me, I knew, and his way of dealing with the threat was to treat me as an *enfant terrible*. In my criticism of Gerry, he, too, felt judged and criticised. "You must develop charity, Brian."

"Yes, Dudley."

"You will, you will."

What worm was it that gnawed him, drove him to self-destruction? Disappointment? It was surely more than that: what was it, in the first place, which had led him to his disappointment, had made him load his talents on to the fragile structure of a game, making bathos inevitable? And *now, as the industrial mists closed, in the floodlights, over Villa Park, the battle had gone not to the swift, but to the persevering, to the team which had made adversity its ally.*

"Did you read Dudley on Saturday? Wasn't it great?"

Did you see Dudley at eight o'clock on a winter morning, overcoat flapping, shuffling along a station platform, under a sooty sky, to catch a northbound train?

"How are you, Dudley?"

"Leave me alone now, Brian, *please*: I mean it. You make too much noise for me, at this hour of the morning." Head bowed, ghastly white, eyes half-closed. "I mean it: will you please leave me alone?"

They lost to Aston Villa. The cruel, cold Villa Park wind came blowing across the stadium, now carrying the ball too fast and far, now holding it suspended in the air like a white balloon. Gerry scored a fine goal for Borough in the first half, getting a pass from Evans, with his back to goal, wheeling on it like a tee-totum, to beat his half-back, and, almost in the same movement, shooting low past the goalkeeper, with his left foot.

But in the second half, the wind was with Villa; McParland, with his raw, tough directness, headed an equalising goal from a corner then, with three minutes left, centred a fast ball which Pace met at full stretch, parallel with the turf, to head the decider. On the platform, afterwards, at Snow Hill Station, I watched the players come slowly down the steps, into the vile twilight of the winter evening, a twilight compounded of darkness, and the dim electric glow from buffet, waiting-rooms, occasional lamps. A train hissed steam like a giant snake, and they made their way, bleakly impassive, through little groups of their own supporters, wearing

blue and white rosettes, blue and white woollen caps, carrying blue and white rattles—"'Ard luck, boys. 'Ard luck,
Cliff, boy." And through packs of boys, scrapbooks open,
pushing pens in their faces, begging, in their ugly, Brummy
voices, "Soign, mister, soign!"

They found refuge of a sort in the buffet, packed tight already with their fans, shouting to one another, drinking
beer at the counter, perilously handing back cups of tea.

"Soign, mister!"

"Not here, son, not now."

Gerry did not come into the buffet; he held court on the
platform to a flattered group of journalists, while round the
outskirts of the group gathered a further circle of grinning,
nodding, nudging fans. "No, no," he said, "we weren't unlucky. Our tactics were wrong. We should have pushed our
luck more in the first half, when we had the wind. I think
subconsciously we were expecting it to stop: it played better
for them than it did for us." Laughter.

A gaunt boy mournfully appeared at his shoulder, scrap-
book extended. "Soign please, Mr. Logan."

"Not now. I'm talking, can't you see that?"

"Oh, please, Mr. Logan." The voice was full of a hoarse
despair.

"No. If I sign it for you, I'll have to sign for everyone."

"No you won't; the others are all in there."

"I said no: send the book along to the ground."

"Ask him to sign," the boy appealed to me, "ask him to."
His pale, plain face bent towards me, involving me against
my will, a face to haunt one's dreams.

"I can't," I said, impotent and guilty, and when he went
away, his dragging step accused me.

After I had eaten on the train, I joined the players in their
dining-car, sitting at a table with Gerry, Cliff Evans and
Ronnie Scott. There was resentment and failure in the air;
everyone was quiet and sullen, even the games of brag were
being played with dull indifference. Jack Westborn, the manager, sat with three directors at the table nearest to the door,
his face set and heavy. Ronnie Scott looked across at him,

drew his mouth into a thin line, and nodded with resigned disgust. Westborn was the scapegoat, then; how often would a defeated team turn and crucify its manager!

"*He's* a tit," said Ronnie.

"He does his best, Ronnie," Gerry said.

"I'd hate to see him do his bloody worst, then," said Cliff Evans. His eyes, dark and shrewd in the weatherbeaten face, rested in their turn on Westborn. There was a quiet intransigence about him; he was the old school professional, a tough anachronism among the grey flannels, white collars, blue blazers. His strong, chapped hand was closed, characteristically, around a glass of beer.

"Fucking talk, can't he?" he had said, when Gerry came to Borough. "Been here three weeks, and I'm still waiting to get a word in. Teaching me how to play."

"What did Jack say after the game?" I asked them.

"What did he say?" said Ronnie, with a wry, secret smile at the others. He picked at the tablecloth with a fork, and at last looked up to say, "Said we lost because we packed up after the equaliser."

"It didn't look like it to me."

"Didn't fucking look like it to us," Evans said.

"He's got to say *some*thing," said Gerry. "He's got to explain it to the Chairman."

"See that wind?" Cliff asked me. "You couldn't move the bloody ball, let alone play football; like kicking a lump of bloody lead. Got stronger in the second half, too. I'm not kidding. It wasn't them that beat us, it was the wind."

Wally Gray, the right-back, bent over our table, pressing on it with his broad hands. "Happy, isn't he?" he said, with a contemptuous toss of the head in Jack Westborn's direction. "I'd like to have punched him one when he said that."

"Yeah, but he don't know what he's saying, do he?" Ronnie said. "Not when we've lost a match, like that."

"Always tell you what to do *after* the match, can't he?" asked Gray. He was a Norfolk man, huge shouldered, well over six feet. His brown forelock hung over his face, combining with the slack mouth, the slack speech, to create a misleading air of stupidity. He, too, was a hard professional. "I've never heard him give a pre-match talk," he said, "not a proper one. He can't even sum a game up at half-time; it's too quick for him. He goes by the result. If you've won, you've played good, if you've lost, you must have been bad. What did he tell us for this match? Nothing!"

"He can't tell us what he doesn't know," said Gerry.

"If you've lost, it means you weren't trying," said Gray. "That's all he *does* know."

"That's all most managers know," Cliff Evans said. They spoke in low, surly voices, like conspirators.

"You want to come to one of our team meetings," Gray told me, "doesn't he, eh, Ronnie? He'll come in and he'll say, 'Right, lads, this week it's Villa,' or 'This week it's the Wolves. I want you to get in hard and make the ball do the work, and don't forget, you're playing for Borough.' Then he'll say, 'Anybody got any questions?' and then Gerry will take over."

"I don't know about take over," Gerry said. "I usually have one or two ideas."

"One or two?" said Cliff Evans. "Is that all it is? You mean a hundred and two, don't you?"

"At least he's *got* 'em, Cliff," said Wally Gray. "It's a good job somebody in the club has."

"I hadn't learned nothing here till Gerry come," Ronnie said. "No one told you a thing."

"Win the League, and he's a great manager, though, isn't he?" asked Evans.

"We make him a good manager, don't we?" asked Gray. "He don't make *us* a good team."

When we reached Paddington, Gerry gave me a lift in his car.

"They're bitter about Jack, aren't they?" I said.

"They're bitter because we lost; you can put up with a bad manager when you're winning. Jack isn't as bad as some I've known, anyway; his trouble is, he's tactless. He's upset, so he says the first thing that comes into his head; afterwards, he's sorry for it. He doesn't consider that the players are upset, as well. Players aren't difficult to handle, if you use a little psychology. For example, I don't treat Cliff on the field the same way I'd treat Ronnie. Ronnie's still a little boy, I'm a kind of father to him, he wants to be told he's done well. Cliff's quite different, he doesn't want to be told anything. He's a sort of Marlon Brando, or that's how he sees himself, so you've got to pretend *you* see him like that, as well. Cliff *knows*, he's going his own way, so I'll say to him, 'That was a good idea of yours, Cliff,' and he'll say, 'What idea?' and you'll say, 'So-and-so and so-and-so'; it wasn't his idea at all, it was *your* idea, but he'll think it was his, and he's forgotten it."

"You'd make a good manager yourself, Gerry."

"I wouldn't want to be a manager; the better you are, it seems to me the less chance you stand. I find I'm getting more and more interested in things outside football. Did you see the Brains Trust on television the other evening?"

"No, I missed it."

"I'm sorry, I think you might have liked it, I'd like to have had your opinion."

My approval.

"I enjoyed it, I was surprised that I enjoyed it so much. I was on with Professor Hodgkinson and this Dr. Rothenberg. They both look at things in this very *dry*, analytical way, and I think if you analyse a thing too long, you lose sight of the thing itself. You tend to see problems where there *are* no problems: it's the same in football. These F.A. coaches are turning a simple game into a complicated one, because the more difficulties they can create, the more need there is for *them*. These professors and people have had opportunities *I* never had, but in a way, I think they've lost something that I've kept. They forget you can look at things in other ways."

"You may be right."

"I think I *am* right. That's why I want to deal with other things than football, I've told the *Daily Gazette* I want to do a general column, I want to write about books and current affairs and show business. Football isn't separate from life, anyway, football is a *part* of life. If you've really lived inside the football world and studied it, it'll help you to understand what's happening outside it, as well."

"I quite agree," I said. "We saw that tonight, with Jack Westborn."

"What do you mean?"

"A manager's a sort of father-figure; players are very ambivalent about him. They don't always see him as he is; they can follow him without much reason, or they can turn against him, as they did tonight."

"I think there's a lot of truth in that," he said. "Charlie Forbes, this season, at Rovers. Everybody knows he's a bad manager, he's been sacked from his last three jobs, but they bring him in in desperation, because the team's at the bottom of the table—and suddenly it starts winning. He hasn't done anything, he's just sat there, chewing his cigar, but he's given the players faith in themselves, they've responded to him. Next season, when the novelty's gone, they could go straight down to the bottom, again."

A month later, he was on the Brains Trust a second time; his companions, now, were Dr. Rothenberg and an intense woman novelist, with beautiful enunciation, and the face of a highly intelligent horse. A question was asked, "Does the Brains Trust agree this country is failing to produce leaders, and if so, why?"

"I'd like to know," Gerry said, "what is a leader? We're always hearing this phrase, a *natural* leader, but I'm not sure they even exist, I think that circumstances create them. For example, in football, a new manager can be appointed, and his team will suddenly begin to play well because he *is* a new manager. Then, as soon as they've got used to him, they may begin to play badly. They may even turn against him, because a manager's a kind of father; they like him, and at the same time, they dislike him : so when things go wrong, they blame him."

He was applauded, that Sunday, by the television critic of one of the highbrow newspapers for his "remarkable Freudian insight into the nature of the relationship between football managers and their players."

Where would he stop!

A fortnight later—Borough had just won the League—he was reviewing in the book pages of the *Sunday News*—Dudley's hand, perhaps—only a sports book, this time, the autobiography of a racing motorist—"a driver faces a perpetual challenge"—but a month after that, the book was the memoirs of a general, and the following week, incredible to see, he was writing the novel column: "This book reminds me of A *Farewell to Arms*, though it hasn't the power and authenticity of Hemingway."

How long would the dog retain its balance?

MARY LOGAN

In the end, I came straight out with it and asked him, "Who is she?"

"Who?" he said.

"Don't play around with me, Gerry," I said. "The girl you're carrying on with. You might as well tell me."

"There's no girl," he said. "Why don't you believe me? This jealousy of yours isn't normal."

"And your lying isn't normal," I said. "You're careless, too, aren't you? You ought to remember what you leave in your suits!"

Then I brought this note round from behind my back and showed it him. It said, "Darling—will see you at 8 to-morrow." His face turned dead white and he said, "You've been going through my pockets."

"No, I haven't," I said. "You asked me to send that suit to the cleaners, and I did. You forgot what was in it, didn't you?"

He said, "Give it me," and snatched it.

I said, "What are you trying to do, destroy the evidence?"

He said, "There is no evidence, there's nothing for there to be evidence of."

"Darling!" I said. "She calls you darling, and there's nothing in it!" And then I couldn't keep it up, I started crying. I said, "Well, I'm not staying in this house, I can't bear it any longer. She'd better move in, whoever she is."

He said, "For Heaven's *sake*, she's somebody I've known for years."

And as soon as he said that, I knew, though it was such a shock to me, I could hardly believe it. I said, "Jenny Cunningham."

He said, "Yes, that's right," and he gave me that innocent look of his, with his eyes opened wide.

"You're still carrying on with her," I said; I was thinking out aloud.

He said, "I never *was* carrying on with her."

"All these years," I said, "and I thought you'd given her up."

"Mary," he said, "will you listen to me for a minute? There was nothing to *give* up."

"I'm not going to stand here arguing about it, Gerry," I said. "This is the finish. I've had all I can stand." Then I turned and went out of the room, into the kitchen, so I could be doing something to distract me, and he followed me in — I remember I thought, how funny, this is the first time *I've* walked out instead of him, and now he's coming after me; maybe I should have tried it before.

He said, "You don't mean that about going, do you?"

I said, "I mean every word of it."

He said, "Don't just think of yourself, think of the children."

I said, "That's marvellous, Gerry, coming from you, that's really marvellous: think of the children! When have *you* thought of the children? When have you thought of *any*one except yourself? The children will be better off without you."

"Mary," he said, "you can talk to her yourself. I'll bring her over. She'll tell you, there's been nothing in it; nothing!"

"Nothing in it for five years?" I said. "Do you think I'm daft? You gave me your solemn word you'd never see her again."

"I'll give it you *now*," he said. "I'll never set eyes on her once more."

"Oh, no," I said, "once bitten."

"Mary," he said, "why won't you believe me? I need you!"

"Not me," I said, "you need your reputation. We've had all that before, haven't we? You got away with it in Rome; people forgot it, but you're much too well known now and so's she, you'd never get away with it in London."

"Listen to me, Mary," he said, "I do need you! Why can't you accept that?"

"Yes," I said, "and you seem to need her, as well."

"Not the way I need you," he said.

"Oh, no," I said, "I understand you perfectly. I'm not your mother, Gerry, I've told you that before. It would be nice if I was, wouldn't it, then I'd let you go off to your little girl friend in peace, whenever you wanted to, and you could come back and see me, when you felt like it. Oh, I'm quite sure you need me, but I don't need you."

He tried to put his arms around me, but I just pushed him away, I said, "You can keep that for Jenny," and he realised at last that I was serious, and he went out of the kitchen, then the front door banged, and he was out of the house.

When he'd gone, I felt completely lost. I knew what I was going to do, but all the meaning seemed to have gone out of everything. All I had was this terrible feeling of bitterness, it was like a block in my throat; I couldn't swallow. I thought, five years, five years, and then—because I didn't care, because everything was finished and I could look at things as they were—I thought, maybe part of what he said may even have been true, maybe he did give her up, until we got back to England, then started up again because she'd got famous.

Because she was a star now, she was always on television, and top of the bill at the Palladium, and she'd even been in three or four films. I thought, *let* her have him, that's the worst thing I can wish her, wait till *she's* got to be his mother, instead of just his mistress. But then I started wondering, what's she got against the world, why's she *doing* this, a married man, with two little children? I'd like to ask her.

I had to fetch Janey from school that afternoon, and she said when she saw me, "Where's Daddy? He *promised* he'd come and fetch me! I think he's horrid, I never, *never* see him."

I didn't know Gerry had made this promise, so I told her, "He would have come, but he had to go back to the football ground and do some extra training."

She said, "But he promised, he promised me," and I realised then how much it was going to upset her if I took her away; she'd be torn between the two of us, maybe for the rest of her life. So I said to myself, I'll make one more effort, one last one. It's no good relying on *his* promises, I'll have to go and see *her*, and if I can put it to her, maybe she'll agree to stop seeing him. I'll tell her, it's not for my sake, it's for Janey.

When I'd got both the children to bed—I'd no one to help me, like I had in Rome—I wondered where I could find her; she'd never be in the phone book. Then I picked up the paper and found she was appearing at the Astoria, in the West End. I phoned up and left a message, saying she was to ring Gerry Logan at our number, at eleven o'clock.

When it got near the time, I was so restless, I couldn't settle to anything; I kept looking at my watch and wondering, will she ring, will she smell a rat? But right on eleven, the phone went, and I had this terrible feeling in my stomach, what shall I say, what shall I tell her, though I must have been through it twenty times.

She said, "Gerry?" in this very cautious voice, and I said, "Don't ring off, Miss Cunningham, I expected you to phone. It's Mrs. Logan, it was me that left the message."

There was dead silence, and I was afraid for a moment she might hang up, then she said, very, very quiet, "What do you want?"

I said, "I just want to see you, that's all. Will you see me?"

She said, "What do you want to see me about?"

I said, "Don't worry, I'm not going to try and scratch your eyes out. I've just got to talk to you; it's as important to you as to me."

You could tell she was still nervous about it, she said, "I don't know, I'm very busy."

"Please," I said. "You must make time for this." So then at last she said, "Oh, all right," but very grudgingly, and I thought, "You bitch."

She said, "I can't tomorrow, I'm much too busy tomorrow, I can give you half-an-hour on Thursday afternoon."

I nearly did tell her, then, but I controlled myself and said all right, I'd come to her flat at four o'clock—it was in Park

216

Lane. Then I suddenly thought, shall I ask her not to mention it to Gerry, but I decided no, that was the very way to make sure she did it.

When I'd put down the phone I just cried and cried, I couldn't stop myself. I must have cried for an hour; I couldn't bear to think that he'd be going to her tonight, so I suppose I did still love him, then; there was still something left, even though I'd got no respect at all for him, any more.

That was the funny thing; the more famous he got, the less I admired him. When I saw him on the television, giving out his ideas on this and giving out his ideas on the other, I wanted to shout at them all, "Can't you see through him? How can you let him take you in?" Because to me, he sounded *false*, he was talking on things he knew nothing about, he was so insincere; but they'd smile at him and listen to him very seriously, as if what he was saying was important. I don't know, I'd think; perhaps it's only me, I just can't see him as he is, any more; but it was the same when I read his articles in the newspaper, I'd think, no, no, it's all just words, you don't mean a line of it, Gerry, you don't know what you're on about.

They'd moved him off the sports pages in the *Daily Gazette*; he was writing on everything, now, things I *knew* he didn't know the first thing about. And yet they went on publishing it, so I suppose there must have been *some* sense in it. What I couldn't understand was the way he could moralise on things, on how badly the footballers were treated, on how unfair it was to chain them to their clubs, on how badly everyone had behaved to Lionel Stone, and yet look how he was going on in his own life, how he was treating the children and me. It baffled me.

It would have been much easier, I suppose, if only I'd been able to behave the way he did, but I couldn't. Oh, I'd plenty of chances, and I know I hadn't been a saint up in Jarrow, but I'd think to myself, what's the *point*? Life was too important now, there was too much to worry about, I wanted something that would solve all these problems, not make them worse than they were.

There was this Welshman, Cliff Evans, who played with Gerry for Borough. I met him at a dance once when all the players brought their wives, so Gerry had to bring me. I'd heard from some of the other girls that Cliff Evans had a terrible reputation, he was carrying on all the time though he was married himself, and he'd got *four* children. He was quite good looking if you liked those sort of rugged Welsh looks, and he pressed up very tight against me when we danced, and I said, "What are you trying to do? Turn me into a concertina?"

He said, "I always dance like this."

"Do you?" I said. "Well, you must be used to complaints."

"No," he said, "I've never had no complaints; they usually like it."

"Well, I don't like it," I said, "so do you mind letting me breathe?"

So he loosened his hold then, and he said, "I think you and I would get on well together."

"What makes you think that?" I said.

"Well," he said, "you're my type, see. All that pretty red hair."

"I'm sorry," I said, "but you're not my type, and even if you were, you'd be no good to me—you've got even more children than I have !"

But you couldn't snub him, he just kept on and on, would I go to the pictures with him one evening? and when I said no, then why not one afternoon, he'd take me for a drive in his car. I said, "It's no use, Mr. Evans, I've heard about you, I've been warned."

"Well," he said, "I heard about you. I heard you were smashing, and you bloody well are."

"Then we've neither of us been disappointed, have we?" I said. "Goodbye !" and I left him at the end of the dance.

Next afternoon, when I got to her flat, she let me in herself. She looked a lot older to me than when I'd last seen her —much older than she did in her photographs, or on television. She still had thick make-up on her face, but she wore her hair cut very short now, almost an urchin cut, where before she'd had it loose and long.

She said, "Oh, come in," in a very flat voice, with no expression on her face, and I could tell she was nervous. She was wearing a very expensive beige leather dress, and she was just dripping jewellery; bracelets, a gold watch, and a diamond ring on her finger—and there was this huge drawing-room with fitted carpets and period furniture, and I thought, she's got so *much*, what does she want to take Gerry away for?

She sat down on a sofa—she didn't ask *me* to sit down—and she took her cigarette out of a big silver box and lit it—she never offered *me* one—and I realised what she was trying to do, she was trying to make me feel like someone who's inferior to her, someone who's asking for a job. Well, I wasn't going to put up with that, so I sat down anyway and I lit a cigarette of my own, and I didn't take the tone I was going to take, because I could see if I did, she'd walk all over me. In fact I didn't say anything, I just sat there smoking until she said, "What have you come about?"

I said, "*You* know what I've come about."

"No, I don't," she said, "I've no idea."

I said, "We could carry on all night like this. I want to know what you mean to do about Gerry—and don't raise your eyebrows like that; it's silly, bluffing; he's told me, himself."

That brought her up short. She suddenly lost this expression, and she really snapped at me, "Told you what? *What* did he tell you?"

"That it's still going on," I said, "that he's still carrying on with you."

She didn't say anything to that, she just sat there, smoking her cigarette, and giving me this look as if to say, well, what are you going to do about it, then?

"I've not come here to have words with you," I said, "it's gone much too far for that; though I must say I don't know

219

why you've done it, why you're trying to take away a man with two little children from his family, when you've got so much, yourself."

"I love him," she said, and she looked at me as though she was daring me to deny it.

"Oh, I know," I said, "you love him, and he loves you."

"He does!" she said.

"Maybe he said he does," I told her, "but *you'll* find out, you'll find out like I found out; Gerry doesn't love anybody but himself."

"That's not true!" she said. "*You* don't understand him!"

"No, of course not," I said, and I even started feeling a bit sorry for her. "But whether I understand him or I don't, we've got two children, and it would break the little girl's heart if she lost her father."

"Has he told you he's leaving you?" she said, and she was so excited she nearly sprung out of her chair. I really did hate her, then.

"No," I said, "I'm sorry to disappoint you, he hasn't. You see, Gerry likes to have the best of both worlds; perhaps that's something I *do* understand, and you don't. *Gerry* doesn't want to leave; things suit him far too well as they are"—she was looking at me as if she could kill me—"oh, no," I said, "it's me, not him, it's me that can't stand any more, and I've told him so. It would be me that left him, not him that left me. But the little girl loves him, and if I take her away, I don't think she'd ever be the same."

"I don't mean her any harm," she said.

"I'm sure you don't," I said. "I'm sure you've never ever thought of her, or any of us. But it makes no difference whether you mean it or not, the harm will still be done."

"Well," she said, and she gave this smirk, "if Gerry and I . . ." and then she didn't have the nerve to go on.

"Say it!" I said; I was really mad, now. "If Gerry married *you*, then Janey could come and live with you. Do you think I'd let that happen? Do you think I'd leave her with *you*, the sort of life *you* lead?"

Well, you should have seen her. How dare I come here and talk to her like that in her own home; *and* when she was trying to help me.

"*You're* no help to me," I said, "and don't you go thinking you're any real help to Gerry !"

"I'm more help to him than you," she said, "at least I do love him."

"Yes," I said, "it's very easy to love him, your way, you don't make any demands on him; but wait until you do ! You've got a few surprises coming to you, I'm sorry for *you* — you're not going to know what's hit you. If you'd got any sense, you'd give him up now, before you start finding out — because things aren't going on as they are, you know. I'*m* not going to stay here any more to be a buffer for you."

"*I* don't need you," she said, "I don't need you, and *he* doesn't need you. I can *see* now what's he's had to put up with, all these years."

"Don't you kid yourself you're saving him from me," I said. "You've only heard one side of it, you've just believed what it suits you to believe. If you'd got a scrap of decency about you, you'd leave him alone, it's the best thing for him and the best for *you* !"

"What difference would it make?" she said, "if it wasn't me, it would just be somebody else."

I nearly let go at her, then; I was getting up to slap her face, and she knew it, because she huddled back in her chair. But then I thought, oh, what's the point, why fight over *him*; she's right, anyway, though *she* doesn't know why she's right. So all I said was, "I'm glad you've discovered that already. I'm glad you've realised it needn't just be you; it could be you or anybody."

"*Oh*, no it couldn't," she said. "Gerry and I have been in love for five years."

"Love?" I said. "You call that love?" and I got straight up and walked out of the flat, without giving her another look.

It was all over, now. I walked up Park Lane to the Marble

Arch tube and I was boiling, half at her and half at myself, thinking, why did I go? I should never have gone! and then, next minute, telling myself I should have kept calm, I'd made a mess of it. But then when I was in the train I thought, I'd never have got anywhere with her, whatever line I'd taken, she's just as selfish as he is; they'll make a good pair.

The only thing that still made me wild every time I thought of it was the way she'd said she and Gerry would look after Janey. My Janey! As if I'd ever let her be taken away from me—let alone by a bitch like that.

When I got home, I sat down and I wrote a long letter to my mother; writing it made me feel better. I put it all down, everything; I'd never told her a thing, before. I said I knew it was going to be a shock to her and father, but Gerry and I were splitting up. I'd decided there wasn't any point in going on; could I bring the children up and stay with them? I could have phoned her, I suppose, but I didn't want to, it wasn't the sort of thing you wanted to spring on anyone over the telephone and besides, I was afraid I might break down and cry. I told her I'd try not to stay too long, I wouldn't be a burden on them both; I'd get a job as soon as I could, and maybe take a flat in Newcastle; but I just had to get out of London.

In fact it was the second time I wanted to leave London and make a fresh start, but this time I was determined I was never going back to it again, it had too many unhappy memories for me. People said that once you'd lived in London, you were ruined for provincial life, but I told myself I'd been used to it once, I'd get used to it again. Besides, how could I live in London with the children, with no family and without any real friends? How could we *make* friends? I'd never *had* a proper social life, with Gerry.

There was only one thing that worried me about going back to Jarrow, and that was the way I knew they'd gossip about me. Oh, wouldn't they be pleased? I could just see their smug faces. *Well*, they'd say, *she's* come back with her tail between her legs, hasn't she? *She's* been taught her lesson.

Mother had told me Joe was still living in Jarrow; he'd married again and he'd got two children. I just couldn't imagine what it would be like, meeting him again. I found it difficult even to remember what he looked like, it was as though it had all been just a dream.

Gerry came in while I was still writing, he said, "Listen, about last night; I was over at Cliff Evans'."

"I'm sure you were," I said.

"If you don't believe me, you can ask him yourself," he said.

"Oh, I don't think I'll bother," I said, "I'm sure you've prepared him well. Anyway, it doesn't matter."

"Why doesn't it matter?" he said.

"Because I'm leaving you," I said, "I'm leaving with the children."

"Oh," he said, "you're starting *that* again, I thought you'd given up all that nonsense."

"No, no, Gerry," I said, "I'm afraid it isn't nonsense, not this time. I'm writing to Jarrow now. As soon as it's convenient, I'm taking Janey and Duncan, and we're off to my parents."

He started shouting at me again, then; I was trying to blackmail him and finish his career—but I just let him go on ranting. Then I said, "It's no use, Gerry. I saw Jenny Cunningham today, and that was the last hope."

"You'd no right to do that!" he said. "You'd no business to see her, without telling me! What did you say to her? What?"

"Oh, I told her a few things I thought she ought to know," I said. "Not that it'll make any difference. She's never lived with you; she'll find out, when she does."

"What things?" he said, and now I got angry as well, because I could see that he was more worried he might lose her than he was at losing me and the children.

"Don't worry," I said, "*she* won't send you packing; not yet, anyway. If you really want to know, I went there to appeal to her, to see if she'd got enough decency to give you

223

up. Not for me; don't think I cared that much, there's nothing more between us—it was for Janey."

"I'll take Janey," he said.

"Oh, no, you won't," I said, "you're not fit to look after any child, and nor's she."

"You can't take my children away from me!" he said. "You're just jealous, because Janey cares more for me than she does for you, and you're jealous of Jenny, too."

"Not everyone's as cheap as you, Gerry," I said. "I know Janey loves you, that's why I want to protect her from you." And then I thought of what she'd said, again, she'd take Janey, and I really lost my temper. "You think I'd ever let *that* woman have her?" I said. "I'd rather she was adopted!"

"That's your spite," he said. "You don't know anything about Jenny; you're doing this because you know it will hurt *me*!"

"Why go on, Gerry?" I said. "Why keep tearing at one another? I've told you, it's over. Let's end it as painlessly as possible."

He went upstairs then, and I heard the bedroom door shut, so I supposed he'd be phoning her; I just didn't care. I finished the letter, then I took it out to post it.

It had been raining since I'd got in, and as I went down the road, little drops of water kept falling off the trees in the dark, and landing on my face. I thought, anyone would think I've been crying, and I laughed, because I couldn't have felt less like crying. As soon as I got out of the house, I'd felt almost happy, because now I was doing something definite. When I got to the pillar box, I held the letter in the slot, half in, half out, thinking, well, shall I or shan't I. But it was only a game I was playing with myself, I knew I was going to send it, and after a while I just let it go and heard that *plonk* it makes when the box is almost empty, and it hits the bottom.

Gerry was coming out of the door as I got back, and he brushed past me without a word, but I just didn't care, it was like a load had fallen off my back. I was a different person, now, I wanted to tease him, and I called after him, "Are you coming back tonight? Ring me up if you decide you aren't staying with her! I want to know whether to put the chain on the door."

He said, "I'll let you know," without turning round; and off he went. He didn't come back, and he still hadn't come back the morning after next, when my mother rang. The poor old dear sounded terribly upset. She said, "You're always so hasty about things, Mary, why can't you talk it over with Gerry first?"

"I've talked to him till I'm blue in the face, mother," I said, "I've been talking to him on and off for the last five years, and all that's happened is we're back where we started."

"Think of the children," she said, "you must think of the children."

"I have," I said, "it's them I've thought of more than anything; I explained it all in the letter." And then I gave up, because what was the use? You *couldn't* explain things to your parents. "Will it be all right if I come up tomorrow, mother?" I said, and she said, "Why be in such a hurry? Give it another day or two, and you never know, it might all blow over."

"Mother," I said, "it will *never* blow over. Now, can we come tomorrow? We'll get the train from King's Cross."

I packed that afternoon. I told Janey and Duncan we were going to stay with their Granny, for a holiday, and they were both of them excited, they loved going there. That evening, Gerry came back again, I heard him come in, then he called up to me from the hall, "What are all the trunks doing?"

"Going to Jarrow with us tomorrow," I said.

He came upstairs, then—I was packing my own suitcase and making sure there was nothing left behind I might want.

He said, "How long are you going to keep this up?"

"It's not a game, Gerry," I said.

"Well," he said, "how long do you mean to stay up there?"

"For good," I said, "I told you, didn't I?"

And then it dawned on him, at last he had to come out of his dream world. He said, "You mean it, then."

I said, "Yes."

"And I suppose when you've gone you'll divorce me?" he said.

I said, "I haven't really thought about it, but anyway, if I did, you'd have your freedom, wouldn't you? You'd be able to marry Jenny Cunningham, then."

"I never *said* I wanted to marry her," he said, but I told him, "Let's not go through all that again."

He said, "You're so cold."

"Not cold," I said, "exhausted. "You've just drained me, Gerry; you've drained me of love and you've drained me of feelings."

He said, "My mother was right, you trapped me."

"Your mother's a bitch, Gerry," I said. "I'm sorry, but I must say it. And if you want to know the truth, I blame her for nearly everything."

I thought that would send him into one of his furies, but it didn't, he was subdued, just standing there like a little boy, and suddenly I found myself feeling sorry for him, and I turned away and got on with my packing, because that was what had happened before, it had happened in Rome, and he wasn't catching me again.

He was very quiet while I was packing, then he said at last, "Will I be able to see the children?"

"Yes," I said, "you can come up and see them. You'll be able to see them when you're playing in the North-East, won't you?"

They were playing out in the garden, cowboys and Indians, they had a wigwam out there, and you could hear them shouting and laughing. He said, "I'd better go and say good-bye to them, then," and he left the room, then I heard him in the garden, and I went to the window.

Janey came rushing to him, like she always did, but Duncan just sort of hovered near him; there was always this "don't touch me, please" about Duncan, even when he was tiny, Gerry was smiling at them as if nothing was the matter,

226

and he picked Janey up and swung her round in the air, and she was laughing and shouting, then he did the same with Duncan, but Duncan just tolerated it, little poker face. Then he kissed them both, and went out by the side gate.

He never said good-bye to me.

GERRY LOGAN

My second season with Borough, we were in the European Cup. I thought we'd do well, especially if we had any luck in the draw, though I didn't think we'd win it. We had a good team, but we were a good *club* team, and Real Madrid were even more than a good *international* team, because their players came from all over the world. They had Di Stefano from Argentina and Santamaria, the big centre-half, from Uruguay, and Kopa, from France, and the little dark fellow, Gento, who was Spanish; he was one of the fastest wingers I'd ever seen.

In the first round, we played a Dutch team, and that was quite easy; we beat them 3-1 on their ground, and 4-1 on ours; then we were drawn against a Czech team.

I'd been behind the Iron Curtain before with Scotland, but that was in Budapest, and Prague was very different. The river was nice and the bridges, but it was a grey city, and everyone seemed to be afraid; there was this feeling in the air. Cliff Evans found a secret microphone in this room, there was this little square hole low down on the wall, hidden by a chest of drawers, and Cliff would kneel there and start shouting down the hole: "Have you searched Jack Westborn's luggage? You want to watch him : he's got a bloody atom bomb in his case, he's going to blow up the President," or, "Everything all right down there, Comrade? Let me know: I'll pour some bloody hot soup down, if you're hungry."

I said, "For Heaven's sake, Cliff, you'll have us all arrested," but Cliff's incorrigible.

We drew that match, 1-1, then beat them 2-0 at Borough. We played well that night, because they weren't an easy team to beat, their defence was very strong, with one wing-half deep the whole time. Ronnie got one goal, and I headed another, just before the end. That put us in the semi-finals, and in those, we got drawn against Milan. I was very pleased, first

228

because we hadn't drawn Madrid, and secondly because I'd be going back.

We played the first match at Borough, and it was a very difficult one. I knew what their plan would be, they'd play on defence, with breakaways; they'd reckon that if they could hold us in London, they could beat us in Milan. They'd have two men on Ronnie, and probably at least one man on me, sticking close to me. The trouble was, you couldn't bring them out of defence by scoring first, because these were home and away games, and if they kept the score down to a goal, that would still make them happy.

Jack went over to watch *them* play, and he came back and said, "They've got this Brazilian centre-forward, Altafini; he's the man to look out for, he's like a tank, and he's clever with it, too. He's always moving well, off the ball."

It seemed to me the only space we were going to get was on the wings, and that was where we'd have to attack. The trouble was, our wingers were very ordinary and in any case, sooner or later you've got to get the ball across—and when you did, there'd be seven of them waiting in the goalmouth. We hadn't got any Nils Petersen, either, to come belting in with his head.

I told Ronnie he'd have to come back and pick the ball up deep, otherwise they'd never give him time to control it. I said to them, "Look, we need an early goal. I've played against these defences before, when I was over there; if you let them settle down, you might as well shut up shop. They're playing away, though, they're in a foreign country, they'll need ten minutes or so to get adjusted, and this is when we must hit them; because if we get even one goal, that could be the only goal, and I know we can draw in Milan."

Well, it worked. Ronnie picked up a ball just on the edge of the centre circle, before he'd had time to get nervous of the tackling, he went past three of them in that way of his, as though they were statues, then he let go with his right foot. Buffon did very well to get to the ball, but Billy Grange, our inside-left, was following up, and he scored.

This unsettled them, just as I hoped it would, and because

we got the first goal, we got another. Ronnie went through again, but this time they panicked and they flattened him, and I scored from the penalty.

Liedholm pulled them round, then, he was still a great player, though he must have been over thirty-five; he was holding the ball and beating a man, then using it—no hurrying—till gradually the others got calm, and they settled down, as well. They knew they needed to pull at least one goal back, so they had to open the game out, and that meant we were more dangerous to *them*, as well as their being more dangerous to us.

This Altafini was a good player, and he gave us a lot of trouble, but their inside-left, Grillo, the Argentinian, he was slowing it down, and Schiaffino could only do it in fits and starts, now.

We both hit the bar in the second half, but there weren't any more goals, and we beat them 2-0.

Everyone was really excited, now; not only did it look like we'd be the first British team ever to play a European Cup Final, but it was unusual to have a London club in the European Cup at all—and *being* a London team, we had all the publicity focused on us. A lot of it was stupid, because the popular papers were so used to making a sensation out of nothing that when there really *was* something, they'd forgotten how to deal with it. It was a marvellous chance for comparing our football with their football, you could have written pages just about our match against Milan, but all you got instead was "Brilliant Borough" and "So-Temperamental Signors" and all the usual "inside" stories.

I'd got no respect for most of the journalists, the best ones seemed to be the ones that weren't on the well-known papers, or the ones that were, but hadn't got the big jobs. With the others, it was all angles and "gimmicks," Arthur Bright, on the *Sunday Globe*, always seemed to me to be the worst of the lot. He didn't write about sport, he wrote about himself, and when he hadn't got a story he'd make one up. He was a very brash little man, and all through the winter, he wore this sheepskin coat, which he'd picked up when he was in Russia.

This was his gimmick, this coat; he was always betting his sheepskin coat this would happen or that would happen, or he'd be so angry he'd boil inside his sheepskin coat. I had a go at him once in my column, I said maybe one day he'd get so angry he'd boil away to nothing, and then maybe the coat would get his job, because after all, it had been waiting a long time. He was a great one for publishing interviews you'd never given him, or ringing you up and talking to you "off the record," then the next day you'd see it all in the paper. When that happened the second time—I was still with Chiswick, then—I wouldn't talk to him at all.

I'd moved into Jenny's flat by this time, and I must say I liked it there, right opposite the park; you'd look out of the windows and you'd see the trees: I'd never lived in the middle of London before. It worked out very well, because Jenny had her career and I had mine, so neither of us minded the other being out at odd hours. I think that's one of the destructive things in marriage, each one making demands on the other; and Jenny understood this. In fact she understood a lot of things, she realised someone with my temperament needed to be left alone a lot, it was no good trying to domesticate them. If Mary had seen that, too, I don't think we need ever have split up, but she couldn't, it wasn't in her.

With Jenny, it was a very different life, a much more stimulating life. I liked the show business world; I always had done; I liked their unconventional ways, because I was unconventional myself. At the same time, I was writing my novel reviews and getting invited to a lot of literary parties and meeting writers, so there was that world, too. There always seemed to be something going on, and I think it was a good thing, because it took my mind off what had happened. You can't be married all these years without it taking a hold on you; you get involved in ways you don't realise at the time, even if later on you and she became incompatible, like Mary and me. You even get used to the nagging, so that when you do certain things, you're waiting for a voice, and when the voice doesn't come, you miss it.

I missed the children, as well, I kept wondering what was

happening to them, especially Janey—Duncan was the cat that walked by itself. It would have been different if they'd still been in London, but they weren't, she'd taken them away up to Jarrow, and if I rang her there, her voice was like ice. I was sending her money every month, so I knew they weren't short of anything, but I felt as if something was being taken from me.

One day I had a letter from her mother saying wouldn't I come up, she'd do her best to help me talk Mary round, she was sure we could manage it, and I thought about it for a few days, but in the end, I didn't answer, I knew it was hopeless.

Jenny was very good about it all, she kept saying she'd be glad to have Janey, we could get a governess for her, and that if Mary wouldn't give her up, we could ask for custody when the divorce proceedings started. Mary hadn't done anything about it yet, though it had all been in the bloody papers, plastered all over the front page, the singer and the football star. Jenny kept saying, "Write to her, write to her," but I couldn't bring myself to do it. She said, "You're always complaining about the gossip columnists; they'll never leave us alone until the divorce goes through and we've been married."

But I didn't know which was the worst, all these references and innuendoes in the papers, or the sort of scandal there'd be in the reports when the divorce did go through, because I knew the way they seized on things and twisted them, especially when anybody was the least well known. So I wanted the divorce, and yet I suppose in a way I was afraid of it.

The first few weeks with Jenny was a very exciting time, it was the first time we'd properly lived together, and there was no tension about it any more, we could both relax, and we were discovering new things about each other. I think physically we got on better than Mary and I had; Jenny was much less inhibited. She was singing at a night club then, and usually I'd be asleep when she came home, so she'd waken me up, but in a certain way; it was something Mary would never have done, but Jenny had this wildness about her.

I loved watching her when she sang, because that was when she was most herself. She had this marvellous rhythm in her body, and she'd move and sway, like one of those Indian dancers. She seemed to have some current going through her, and the audience would feel this, too; she seemed to hypnotise them, even in a big theatre; she could make them do anything she liked; clap, sing, laugh, cry. She was a different person, then; somebody I didn't know and who didn't know me. I admired her, but at the same time, I'd almost feel I'd lost her. She told me once I made her feel the same when I was playing football.

I'd agreed to review novels for three months, that was another thing that occupied me, but when they were finished, I gave it up, it was too much work for me, though I told them I'd still do occasional books. Besides, I was going on with my column in the *Daily Gazette*, though I wasn't so happy about it any more, because they kept trying to dictate to me what I'd write, and I wouldn't put up with that.

We weren't doing so well in the League this season. I think it was because, subconsciously, we were all bound up with the European Cup, and we knew if we were going to win it, we had to give it everything. We went out of the F.A. Cup in the Fourth Round, Spurs beat us at White Hart Lane, and I wasn't sorry about that, either, because I believe a team can only take on so much, unless it's got two complete teams of equal strength, and we hadn't even got a team and a half.

We played the return semi-final in Milan, and it was a strange feeling, going back again, walking through the Piazza della Scala, speaking Italian, having lunch with the old President of Ambrosiana—we were still on good terms. All Cliff Evans wanted to know was, "Where's the knocking shops, where's the bloody knocking shops I've heard about?" but I told him, "You wait till *after* the match; if we win it, then I'll find you one."

Well, we didn't win it, we drew, but that was as good as a win, because it put us into the Final. The game was a fight, because this time *they* got an early goal; Altafini headed it from a cross from the right wing that our goalkeeper lost in the floodlights; but the defence stood up to their pressure very well, and a quarter-of-an-hour later I put Ronnie Scott through, and he danced past Buffon and equalised.

They threw in everything in the second half, but they weren't as fit as we were, and in the last quarter-of-an-hour, we could easily have had another goal or two. I hit one on the turn against the foot of a post, after doing a scissors with Ronnie, and Buffon only just beat Ronnie to another through ball, from Cliff.

In the other semi-final, Real Madrid knocked out Hamburg, so that meant we'd be playing *them* — in Rome, at the Olympic Stadium.

I wrote in my column that I regarded this as the most important match of my life. I said that I knew that on paper we were the underdogs, but this was an advantage, and as far as I was personally concerned, playing at the Olympic Stadium was as good as playing at home.

It seemed to me the climax of my whole career. I didn't think we'd reach the Final again, even if we won this one and qualified for the following year, because I knew we'd played above ourselves. As for the World Cup, which was the only competition that meant more than this one, I knew I'd be too old by the next one, although I was back in the Scotland team, now; and besides, though I hadn't told anybody, I was beginning to feel the strain a bit, at inside-forward. Even though I'd learned how to save my energy in Italy. I still got through a hell of a lot of running, and I didn't think I could keep it up much longer; I was thinking of eventually dropping back to wing-half, like Liedholm had, and then maybe I could carry on as long as him.

I knew this Final was a game we'd have to plan, and I had long talks about it with Cliff Evans, and with Jack Westborn, too. He'd no ideas of his own, but if I kept on hammering away long enough, I could persuade him in the end that mine were his.

The thing that was vital was to counteract Di Stefano, because without him, the team was nothing; he *was* the team. He was almost as useful to the defence as he was to the attack.

We got films of all their previous Finals and we studied them; it seemed to me that what we had to look out for more than anything was the move when he gave a quick ball, then went through like a bomb for the return; there was only one way to stop that, and that was always to have someone going with him. I was pretty sure we could get goals up their end all right—a lot of teams had; what worried me was seeing they didn't get goals up *our* end. Jack was all for putting a man on Di Stefano to go with him everywhere, but I didn't like that, not just because it wasn't football—we couldn't beat them on football, anyway—but because I thought it would do us harm. It meant that whatever man we used was lost either to the general covering, if he was a defender, or to the attacking build-up, if he was a forward. Besides, it was a negative approach; psychologically, you were approaching the match in the wrong frame of mind, you were giving them the initiative.

What I suggested was that we should use two men, a defender to stay on him when he was in our half, and a forward who'd mark him when he dropped back in his own. I thought Billy Grange could be the forward, because he was the least important of the three insides, and we didn't want to sacrifice a winger. In defence, it could be our left-half, Johnny Briggs, who was defensive minded anyway, and this was the sort of job he did best. That would leave our centre-half, Joe Finch, free just to take whoever was coming through the middle, whether it was Di Stefano or one of the inside-forwards, because this was what *he* did best. Once he had to mark a centre-forward who moved around as much as Di Stefano, he had to start thinking, and Joe wasn't a thinking player, he was a hard player, he'd have been pulled all over the place.

Another thing was Gento, their left-winger, I didn't think Wally Gray had the speed to hold him, and he was too slow on the turn. Gento wasn't clever, he was just fast, and all he wanted in my opinion was a back who'd stand off him and let him run, then run with him. What I wanted to do was use our young right-half from the Reserves, Peter Clapham, because if there was one thing he could do it was run like blazes, and we could give him a run in the League team to get him used to the position. But Jack didn't want that, because he said it would upset Wally and be bad for the team's morale. So I put up another idea, a compromise; switch the backs, put Wally on the left and use Frank Dickson on the right. Wally could use his left foot quite well, and although Frank's right foot was his swinger, he could give Wally a good few yards in speed. Jack hummed and hahed a bit, but in the end he agreed.

I told Ronnie Scott to pick the ball up deep again, not because he'd have two men on him this time—Real didn't play like that—but because I knew Santamaria was hard, and if Ronnie took a knock or two early in the game, he was liable to hide out on the wings, where he wouldn't be any use to us.

We played badly in the League after we'd qualified in Milan; we only won another three matches, and we finished seventh. We weren't deliberately not trying, but the League didn't mean anything now, and everybody knew it, so when the papers started writing we hadn't a chance against Real, we were playing so poorly, it didn't worry us, because we knew from what we'd done already that we could turn it on when we really had to.

We flew out to Rome the day before the game. It was just the beginning of their Spring, and it hit me harder than ever, I wondered how I'd ever been able to leave a city like this, and I had to keep reminding myself what had happened when I was there. In fact, I didn't have to try very hard, because I'd hardly got into the hotel when the phone went in my room, and it was somebody from Flaminio. Very secret—could I meet him that afternoon in a café up near the Piazza Risorgimento. No, I said, I couldn't, I was very busy. But this was important, he said, I'd be very interested in what he had to tell me. Flaminio could make me a very good offer. They weren't like Trastevere, they were a serious club, I'd be happy with them. I said, "I'm happy where I am, thanks, and I'm not coming back," then I put down the phone.

The hotel was just above the Spanish Steps, I'd suggested it to Jack Westborn, myself, and after dinner, when the others were mostly playing cards, I went out for a stroll by myself in the Villa Borghese. That was something I could never understand about footballers, it was cards, cards, cards all the time, whether they were on the train and killing time, or whether they were in Rome, like they were, now.

I leaned over the parapet up there, like I used to when I first came to Rome, and it was very quiet, you could hear people moving through the dark like ghosts, and just the occasional sound of their voices. And I started thinking about all the things that had happened to me since I'd been here; I thought, the last time I was here, Mary and I were still married, and for a moment I couldn't believe we still weren't. I'd go down the hill in a minute and pick up my car at the bottom, then I'd drive down the Via Babuino and through the Piazza del Popolo, under the arch, out along the Via Flaminio, and up by the old stadium, for home. I felt . . . it was almost like an ache, for a minute, I felt I'd lost something. I'd lost Mary, I'd lost the children, and then I remembered Jenny would be over the next day, she'd be flying out in the morning for the game, then she and I were going to stay on, for a holiday; she'd never been to Rome.

We'd trained in the Olympic Stadium that afternoon, and I'd looked around all the empty green seats and pictured how it was going to look the next day, and wondered what would happen. It was strange seeing these goals again, they're not like British goals, the nets are pulled down very tight behind the crossbar, and I wondered, how many times are we going to put the ball there?

When I'd stood at the parapet awhile, I started walking through the Pincio, but after a time, I got lost. There's this thing about it at night, every alley looks like all the others; you keep thinking you've found the way back, but you haven't, you're drifting farther and farther away. In the end, I did find myself at the edge of the Villa, but I'd no idea where

I was, it was a street I'd never seen before, without a taxi or a bus stop in sight. So I went on walking until at last I came to a road with traffic, and got a taxi to take me back to the hotel.

I was glad to get back there and be with the boys, because this walk had done something strange to me. I kept wishing all the way in the taxi Jenny was here, and once, while I was in the gardens, even Mary: you know how these thoughts can spring into your head when you're in the dark on your own, and you're walking.

Most of them had gone to bed, but Jack was down; he looked up at me as I came in and he said, "Where have you been?"

"Just walking," I said, "I've been in the park here," and he looked at me a moment as though he didn't believe me, but he said nothing. I played a few hands of brag with Ronnie Scott and Wally Gray, and then I went to bed.

The next day, there were a good ninety thousand in the stadium. A lot of our own supporters were over, they'd come in special planes, there were these patches of blue and white in the crowd, and you could hear the rattles whirring, which was something you never heard in Rome. The crowd gave us a very good reception, they were shouting, "*Bravo, Loggan!*" and I got the impression that they were going to be on our side, partly because I was somebody they knew, and partly because it would be more exciting if *we* won. It didn't worry me too much, one way or the other, but I was pleased, because it might help some of the less experienced players in our side, the nervous ones. It could be very disheartening for someone who wasn't used to it to score a goal, and hear nothing but dead silence, so he'd think to himself, have I scored or haven't I? Maybe I was offside?

Jenny was up there somewhere, in the tribune of honour. She'd come round to the hotel when she arrived; Rome had excited her, as I knew it would, and she was excited about the game, as well; in fact she was more excited than I was.

I wasn't too worried about getting a quick goal today, because Real were a great team, you couldn't demoralise them, and besides, they didn't play on the defensive; what worried me was that *they* might get one. So in the first ten minutes or so, I stayed quite deep, I wanted the boys to play themselves in, I wanted to give us confidence so when I got the ball for the first time, I deliberately stood still with it, letting their inside-left come to me, then I sold him a dummy, took it up to the left-half, and beat him as well, then let him come again. It wasn't progressive, but it wasn't meant to be, it was just meant to show the boys, we're as good as *they* are. In the end, I just gave a square ball to Billy Grange.

Di Stefano was moving all over the place, from the very beginning, but Johnny Briggs was sticking to him well. Once, he put Gento away with that beautiful backheeled pass of his, always dead accurate, as though he'd got eyes in the back of his head, and Gento thought he'd run Frank Dickson with it. But Frank was already moving when he got the ball, like a relay runner, and he caught Gento near the corner flag.

When Di Stefano found that Johnny was following him everywhere, he naturally dropped back, to shake him off, but there he was picked up by Billy Grange, and I could see he didn't like it.

Cliff Evans was playing a great game, he was getting in very quick on their inside-left, Rial—who was another Argentinian—then giving the ball beautifully, sometimes just short to me, sometimes inside the back to Mike Redfern, our outside-right, and others, right across field, to the opposite wing. It was a game of chess, like all the best games; it almost seemed to me that I was playing Di Stefano and that the chessmen were the other twenty.

There was no score for twenty-six minutes, and by that time I knew we'd settled down, the boys were convinced this wasn't a super team we were playing, it was a team we could beat. Then Di Stefano went right back deep, helping his defence, as he liked to do, and he got the ball down just by the left hand corner flag. He had Billy Grange right on him, but he could have got out of trouble by giving it short to his right-back, and moving for a return. But instead of that, probably for personal reasons, he tried to beat Billy, and he didn't succeed. Billy took it off him, and pulled it back across the field, to me. It was about twenty yards out, and I was moving in on it. I could see if I stopped to control it, or took it on into the box, there'd be three men would move across to block it. So I took a chance, I hit it first time, and the moment I hit it, I knew it was going. Their goalkeeper, Alonso, didn't seem to me to move, though afterwards I saw photos of him flying through the air, when the ball was already past him. It went across him, just inside the far, top corner, and then everybody was dancing round and hugging me and shaking my hand, and the crowd were giving that tremendous Roman roar, that's louder than anything you hear outside Hampden. I knew they'd be with us now the rest of the game, because if there's one thing a Roman crowd likes, it's to cheer an underdog that turns out to be the upper dog.

That goal really stung Madrid, and they came back at us right from the kick-off. Di Stefano pushed the ball to his inside-right, the inside-right backheeled it to the right-half, and I could see what was coming. Di Stefano went off like the clappers, and the right-half put the old long ball straight into his path. But Johnny had gone with him, thank goodness, and he slide-tackled him, just as he was crossing the eighteen yard line.

Then little Kopa started giving Wally Gray the run around, on the right wing. He was one of the best balanced players I've ever seen, and he was beating him on the outside and on the inside, he was doing just what he liked with him; and of course, Wally was getting no support from Johnny Briggs, because John was looking after Di Stefano. Di Stefano could obviously see all this, because he was going left and taking Johnny with him, making it worse. It was a risk I'd known we'd have to take, but I thought it was worth taking, because Kopa on the right wing couldn't do the damage of Kopa in the middle, when he was playing for France. I shouted at Wally, "Keep him out there, stand off him; just make him centre," but I was worried about it. If it went on, I'd have to release Johnny Briggs and maybe put Billy on Di Stefano in both halves of the field, which was something

I didn't want to do. Or I could switch the full-backs, but I didn't want to do that, either, because Frank was playing Gento so well.

I thought we'd had it, just about five minutes from half-time. Kopa sent Wally the wrong way, came inside him, and brought the ball in so close Joe Finch had to go to him, then squared it for their inside-right, Mateos. Mateos barely got time to hit it, though; I've never seen a keeper move quicker off his line than Norman James, our youngster, he'd only come in this season. He flung himself like a maniac and blocked the ball with his body. Fortunately it ran loose to Wally Gray, who was coming back, and we were safe.

After that, though, he began to get on top of Kopa, and the defence got organised again. In any case, they had problems with *our* attack, especially when Cliff came through in support. Ronnie very nearly scored when I gave him a short pass, expecting a quick return, instead of which he turned on it like lightning and hit it with his right foot, almost in one movement—like Puskas with his left—and the ball went a foot wide of the post.

At half-time I told them, "We can do it, don't relax, that's all."

Jack Westborn said, "We've got to hold that lead, that's the only thing that matters. I want Billy to play back in defence this half."

And I argued with him, I said, "We're a goal up, our plans are working well, we've as much of the play as they have—why throw all our advantage away?"

He said, "I want *you* deeper, too, you're leaving gaps there, Cliff's going up too far, behind you."

I said, "Why don't you make us all stand under the cross-bar, then we can *really* concentrate on keeping them out."

He said, "I've told you before, I'm the manager. If you don't do what I tell you, you'll regret it."

And I thought suddenly how ridiculous it was, here we were a goal up on Madrid in the European Final, arguing like hammer and tongs. And I laughed and I said, "It's just like old times in this dressing-room, only then we usually had it in

241

Italian." Then I said, "Let's compromise, Jack, let's play the first half-hour as we are, then if we're still just one goal ahead, we'll shut up shop for the last fifteen minutes." He looked for a minute as if he might go on blustering, then he said, "Right, but as soon as I tell you to change, you'll change."

Looking back now, perhaps what was really in the back of my mind was that I didn't want to kill the game, it had been such a great game. But I still don't think Jack's tactics would have worked, not for a team like ours. We weren't used to playing *catenaccio* defence; if we'd been an Italian team, it would have been another story.

When the game began again, there was a bit of needle in it. I don't think Real liked the idea of this London team who'd just come over to be beaten not only giving them a run for their money but looking like beating *them*. Both our wingers were kicked up in the air in the first five minutes, then Ronnie was body-checked as he was going through and Bob Main, our trainer, had to come on and give him treatment. Ronnie was giving them a lot of trouble now, because I think he realised he was quicker than Santamaria. He was doing cheeky things, too, which were a sign that he was confident. Once, he flipped a centre from Mike Redfern over his head, and it only just cleared the bar.

I was covering a lot of ground, taking advantage of the space Billy left, whenever he went with Di Stefano, and Cliff was finding me with some lovely diagonal balls, from right to left. The crowd was really excited now, another twenty minutes had gone, and Real still hadn't scored. They couldn't pronounce our name, Borough, so what they did was shout for England: "*In-ghil-TERRA, In-ghil-TERRA.*" I turned to Cliff and I said, "Do you know what they're shouting? They're shouting, come on England!" and he said, "Tell them if they keep that up, I'll start playing for the other side!"

I was remembering what I'd promised Jack, and hoping we could get that other goal; or, if we couldn't get it, wondering whether I might just defy him. He'd have no come-back if we won.

Then Cliff Evans came dribbling through on his own. He beat two of them nicely, and they were funnelling back, all watching him; they were obviously afraid he'd have a bang at goal.

When I saw that, I started moving as quickly as I could from right to left, and Cliff saw it, too. He took the ball on another couple of paces, then he sent over this perfect chip. I got my head to it without breaking stride, Alonso touched the ball, but he couldn't stop it, and it was over the line when the left-back came rushing in, and belted it out. I was down on the ground, waiting for the referee to give a goal, but instead of that the game just went on, I couldn't understand it; there was the referee, trotting away upfield, as if nothing had happened.

Two of our boys went running up to him, but I shouted at them, "Get on with the game, get on with the game!" The crowd were going wild, there were bottles and cushions coming on to the pitch, and the policemen were forming up, ready in case they tried to jump over the wire. I could see Jack Westborn, he'd got up from his bench by the side of the track, and he was leaping about and flailing his arms like a madman.

When the ball went out of play for a goal kick, at our end, I told young Norman to hold it. I went up to the referee—he was an Italian—and I told him in Italian, "That was a goal, why didn't you give it? The ball was over the line."

He said, "I couldn't see."

I said, "If you couldn't see, you've got a linesman there: ask *him*!"

Some of the other boys were crowding round, but I told them, "Go away, go away, you'll only confuse things." The Real players were mobbing him as well, and I was being jostled in the middle there, the crowd was whistling, and it was just what I'd been used to when I'd played here, except then, I wasn't in the middle of it, I used to stay outside.

In the end, the referee did go to his linesman, with us following him fifty yards across the field, and the linesman said *he* couldn't see, either. I told them, "You're a very good pair, you ought to have a couple of guide dogs with you," and the referee threatened that he'd send me off.

In the very next minute, they equalised. Gento had changed his tactics, instead of trying to beat Frank Dickson straight down the wing, he was going in for those little, short, diagonal bursts. He'd move ten or fifteen yards in from the line, take a shortish ball from Rial or Di Stefano, then go like hell towards the touchline or the goal line, just so he could lose Frank and give himself space.

This particular time, he went past Frank and stopped a few yards from the corner flag, turned on the ball, pulled it back quite low, and Di Stefano flung himself at it and turned it in with his head, while he was still in mid-air. It was a great goal, but it should never have *been* a goal, and coming when it did, for the next ten minutes it knocked the heart out of the team. I couldn't blame them, because I felt really depressed, myself.

In those ten minutes, they were all over us, they hit the post, Wally kicked off the line, then Kopa came into the middle and gave Di Stefano one of his long balls. Johnny was with him again, but this time, Di Stefano got his shot in as soon as he caught up with the ball, it went off Johnny's foot, changed course completely, and curled high over Norman's shoulder, into the goal.

We came back, then, we put everything we had into it. Cliff was up there, Billy forgot all about Di Stefano, even though he was back in defence the whole time, now, and Ronnie had a shot after a corner which hit Alonso's foot and went over the bar. When the whistle went, I never heard it, I suddenly realised everyone around me had stopped playing and some of them were shaking hands. Di Stefano came up and I shook hands with him, we put our arms round one another's shoulders and I said "Well played," but I felt near to crying. The other lads were walking off the field with their heads bent, but I called them back and made them line up in the middle of the field to salute the crowd, and the crowd gave us a terrific ovation.

Jack came into the dressing-room and said, "Hard luck, boys," and I thought to myself, If he says anything now, I'll hit the ceiling. But he was as down as the rest of us and all he said was, "That ball was over the line a bloody foot, wasn't it?"

I said, "A foot? Two foot! When he cleared, he must have caught his foot in the netting."

Everyone was very quiet in the showers, and I was too disappointed to try and cheer them up. I just said, "Everyone did well, you all did well," and Ronnie said, "Yeah, the fucking referee did well and all, didn't he?"

Jack looked into the dressing-room again when most of us were dressed and said, "The Press want to come in," and one of the boys said, "Fuck the Press."

"Oh, let them in," I said, though I didn't want to see them, either, all the Italians grinning round and wanting me to recognise them, and all the English putting on those long faces they put on when they think they ought to be looking sorry.

I'd been especially fed up with Arthur Bright, he'd written a piece that morning about Borough's brave lambs being butchered to make a Roman holiday, the usual bloody rubbish, and when he came into the dressing-room with the usual insincere smile all over his face—saying, "Hard luck, boys, hard luck," though you could see he didn't care a damn, I went for him. I said, "Did you enjoy your Roman holiday?"

"Very nice," he said, "great game, I only wish you could have won it."

I said, "We didn't play badly for lambs, did we?"

"No," he said, "no, you played very well, you were the better team."

"I'm glad even you could see that, Arthur," I said, then the Italians just swept him away, smiling at me and shaking my hand and saying, "Mi dispiace, mi dispiace." But them I didn't mind so much, at least they believed in what they were doing, even if they might change their beliefs three times a day. Beppe Valentini was there, too, looking all sorrowful, like a spaniel, and taking my hand in both of his to say what a shame it was, but I didn't want sympathy, all I wanted was to get away and be by myself—or with Jenny.

I didn't mind losing; what I did mind was being cheated.

I SOMETIMES wondered, had they won that Final, whether he would have retired. In some sense, the rest of his career seemed an anticlimax, just as the result of that match seemed an anticlimax, too. I never asked him directly, so could never know: yet perhaps, even if he hadn't planned it, he might in the glory of the moment have seen retirement as a grand gesture.

For what was left, now? He would never play a finer or more famous game, he had matched Di Stefano skill for skill, strategy for strategy, had swept an essentially moderate team to heights it could never have achieved without him. When his header had gone past Alonso, I had leaped to my feet in the *tribuna stampa*, with everyone else, shouting, "Goal! Goal!" discounting the lunging, desperate full-back. If the ball could have gone into the net, the moment would have been better, more climactic, still, but nets were irrelevant; a goal was a goal.

And then, the awful succeeding moment of cold shock; the game continuing, the referee turning his back, the protests, the eventual, token, consultation, coming far, far too late to put things right.

Yet even though they'd lost, this was still the moment to retire; before his legs began to go, before the highbrows found him out, before the divorce burst in public like some noxious boil. Now, while he was still a hero, on the field and off it, while even the facts of his marriage were no more than postulated, guessed at. Again and again, as the weeks, the months, the very seasons, passed, I wanted to tell him, "Stop now . . . now. Stop while you're still a giant, stop while you're playing well enough to keep afloat"—float the public image, float the whimsical paradoxes. One wanted to play slave to his Emperor, to stand at his elbow, reminding him he was mortal, doubly so as a footballer. For if man begins to die as soon as

247

he is born, how much more imminent is the end of a footballer, with his few years at the top, followed by the many
spent in the stale odours of a public house, sweeping up lint
and bandages, in dressing-rooms; spent at a factory bench, on
building sites, in youth hostels. Gerry wouldn't come to that,
but then, what would he come to?

"You can't tell Gerry," Charlie Barker had said, in their
days at Chiswick. "He knows it all, Gerry does."

He had, to an extent, been discovered already. His honeymoon with the football writers was over, for one thing; he
was competing with them, critical of them, and their ranks
closed against the amateur. There was the end of his marriage,
too; the football world had forgiven it, without condoning it.
The very fact that he had run off with a "celebrity" seemed,
ironically, to palliate the deed, at the same time that it pub-
licised it. Men winked at one another; they themselves—managers, players, journalists—would like to be in his shoes.

When I met Jenny Cunningham, myself, I did not warm to
her. She seemed lightweight—the more so, by comparison
with Mary—and I was irritated by her show-business gloss.
There were too many automatic enthusiasms, too many moments when the eyes went dead while the smile stayed, while
she looked off into space sure that nobody was watching
her : there was a blankness there. Nor did I like her singing.
She seemed to me a weak parody of the Americans, with a
phoney accent, a phoney animation.

I wondered what would happen when Gerry was no longer
a star. For the moment, there was a certain parity between
them, a mutual admiration, even if she earned more money
than he; but a singer must long outlast a footballer. Besides,
what I detected, when they were together in a football con-
text, was not the admiration Mary had first shown, but pro-
prietorship. Look at him, her smile seemed to say; look, he's
mine, as well.

Once, after a match at Borough, while I was sitting behind
them in his car, she asked with sudden sharpness, "Which
way are we going? Where are you taking me?"

248

"Back to the flat," he said. "I thought we'd maybe have a cup of tea there."

"But I want to go to the Colony," she said, "you know I'm singing at the Colony," and laughed immediately, for my sake.

"Can't bloody make him out, Gerry," Cliff Evans said to me, about that time. "I mean, we all do it, don't we? We all have it now and again; in, out, and then it's over. Not with Gerry, though; with Gerry, it's got to be bloody permanent."

I thought that it was probably true, or perhaps the truth was that he needed what Mary had called bitterly "the best of both worlds," a mother figure and a mistress—and if he did, could he himself be blamed?

Mary had sunk like a stone. She was in Jarrow now, with both the children, and I could never see Jenny without thinking of her. She had vanished, with her insights and her bitterness, her righteous grievance, which was so hard to bear because you could say nothing to assuage it. At times, I despised myself, detecting a sense of relief.

Gerry no longer wrote his novel column; it had lasted for only a few months, and to me had seemed facile and impertinent. "I hadn't the time," he told me—which was believable —"I told them it was too much for me." At the beginning of the new season, he quarrelled with the *Daily Gazette*, and left them too—"I'm disillusioned with journalism, Brian." One couldn't blame him for that—who wasn't disillusioned? —but the protest had come a little late, there were conflicting stories of what had really happened. Where did principle end, and discipline begin? He was a good columnist, but where would he now find a column?

Dudley Welsh remained loyal: "I'm trying to persuade our people to give him the same kind of column; he was wasted on the *Gazette*, he was far too intelligent." And as for the divorce, "He's a troubador. I loved his wife, she's so *sympathique*, but being married to a troubador was too much for her. You couldn't blame her; you couldn't blame either of them. I think he'll be better with his new wife; she's temperamentally similar to him. Have you heard her sing? Marvellous! Not pops, she hates pops; jazz singing. They were round at my flat; she sang and sang all night, she was magnificent!"

Gerry began the new season badly. It had been a dry, hot summer, and the hard-baked grounds were anathema to a ball-player. Besides, he looked tired, to me, as though the last, amazing season had taken too much out of him, as though he were still floundering in the moral backwash of that defeat in Rome.

He was frank about it all: "I may be finished as an inside-forward. I thought I'd have perhaps two more seasons there, and then drop back to wing-half. Now, I'll just give it to November, when the grounds are soft, and if it's still no better, I may make the change."

It was very little better, and he did change: to left-half, so that Cliff Evans could remain on the right. The move was tactfully arranged; he dropped back when Briggs, the usual left-half, was injured, then stayed there, settling there at once, with the versatility of the great footballer. Yet as a pair, he and Evans were too much alike, each an attacker, anxious to go upfield, so that though Gerry was immensely more talented than Briggs, the sum of his partnership with Evans was less than Evans' partnership with Briggs. Besides, who was to take his place in the attack? The team had pivoted around him, been brought to life by him, and now, however well he played, it must be in a subsidiary position. The club tried various reserve players at inside-right, but none was more than adequate. For a while, when the team was in the bottom half of the table, they moved Gerry back again, and he played a brilliant game, at home to Manchester City. But his next two games were mediocre, and at his own instance, he returned to left-half.

His eclipse as a forward had been sudden and startling though he, inevitably, had an explanation for it. "I was playing on nervous energy, last season. Physically, I was tired, but the European Cup was such a challenge that it didn't affect me."

There was no doubt that, as a half-back, some of his glamour had gone, partly because he no longer directed play, partly because he seldom scored a goal. Ideally, this should not have mattered; yet it did, for there *is* a glamour about goal-scoring, the moment of ecstatic shock when the ball tears into the net; there is a significance about the man who puts it there, even if his goal is a gift.

The divorce case came, and was uncontested. Jenny Cunningham was co-respondent, Mary kept both children, the newspapers had nothing to put beneath their headlines but this. Borough reached the Sixth Round of the Cup, came fourteenth in the League, and in the summer, transferred Cliff Evans to Headingford United in exchange for Eddie Oakham, the English international inside-right. The following season, Gerry moved across to right-half, where he won back his place for Scotland.

"I'm over the hill, of course," he'd say, but he wanted to believe it only intellectually. Besides, his combination with Oakham, a hard little player, with the appearance of an errant cherub, was as fruitful, in reverse, as his previous partnership with Evans, behind him.

"Liedholm could do it," he said. "Liedholm played in a World Cup Final when he was thirty-eight."

"Will *you* play till thirty-eight?"

"I don't know, Brian, I haven't decided."

And I remembered what Mary had once said to me: "Gerry lives in a dream world." Of course he would set himself no time limit, he was like a man who suffers from an incurable disease, half suspects it, but will never acknowledge it. As long as he played, so long could realities be kept at a distance.

In railway carriages, in diners, rolling between London and Birmingham, Manchester and London, we football writers wondered how long he could keep on. There were periods when he would seem at the end of his tether; weary, struggling to keep up with the tide of play, humiliated by fast young inside-forwards. And then, he'd come back again, finding energy from some secret reservoir, becoming again the dominant man on the field.

Charlton offered him their managership, but he turned it down: "When I go out of football, I'll go out of it altogether."

Would he change his mind, when the chips were down?

"Och, who'd *have* him?" asked plump McDonald, of the *Inquirer*. "He's talked himself out of management, the same as he's talked himself out of journalism."

The divorce was made absolute, and he married Jenny. The wedding took place obscurely: at Gerry's insistence, I was sure. Borough came second in the League that season, and reached the semi-final of the Cup. He was over thirty-five now; like Stanley Matthews, he might play on into his forties.

"Yeah, but Matthews is a winger," said Rainford, of the *Daily Courier*, thin and pale in his carriage corner. "Matthews can take rests."

And yet there was something indestructibly young about Gerry; the lean body, the abundant, flaxen hair, made the very thought of his retirement absurd. Still, there were matches, moments. A vile November day at Borough, the cold rain swirling across the floodlights, the pitch a Passchendaele of mud, and Gerry dragging his slim, tired legs across it like a lost explorer, stumbling through the sand, falling, while the crowd shouted, "Get up, Logan, get on with the game, Logan! Why don't you pack it in?"

And he, smiling, shook his head, got up, and did go on with the game. What else could he do?

GERRY LOGAN

PEOPLE ask me all the time, when will you retire? Or, what'll you do when you *do* retire? And when I tell them I don't know, they look at me as though they can't believe me. But of course it's perfectly true, I *don't* know when I'll give up football, that's something only my body knows. It may be this season, it may not be for another five years.

In the same way, I don't know what's going to turn up, when I do retire. I wouldn't be a football manager because, as I've said before, the better you are, the less chance you've got, like Lionel, and I won't be a sports journalist, because a journalist is a puppet, he does what he's told.

It may be something in television, television appeals to me; or it may even be something with Jenny, in show business— I'll worry about it when I finish playing. I've still got ambitions left in football, anyway; we could win the League this season, and that would put us in the European Cup again. We'd have a chance, too, because Eddie Oakham is a good little player, and now I'm playing half-back, I find I can influence the defence, as well as the attack.

I said to a journalist the other day, I'll retire when Borough win the European Cup, and Scotland win the World Cup.

There's only one thing certain; I'll go out while I'm still on top, no sliding down through the Second and Third Division, I've never played there yet, and I never will.

After that, I'll see, because I don't believe in planning life, a man who plans his life has no freedom. Football's one challenge, retiring is a *new* challenge; I've faced one, and I'll face the other. When you stop facing challenges, that's when you stop living.

8386228R00152

Printed in Germany
by Amazon Distribution
GmbH, Leipzig